Flames of War

Based on Historical Events

David Lee Corley

DEDICATION

Dedicated to all the men and women that fought and
sacrificed for their country.

Table of Contents

"The first casualty of war is innocence."

– Oliver Stone

The Most Wanted Man in Laos

January 1, 1967 – Mountains, Laos

The headlights on Chau's truck snaked their way through the dark mountains on a winding road, if you could call it that… a road. The nonstop rain had washed out much of it. What was left was precarious at best. Chau had grown used to the difficult terrain over the years. She had it memorized and knew where to watch out.

The North Vietnamese work crews labored day and night to maintain the road. Picks, shovels, and wheelbarrows were their tools of trade. A bulldozer was just a distant dream in this part of the Ho Chi Minh Trail. As loyal patriots, they tried to keep the road open and the supplies and troops flowing into the South. It was a constant losing battle. If it wasn't the rains that turned the road to mud, it was the American bombers that pounded the road to dust.

The Americans… she thought. As a young woman,

she had befriended them and slept with many before she knew them as the enemy. She may have even loved one – McGoon. She didn't talk of those times with her comrades. It was too dangerous. They wouldn't understand. Communist dogma was black and white with little room for compassion or tolerance. When she joined the North Vietnamese Army, it was her communist instructors that had taught her to hate the Americans. They were invaders determined to take over Vietnam, her country. She would sacrifice everything to keep that from happening. She was a flag-waving nationalist.

She was also lucky and honored to be driving the lead truck in the convoy. She knew the road better than any of the other drivers. As the lead vehicle, she was allowed to use her headlights. Everyone else had to follow the truck in front of them. That wasn't easy, especially when a truck drove off the side of a cliff. Unable to see the road clearly, several trucks behind the vanished truck would usually follow it over the edge. Few survived such a fall. Of course, most of the supplies could be recovered if there was no fire from the crash, but that did little to comfort the families of the dead drivers and soldiers. Chau had learned not to get too close to anyone that drove the Ho Chi Minh Trail. She avoided remembering her comrades' names and rarely asked about their personal lives. There was no time to mourn when someone was lost. The convoy had to keep moving… no matter what.

Chau was approaching the most dangerous section of the road that often washed out during heavy rains. The road had been carved into a steep slope. All of the trees and vegetation had been swept away long ago leaving exposed soil that sopped up the rain. When it was saturated and grew too heavy, the slope let loose creating an avalanche of mud and rock that took out the road. It was raining, but not heavy. It gave her hope that the road would remain intact as the convoy passed. Even so, she forced herself to focus on the road and watch carefully as she continued. As the lead truck, everyone behind her depended on her eyes and experience.

Watching the approaching convoy through binoculars, Blackjack could feel his pulse rising. This was the fun part of what he and his team did. It was also the riskiest. All the preparation and work led up to the few minutes that would follow the detonation. The SOG team and their Montagnard warriors had placed a series of C-4 charges high on the upside of the slope above the road. The way to create an effective avalanche was momentum. Start high and the rocks and mud would collect more rocks and mud as they traveled down the slope gaining speed. The avalanche would block the road and trap the rest of the convoy. Easy pickings for the well-armed Montagnard.

The SOG team and the Montagnard often attacked enemy units two to three times their size. The surprise and ferocity of their assault gave them an advantage. It wasn't rocket science. It was momentum – getting the enemy running and keeping it running. The enemy cannot counterattack if it's running in the opposite direction. Simple really. Simple plans were almost always better than complex plans when it came to war. There was less to go wrong. Even the best plans go out the window once the battle starts.

Blackjack watched as Chau's truck passed the location of the first C-4 charge. He waited. He wanted as many trucks as possible to be caught in the avalanche. It was about timing. He could feel the rush of adrenaline coursing through his body. He hated the idea of being addicted to anything, but adrenaline was different. It made his reactions quicker. His mind was more focused. His muscles were stronger. There was no denying it. Adrenaline made him Superman. He willingly let it take over. His eyes narrowed. He was a hunter. He picked up the detonator…

Chau was grateful that the road was intact. As she approached the far end of the slope, her hopes were dashed when she heard a large series of explosions above. She didn't know what it was, but it didn't matter. The convoy was in trouble. Her head jerked around, and she looked up the slope. It was hard to see in the dark. Her irises had closed from the bright flashes of the explosions and her vision was limited. But she saw enough – the earth was moving toward her.

She stomped on the accelerator and the truck picked up speed. The end of the slope wasn't far. With luck, she could reach it before the rocks and mud reached her truck. But she wasn't lucky that night. She felt the first boulder slamming into the side of her truck, forcing it toward the edge of the road. She steered back toward the road, but it was too late. More boulders and mud hit the side of the truck as the wheels left the road and it tipped on its side. It tumbled down the slope.

She was helpless, trapped inside the cab. She held on to the steering wheel as it lurched from side to side. A boulder smashed into the roof, crushing the cab, the windshield, and the driver's door window shattering.

Mud and rocks entered the cab, hitting her in the face and arms. Her hands were forced from the steering wheel. She was in freefall banging her head, her arms and legs flailing out of control as the truck continued its journey down the slope. She struggled to keep her mouth and nose clear of mud. She wasn't afraid. She was angry at herself for letting this happen. She was responsible for the safety of the convoy. She should have spotted the ambush. A fist-sized rock hit her in the side of the head, and she blacked out. Mercy at last.

Above, five trucks had been caught in the avalanche and were pushed over the side of the road. Troops and supplies were ousted out the back of the trucks as they tumbled downward and were scattered among the cascading mud and rocks. The bodies of the soldiers twisted in the muddy flow like ragdolls. Legs and arms were fractured; some had their necks broken. They were helpless against the momentum of the slide.

The convoy came to an abrupt stop. With no room to turn around, the trucks still on the road were trapped just as Blackjack had predicted. A parachute flare launched from a mortar lit up the convoy creating clear targets. The Montagnard sprung up from their hiding places on the uphill side of the mountain slope and opened fire. The SOG team had assigned targets designed to decapitate the convoy's leadership and create mayhem. Officers and NCOs were singled out and dispatched.

The fusillade of gunfire put out by the SOG and the Montagnard was intense. There was no reserve. Everyone fought. The NVA troops being transported south easily outnumbered the SOG and Montagnard, but they were leaderless and in complete disarray. The warriors on the hillside pressed the attack. As much as they wanted to run down the slope and fight hand-to-hand, they were disciplined and kept their firing positions. Once their enemy was depleted, the signal to charge would come. They had learned from their American SOG advisors and fought as a cohesive unit. That strategy brought them victory which the Montagnard loved. Victory was like revenge… sweet.

One by one, a recoilless rifle manned by two Montagnard took out the trucks on the road, destroying their cabs and engines, and setting them ablaze. American-made grenades arced across the night sky to destroy more trucks and killed those defending them. The convoy was burning. The ammunition they carried exploded killing the NVA using the trucks for cover. Unable to determine the size of the force attacking them, most of the NVA broke and ran down the slope. Some were caught by the mud and rock of the avalanche that was still moving, but slower. Those that remained were quickly overwhelmed by the Montagnard when the order to charge was given by their village chief. It was a massacre with over seventy-two NVA killed. There were no NVA wounded. The Montagnard had three wounded and two killed. After the Montagnard had taken what they wanted, fifty-two trucks were destroyed which included the supplies and ammunition they carried. It was a big victory for the SOG and Montagnard. Blackjack would be buying his warriors and their families several pigs for a feast when they returned to their village several days later.

Chau awoke in darkness. She tried to move but could feel that her legs were buried in mud and rock pinning her down. The pain in her left forearm was intense. She felt along her arm until she discovered the broken bone sticking through her skin. With her good arm, she retrieved the cigarette lighter from her uniform's shirt pocket. It was a Zippo lighter she had "borrowed" from McGoon. She opened the lid and spun the little wheel until it lit. What remained of the cab was illuminated. She was almost completely buried beneath mud and rock. Only the cab's crushed roof had saved her life. There wasn't much room in the tiny cavern and that meant there wasn't much air. The flame from the lighter was using oxygen, but she needed to find a way out if there was one.

She glanced at the broken bone in her arm. It was as she expected – lots of blood, torn flesh, and pain… a lot of pain. While she was unconscious and still, the blood had coagulated which had slowed the bleeding to a trickle. Moving her arm would break up the clotting and it would most likely start bleeding heavily again. She forced herself to ignore her forearm for the moment. She knew it was bad and didn't need to use valuable time to examine the wound more closely. If she could not escape the cab she would suffocate, and her broken arm wouldn't matter.

The flame flickered and dimmed from lack of oxygen. She had no idea how long she had been unconscious using up oxygen, but however long it was she figured she was lucky to wake before dying. At least she stood a chance of escaping before her oxygen ran out. She extinguished the flame, and the cab went dark once again.

She remembered the toolbox beneath the seat. There was a clawed hammer that could be useful for digging. Feeling her way in the darkness, she used her good arm to move the mud and rock off her legs. It took valuable time, but she had no choice. After two minutes of digging, her legs were finally freed, and she had created a space in front of the seat. She cleared away more mud and rock before reaching underneath. She found the toolbox and pulled it out. When she opened it, she felt inside and found the hammer. She also found a ball of string that would help her determine which way was up. She could feel the gravity pulling her down toward the passenger door and imagined the truck was on its side, but she needed to determine the shortest path to the surface. Once she started digging, she guessed there wouldn't be much time before she was buried alive. Up was critical. She unwound some of the string and let it dangle. She relit the lighter and studied the angle of the string for a moment. She knew which was up and determined the shortest way to the surface was through the broken windshield. She wasted no time.

She switched hands holding the lighter. It was extremely painful, but she had enough power in her mangled arm to hold the lighter and keep the flame from going out. It was getting harder to breathe and each new breath was a struggle and shorter. Her energy was diminishing by the second from lack of oxygen. She knew she needed to make her attempt at escaping while she still had power in her muscles.

She moved her body up as close as possible to where she would attempt to exit the cab. She had no idea how much mud and rock was between the truck and the surface, but she wasn't going to die without trying to free herself of the muddy tomb. She gripped the hammer's handle and struck the mud in front of the hammer's claw. As she had calculated, the mud and rock fell into the cab but created a small space in front of the cab. She pulled herself inside the space and struck the mud again and again, each time pulling herself upward. The mud and rock started flowing faster without hitting it with the claw. Each time, she planted the claw in the muddy tunnel wall and pulled herself upward as fast as she could. Then, the flame flickered out. She was out of oxygen. With her remaining strength, she pulled herself upward in the darkness. Once, twice, three times… then she felt herself out of breath. Her head was spinning. She couldn't remember what she was doing. She stopped. The mud and rock kept moving through the tunnel into the cab. She could feel it but couldn't see it. It didn't matter. She was sleepy and closed her eyes. Her struggle was over as the darkness consumed her.

A minute later, her eyes flickered open. She was conscious again. She could breathe. She still couldn't see. She felt for the lighter. It was gone. Lost somewhere in the mud below. *The mud below*, she thought. The mud and rock in the tunnel she had created kept flowing downward even while she was blacked out. She imagined that enough soil had moved that the tunnel had reached the surface to open a passageway for the oxygen. She couldn't see it, but she used the hammer like a mountain climber's axe planting it in the soil and pulling herself upward to where she thought the surface might be. She could feel the mud flowing past her filling up the tunnel and trapping her legs. She couldn't give up now. She was so close to freedom… close to life. She kicked and pulled her knees up. Her good hand gripped the hammer as she embedded it in the side of the tunnel and pulled. She felt herself moving upward as the mud filled the space below her and she could push with her legs. She was exhausted but didn't give up. Her muscles ached. Her broken forearm throbbed.

Another couple of lunges upward and her head pushed through an opening. She could feel the night's air filling her lungs. She knew she couldn't stop to rest. She planted the hammer one more time and pulled herself out of the tunnel. It was a miracle. She was free.

She lay on her back gasping for air and laughing. Life never seemed so precious. Her arm was filled with pain, but she didn't care. It would heal in time, and she would be whole again. All that seemed to matter to her was a chance of revenge against the enemy soldiers that had done this to her and her comrades. Transporting more reinforcements and supplies into South Vietnam would be that revenge. She wanted to heal as fast as possible, so she could once again get behind the wheel of a truck and carry out her duty. It wouldn't be the same as pulling the trigger, but helping the war effort was the best she could do.

She gave herself one minute to celebrate, then carefully rolled over on her stomach and looked up the slope. She saw the convoy burning on the road above. Secondary explosions of fuel tanks igniting and ammunition cooking off lit up the surrounding area. She wondered how many of her comrades escaped. She wondered if the enemy was hunting them… and her.

She realized it would be light soon, maybe an hour or so. She had to find cover to hide and hopefully tend to her broken forearm before setting out to find the supply depot seven miles away. Once she reached it, she would be safe, and her comrades would take care of her. She knelt, then used her good arm to push herself up to her feet. Keeping low, she moved across the avalanche slowly, careful not to start another slide.

When she reached the edge of the slide area, she entered the jungle. She found herself a good hiding place between the massive roots of a tree. She couldn't see well enough to tend to her wound, but she also knew it didn't matter much since it was full of mud and bits of rock and glass from the broken windshield. She had no water with which to clean the wound. She used her teeth to cut the bottom of her mud-caked shirt and ripped a long strip of cloth. She fashioned a basic sling to hold her broken arm and keep it from getting damaged further. It wasn't much, but it was all she could do at the moment.

She decided to rest until dawn. She would need her strength for the trek back to the supply depot. She lay back into her tree root cradle and closed her eyes. Exhausted, she was asleep in less than twenty seconds.

After tending to her wound, the young doctor at the supply depot had ordered her to return to Hanoi where the surgeons were more experienced. He had done what he could to clean her wound but was not comfortable setting the bone which was broken in several places without an x-ray. He feared infection. He knew that once Chau arrived at the hospital, the doctors would need to rebreak the bones to set them properly. He decided not to warn Chau of the painful procedure. It wouldn't do her any good to worry about it. She needed to be able to sleep to regain her strength and allow her body to fight any infection.

Hanoi, North Vietnam

It took almost a week for Chau to reach Hanoi by

truck. Many of the roads were bad in North Vietnam, especially in the highlands. It was an uncomfortable journey. Her wounded arm bounced up and down. Each bump sent a stab of pain through her body. In the middle of the journey, she contracted chills and a high-grade fever. The wound had become infected as the doctor had expected. It would only be a matter of time before it killed her if she didn't get treatment.

The surgeons in Hanoi had done a good job saving her arm. It took almost an hour to get the last little bits of dirt, rocks, and glass out of the wound. Rebreaking and resetting the bone took two more hours. She slept in an opium haze during the surgery and didn't mind one bit as the doctors probed and pulled at her wound. The resetting of the bone brought pain, but she didn't remember it. She didn't remember any of it.

She woke up with a cast on her arm and could feel the throbbing of her flesh and bone inside. It was like a series of clamps was holding her bones in place. She still had a fever, but it didn't seem as bad as before the operation. Maybe she was healing as she had hoped.

An intelligence officer sat in a chair waiting for her to wake. She suspected she would be court-martialed for losing her truck and abandoning the convoy. It wasn't her fault, but she doubted that would carry much weight in her sentencing. Instead, he interviewed her about the attack on the convoy. She told him what she remembered, but she had spent most of the attack buried in her truck and never saw the men that carried out the ambush. She wished she could be of more help. The officer assured her that the other survivors had filled in the blanks. He called her "a very brave woman" and left without any word of court-martial.

Chau was relieved. She wanted to return to Laos and continue to drive on the Ho Chi Minh Trail. A court marshal would have prevented that.

It would take three months for her arm to heal enough that she could drive a truck. While she waited to be cleared by the doctors at the hospital, she was allowed to travel around the city and visit the places that she once visited with her friend Nguyen and her lover, McGoon. She rarely had time off when she was driving. She felt guilty but there was little she could do but heal. Besides, the fresh air in the capital's beautiful parks did her good and lightened her mood.

For the first time in a long time, Chau thought about Nguyen. She wondered if her friend was still alive and what she might be doing. After McGoon had died at Dien Bien Phu, Nguyen and she went their separate ways – Nguyen to the south and her staying in the north. She pondered if Nguyen was a communist and helping the Viet Cong. Maybe she married and had children. Chau had not had time for romance since she started driving the Ho Chi Minh Trail. But maybe Nguyen had been luckier. Maybe she was even rich and lived in a mansion. Even with all of its problems, Chau had heard that anything was possible in the South.

After reporting the results of his interviews with the survivors of one of the worst convoy raids since the Ho Chi Minh Trail had been built, the NVA high command decided to take action. A young Montagnard warrior had been captured during one of the raids. After weeks of interrogation and torture, the young tribesman gave up the names of the American SOG team members, including their leader. The terrorist named "Blackjack" and his SOG team had to be stopped. Leaderless and without American support, the Montagnard would revert to the peaceful tribal ways and no longer attack the supply and troop convoys on the Ho Chi Minh trail.

After much discussion between the politburo members and the NVA generals, it was decided to assemble an elite unit to hunt down the Montagnard and capture the SOG team. Led by a special operations commander, the new team would be given all the resources it required to complete its mission. Even the Pathet Lao would be asked to support the NVA special operations team. From that point forward, Blackjack had become the most wanted man in Laos.

Bolo

January 2, 1967 – North Vietnam

In 1966, the bombers in Operation Rolling Thunder sustained heavy losses from the Vietnam People's Air Force (VPAF) that had consistently evaded USAF escorts. Because of the long flight from their base in Thailand, the American fighter-bombers were forced to fly the same path to conserve fuel and became predictable. The enemy fighters found the American bombers laden with heavy bomb loads and unable to maneuver effectively if attacked. They were easy pickings for the MiGs and losses of American bombers were substantial. Once a fledgling air force, the VPAF became a force to be feared as its pilots gained experience and more advanced fighters came online.

According to the rules of engagement, the USAF jets were required to make visual contact with the enemy before firing their air-to-air missiles. The policy was designed to avoid friendly fire against other allied aircraft, but it took away the Americans' main advantage – the medium-range AIM-7 Sparrow missile that could take out a target without ever seeing it. Something had to be done and fast.

USAF Colonel Robin Olds was the commander of

the 8th Tactical Fighter Wing based at Ubon Royal Thai Air Force Base, Thailand. The 8th TFW (Tactical Fighter Wing) was nicknamed "The Wolf Pack" because of its pilots' aggression and the use of teamwork to defeat the enemy. Olds was an experienced pilot that served two tours in Europe during WWII and became a double ace when he shot down ten enemy aircraft.

Sent to Vietnam to revive the performance of the 8th TFW, Olds was confident that with training his pilots could prevail against the enemy MiGs that had taken their toll on so many of the bombers this past year. The wing's new commander led from the cockpit and flew with his men whenever practical. The wing's primary fighter was the Phantom F-4C. The major drawback to the Phantoms was that they had not been equipped with QRC-160 radar jamming pods like the F-105 bombers. In other words, the Phantoms were vulnerable to SAMs. Any plan to defeat the enemy had to take this deficiency into account.

After reviewing the wing's past missions, Olds, a skilled tactician, came up with a strategy to ambush the small and more maneuverable MiG-21s. To execute his plan, he needed his pilots to draw the MiGs into aerial combat on an even playing field. The concept behind Operation Bolo was simple: make the Phantoms look like the cumbersome bomb-laden F-105s, then lure the MiGs into a protracted dogfight with the American fighters that emptied their enemies' smaller fuel tanks. Running low on fuel, the MiGs would lose their ability to maneuver and become prey to the Phantoms. To extend their flight time, the American jets would use drop tanks that would be jettisoned as soon as they engaged the enemy aircraft. It was a risky strategy that would put many of his best pilots in harm's way. But Olds knew that almost any victory required risk and often resulted in losing the lives of some American pilots. He would do everything in his power to keep his aircrews as safe as possible, but shrinking from a fight because it might require sacrifice was not an acceptable pretense. Pilots were paid to fight the enemy. It was their duty.

Olds assigned the mission planning to a group of veteran junior officers: Capt. John Stone, 1st Lt. Joseph Hicks, 1st Lt. Ralph Wetterhahn, and Maj. James Covington. They worked under tight security and didn't brief the pilots assigned to fly the operation until two days before the operation and only after everyone had been restricted to base. The plan involved two air wings – the "West Force" would be the 8th TFW at Ubon, while the "East Force" would be the 366th TFW at Da Nang Air Base in South Vietnam. With seven flights of F-4Cs, the West Force was the bait and would simulate a heavily loaded F-105 strike force coming out of Thailand. The East Force would be made up of F-105s, EC-121s, and EB-66s from Da Nang and four flights of F-104s from the 435th TFS from Ubon. The East Force would render the enemy's SAM sites ineffective by jamming their radar and cutting off the MiG-21s' retreat if they broke off their attack and headed for their alternate bases in China where they would be safe from attack.

The operation planners calculated that the MiGs would have a maximum of fifty-five minutes of flight time from takeoff to landing. They decided to stagger the arrival times of the F-4C flights passing near the targeted airfields. The idea was that every five minutes a new flight would enter the battle area and engage the enemy jets. They hoped to run the MiGs out of fuel by continuing engagement and preventing them from landing. It was also decided that no other US aircraft would be allowed in the area, so the first three flights of Phantoms would be "missile-free" and could engage the enemy jets at a distance without having to first identify them visually. The Seventh Air Force rules of engagement were to be set aside for Operation Bolo.

The entire plan hinged on the MiGs taking the bait and engaging the strike force. To deceive the North Vietnamese, the Phantoms from Ubon would fly the same routes, altitudes, and speeds as the F-105s had been using. They would even use the same air refueling tanker tracks and altitudes. The Phantom pilots were instructed to use the F-105 jargon when they radioed one another. The F-4Cs were temporarily fitted with QRC-160 jamming pods normally used by the F-105s so their electronic signature would appear the same. The Phantom pilots flew line-abreast pod formations like the F-105s flew to maximize pod effectiveness. Operation Bolo was named after the sharp and deadly cane-cutting machete used by the Filipinos. The bolo does not appear to be a weapon until the enemy is drawn in and it's too late.

The mission was delayed one day because of bad weather. With Olds as the flight commander, the first flight of F-4Cs took off from Ubon Air Base in the early afternoon. Several hours later, Olds' flight arrived over the enemy's Phuc Yen Air Base, and nothing happened. It looked like the North Vietnamese were not fooled and would not engage the Phantoms. Olds looked down and saw only a thick layer of clouds that obscured the air base and its runway. He could not see if the MiGs were taking off or still on the ground. Frustrated, Olds reversed course and flew northwest. After three minutes and still no contact, Olds canceled the missile-free option. The second flight of Phantoms was approaching, and he didn't want any friendly fire to hamper the mission.

Just as the second flight arrived over the air base, the first MiGs emerged from the clouds covering the runway. The enemy had taken the bait and it was time to play ball. Seeing the MiGs, Olds dropped his fuel tanks and engaged his afterburners. The aircraft in his flight followed, dropping their wing tanks, and speeding toward the enemy. Olds fired three times at the MiGs and all three of his missiles failed to launch or guide. His cursing was memorable.

As Olds watched several more MiGs emerge from the clouds below, one of the enemy aircraft pulled up behind his Phantom and lined up his sights on the Phantom's engine. It would be an easy shot. Olds knew there was little hope of surviving such a shot. Fortunately, one of the Phantoms from the second flight was close and saw Olds' predicament. The Phantom pulled up behind the MiG diverting the enemy pilot's attention away from Olds. The MiG broke off his attack and headed back into the clouds. Olds was going to buy several rounds at the officer's club for the pilot that just saved his life. Olds wasted no time looking for another target to engage.

It was Ralph Wetterhahn, one of the mission planners and a member of Olds's flight, that scored the first kill using an AIM-7 Sparrow to down a MiG. The enemy pilot ejected from his badly damaged fighter and floated safely to the ground.

Another MiG appeared behind Olds's fighter and

engaged. Olds immediately broke to the left to get out of the enemy jet's line of fire. Then another MiG appeared from the clouds in front of Olds and turned wide at a distance of 2,000 yards. Olds followed as the MiG disappeared once again in the clouds. Its vanishing was followed by more cursing.

Still, another MiG emerged from the clouds heading straight at Olds's aircraft. Instead of breaking off, Olds again engaged his afterburner and reared his aircraft at a forty-five-degree angle which placed him inside the enemy's turn. The enemy was turning left, so Olds barrel rolled to the right. Olds found himself above his enemy and half upside down. Timing was everything at that point. Olds held his position until the enemy completed his turn, then dropped in behind him. He had a deflection angle of twenty degrees with a distance of 1,500 yards. Olds was behind and lower than his enemy's aircraft. The pilot could not see him and didn't even know he was there. Olds launched two sidewinders at the silhouette of the enemy's aircraft. One of the missiles found its target and blew off the enemy's right wing. The MiG spiraled downward and disappeared in the cloud cover above the air base. Celebratory cursing.

The third flight of Phantoms entered the target area and engaged the enemy aircraft. Capt. Walter Radeker from Olds' flight saw a MiG tracking his flight leader and maneuvered to engage the enemy aircraft. Even with the enemy in his sights, Redeker was unable to get a good tone to achieve missile lock. He fired a Sidewinder anyway hoping it would guide and find its target. It did. The missile hit the MiG in its tail and exploded. The MiG went into a spin and the pilot ejected. Another MiG down. Olds' flight had destroyed three MiG-21s before hitting its fuel consumption limit and the pilots were forced to disengage. They headed for home as the air battle continued.

The two remaining flights engaged the enemy while more American flights were on their way. The second or Ford flight was led by Colonel Daniel "Chappie" James, Jr. At 3:04 PM, the Ford flight was attacked by three MiGs. James was focused on the two MiGs in front of his flight approaching head-on. He didn't notice the MiG behind him maneuvering to attack his number three and number four from the rear. Fortunately, James's wingman, Captain Everett Raspberry warned James of the threat. James turned left then right and spotted the MiG behind him. He radioed the pilots of his number three and number four and ordered them to break right. As they broke right, the MiG behind broke left. For a split second, James and the MiG pilot were side by side. The two pilots were close enough to see each other's faces.

James went into a horizontal barrel roll to get away from the MiG and into firing position behind the enemy aircraft. Once in position, James achieved a steady lock tone and launched a sidewinder. The missile missed when the enemy pilot suddenly broke left at full throttle. But as the MiG turned, it passed in front of Cpt. Raspberry's Phantom. Realizing his mistake, the MiG pilot descended toward the clouds over the air base. Raspberry followed performing a barrel roll that put him in perfect firing position. He launched a Sparrow which slammed into the enemy's tail section. The badly damaged MiG-21 shook violently and fell into a spin. Its pilot ejected before the fighter crashed into the ground.

Ford flight fired on the enemy MiGs several more

times, but none of the missiles made contact. Reaching its fuel limit, Ford flight left the battle without any losses of its own and one enemy MiG-21 kill. Much of the Americans' success was due to the Phantoms' high-speed maneuverability.

Rambler flight was the third to arrive in the area. Led by Captain John Stone, one of the architects of Operation Bolo and the wing's tactics officer. When they arrived, Stone immediately spotted a pair of MiGs in a break in the clouds below. He dove his aircraft, achieved tone, and launched an AIM-7 Sparrow. Once released from the wing's pylon, the missile failed to ignite. Wasting no time, Stone fired a second Sparrow. The missile guided to one of the MiGs and exploded destroying the aircraft. Stone observed another MiG approaching from behind and moving into attack. Stone didn't panic but instead steered his aircraft into the line of fire of Major Philip Combies, Rambler No. 4. With the enemy aircraft less than 2,000 yards, Combies used his aircraft's reticle to line up his shot and fired two missiles. Only one missile ignited, but that was enough. The missile hit the tail section of the MiG-21 and created a huge orange ball of fire.

Seconds after Combies's kill, another MiG-21 crossed in front of Rambler No. 2 commanded by 1st Lieutenant Lawrence Glynn. With the enemy aircraft in his sights, Glynn immediately fired a Sparrow. The missile hit behind the MiG's tailfin and exploded destroying the enemy aircraft. SAM missile launches threaten Rambler flight. With three kills and no losses, Combies ordered his pilots to disengage and head back to base.

The four remaining flights arrived to find that the surviving MiGs had had enough and disappeared into the clouds. With the threat of more SAM sites, they headed back to base.

When the Phantoms landed at Ubon Air Base, the ground crews gathered along the runway. The pilots opened their cockpits as they taxied and raised their fingers indicating their kills. The ground crewmen went wild each time a kill was identified. The officer's club was full that night and poured through the entire inventory of the top-shelf liquor as one pilot after another bought rounds for the entire bar.

In all, the eighth TFW had achieved seven MiG-21 victories with no losses of their own. Operation Bolo was considered a huge success and led the USAF to plan similar missions to engage the MiGs through deception. The American airmen were back in business.

Losing so many of the best aircraft in such a short amount of time, the North Vietnamese were forced to disband their assets by grounding their MiGs for four months. During that time, they retrained their pilots and devised new tactics to take on the Americans.

The Ban Naden Raid

Villages in the northwestern mountains of South Vietnam near the Laotian border were few and far between. Blanketed in triple canopy jungle and steep mountain slopes, it was a harsh territory with little open and level land for farming. Any fields needed for crops had to be hacked out of the dense undergrowth. Most villagers survived by hunting wild animals and fishing the streams that flowed from the mountain ranges.

Laying on his belly at the edge of a tree line, Granier watched a village through his detached rifle scope. Lined on both his sides were ten Phoenix trainees all holding their rifle scopes, binoculars, and distance-finding scopes. The trainee directly next to him on the left side yelped when a fire ant bit him on the leg. Granier reached over whacking him on the head and said, "Suck it up," in a menacing whisper.

The trainee obeyed and kept his pain to himself. It wasn't the fear of Granier's long reach and callused hand that kept the trainees in line. It was the awe of his reputation. He was a legend, and nobody wanted to disappoint a legend. They hung on his every word and even mirrored the way he dressed and walked. He was a real-life Clint Eastwood in their eyes – tough as nails and meaner than a scorpion. They had all memorized lines from Clint Eastwood's movies and mimicked

Granier with his unique mannerisms saying the lines at night when he wasn't around. It was an honor to be part of his team even if it was only training.

Granier thought hero worship was bullshit. A true warrior had to be anchored by his own skill and quest for perfection, not admiration of somebody else's talents and accomplishments. He wanted his trainees to develop confidence in their own abilities, not his. He would drill that into them time and time again and even punish them if they complimented him. The Phoenix program didn't need fanboys. It needed effective operatives. That was his mission.

Granier spotted what he was looking for – the village chief getting ready to lead a hunting party into the jungle. The hunters would use blow-darts dipped in concentrated poison frog venom to silently take down wildlife hiding in the branches of trees. Even a scratch from the dipped dart was enough to paralyze the prey causing them to fall to the ground. Granier had learned how to aim and shoot a blow-dart gun, but he wasn't much good at it. He preferred using a knife or crossbow when silence was required.

Granier used hand signals to instruct the trainees to follow him. He moved quietly to where he thought the group of hunters might be heading. His trainees followed, also quiet. To even be accepted into Granier's Phoenix course, the trainees needed extensive fighting experience and jungle training. He didn't have time to teach everything required to be an effective operative in Vietnam. His was a polishing course – tips and tricks. He taught by example taking them on snatch-and-grab missions.

Hidden in the dense vegetation, Granier and the trainees waited until the hunters had passed their position, then pulled up behind them following at a distance. Granier did not want to fight the hunters. He didn't want to lose any of his trainees which he was sure would underestimate the fighting skills of the villagers.

The villagers stopped at the base of a large tree and looked up studying the various wildlife in the branches. The chief pointed to a leopard hidden in the shadows. He wanted its pelt for a cape. Each warrior took his turn firing a blow-dart at the leopard high in the tree. All missed. It was the chief himself that finally took the predator down with an almost perfect shot hitting the beast's shoulder. After a few moments for the poison to take effect, the paralyzed leopard hit the jungle floor with a thud. Groggy from the poison but still conscious, it hissed at the warriors gathering around it but couldn't move. The beast was no danger. The chief stabbed the leopard in the throat with a spear, killing it but not damaging its beautiful fleece. He drew his long knife and went to work skinning the animal.

The barks of several monkeys in nearby trees caught the attention of the villagers who wandered off leaving the chief with his trophy. Moments later, Granier and his trainees emerged from the jungle and surrounded the chief. When the chief looked up, Granier used the butt of his rifle to knock him out. The trainees grabbed the unconscious chief, tied his hands and legs, then used a pole to carry him off deeper into the jungle like he was some sort of slain animal ready for the cooking pot. Granier took up the rear to make sure none of the villagers followed.

After moving to a clearing, the trainees took up defensive positions, while Granier stayed with the captive. The chief woke from his unintentional slumber and groaned. His eyes blinked open. Granier pressed his finger to his lips and motioned for the chief to remain silent. Granier glanced at his wristwatch. It was almost time for their rendezvous with the helicopter that had originally inserted the team. Granier didn't like using a radio if it could be helped. He felt it could give away the team's position. Preset rendezvous were better if he had good control and could define the time needed to complete the mission. In this case, he did.

Hearing the whoop-whoop of approaching helicopter blades, Granier signaled the team to be ready. The helicopter appeared over the jungle and swooped down. It would be on the ground for less than a minute while Granier, the captive, and the trainees loaded up. The engine groaned against the load as the helicopter once again lifted into the air and disappeared.

The chief had never ridden in a helicopter but didn't seem afraid as he watched the jungle canopy sweep below. One of his tribesmen had informed the SOG that the chief had been collaborating with the Viet Cong and storing supplies for them. He had even encouraged his younger warriors to join the Viet Cong to fight the American invaders. The SOG had turned the intel over to the CIA who in turn assigned the snatch-and-grab mission to Phoenix. Granier had liked the mission because it involved an indigenous tribe that his trainees needed to learn about.

The chief squirmed, then showed the trainees sitting between him and the open door that the rope that bound his hands was cutting into his wrists. The trainee reached over and tried to loosen the knot but to no avail. The trainee took out his K-bar and used the tip to loosen the knot. Granier saw what the trainee was doing and said, "No. Don't do—"

It was too late. The chief elbowed the trainee in the face and grabbed the knife. Stunned, the trainee leaned back, lost his balance, and tumbled out the open helicopter doorway falling through the canopy below. The chief wasted no time, cutting himself free using the trainee's knife, then leaping out the doorway and falling through the jungle canopy. He was gone, swallowed up by the jungle. "Shit," said Granier as he signaled the pilot to turn around.

Granier grabbed a map, located their position, then pointed to the closest landing zone three miles away showing it to the pilot. Tying off a long coil of rope and throwing it out the door, Granier could see his trainees getting ready to follow him. He put his hand out like a dog trainer and said firmly, "Stay."

He was pissed and in no mood to play wet nurse to his trainees. As the helicopter approached the point where the trainee had fallen, Granier slung his sniper rifle over his back, grabbed the rope, and rappelled down through the jungle canopy. He was gone.

Hitting the ground with a thud, Granier drew his sidearm from its holster and wasted no time searching for the trainee. After a few minutes, he found him, dead. His neck had been broken when he hit a branch headfirst. Granier cursed silently, then searched the trainee and found his sidearm was missing. Granier cursed again. The only good news was that the escaped chief that had stolen the pistol was probably close and watching. Granier looked around for signs of the fugitive. There was nothing. Not even footprints. *This guy is good,* he thought.

Granier considered for a moment, then surmised that if the chief left no footprints, he must have used the tree roots to travel across the jungle floor. Smart. Very smart. He studied the possible routes across the tree roots in the area. There were too many leading in different directions to be of much help. Granier took out his compass and glanced at it before returning to survey the jungle. The chief would head back to his village where he would be protected by the other villagers. But Granier doubted he would go directly back. That would be too obvious and dumb. This guy was neither of those.

Granier determined which tree root path was most likely and followed it. He knew he was being watched. If he was heading in the right direction the chief would have no choice but fight or run. Staying put was not an option. Granier kept his sniper rifle shouldered. He was good with a pistol, just not as good as he was with a rifle. Granier was highly trained for this type of hunting. He knew that in a straight-up firefight with pistols, he would be victorious, and the chief would be dead. But that wasn't what he wanted. He wanted the chief alive. He wanted what he knew and who he knew. That was the whole concept behind Phoenix – expand its knowledge base of the enemy network until everything was exposed, then kill it.

Although Granier's eyes mostly focused on the path ahead of him and the surrounding jungle, he took time to glance up at the canopy. Anything was possible. The chief knew this environment far better than he did. He was prepared for anything in any direction. His senses were heightened. Adrenaline kept him safe from surprise.

Granier had been right. The chief was close and was watching. While Granier wasn't heading straight for him, he was advancing in his general direction, and it made the chief anxious. How could this American know where he had gone? He left no footprints. He wondered if the man was some sort of ghost that he didn't know about. Maybe a new American weapon. He wasn't sure but didn't want to find out. The chief was sure he could outrun the American. This was his jungle, and he knew the ground. He bolted from his hiding spot and sprinted through the trees and foliage.

As soon as the chief had moved, Granier spotted him and took off at a full run chasing his prey through the dense jungle. Roots stretched across the jungle floor. Vines hung down from the trees and curled up on the ground like coiled snakes. After four hundred yards of hopping over giant roots, fallen trees, and man-sized boulders, Granier lost sight of the chief. He slowed, then stopped. The valley had narrowed and there were steep slopes of lush green on both sides. A mountain stream flowed through the jungle with foot-high waterfalls and pools of swirling water. The air was thick and hot. He listened, separating the individual sounds of flowing water, bird calls, and the clicks and thwacks of oversized insects. He moved his head around slowly allowing his ears to focus on different areas of the rainforest. He saw nothing. He heard nothing. The chief was close… he could feel him. But where?

Holstering his pistol, Granier unslung his rifle and chambered a round. He was unsure what he was going to do with the weapon, but it felt right. A rifle in his hands always felt right. Granier heard a branch crack above. His attention turned skyward as the chief dropped out of nowhere and hit him in the chest with both feet. Granier fell backward landing on a giant tree root. He had the wind knocked out of him, but he kept moving and climbed to his feet gasping for air. It was the only way to survive. His rifle was gone from his hands, hidden among the tree roots. The chief was in front of him and aimed his pistol. It was an easy shot just a few yards away. The chief pulled the trigger, and nothing happened. Whoever taught him to shoot, must have been using a revolver and didn't teach him about semi-automatics with their need to chamber a round before being able to fire. Granier pulled his sidearm, chambered a round, and aimed at the chief's face. The chief dropped his pistol in surrender.

Granier had lost one of his trainees and was annoyed. He considered shooting the chief to balance the scales. He knew it would be counterproductive, but it would bring some justice to the dead trainee. He decided it was a stupid thought. The trainee was dead and killing the chief wouldn't bring him back. Granier always attempted to leave emotion out of his decisions. Emotions were undependable. But then again… the chief didn't know that. Putting the fear of God into the chief might help things along with the coming interrogation.

Granier walked over and pistol-whipped the chief across the face knocking out two of his rotting teeth. The chief fell to the ground. Blood flowed. He looked up at Granier who looked like a forest demon. Granier grabbed the chief by his animal claw necklace and prepared to hit him again with his pistol. The chief said, "American pilots" as clear as day as if it would stop Granier. It did.

The helicopter blades were still, as was the rest of the aircraft sitting in a jungle clearing. The trainees and aircrew had taken up defensive positions around the clearing each pointing their weapon toward the trees. A voice pierced the silence, "If you shoot me or my captive, I won't be happy."

Moments later, Granier appeared from the jungle with the chief walking in front with the dead trainee's body over his shoulder. Everyone was relieved to see Granier. Nobody wanted the legend to die on their watch. Their joy was tempered by sadness from the sight of their dead comrade trainee. "Just remember," said Granier. "This is what happens when you don't use your common sense and do stupid things." They moved forward and took the trainee's corpse from the chief and carried him to the helicopter. "Is your radio secured?" said Granier.

"Sure," said the pilot. "What's up?"

"The chief says there are three American pilots in a prison camp forty-two miles to the northwest in Laos."

"And you believe him?"

"No. But he gave me the prisoners' last names. It should be easy enough to verify if he's telling the truth. Who knows? We may have gotten lucky."

January 9, 1967 – Ban Naden, Northern Laos

The names of the captured pilots given by the chief matched three American personnel records including an Air America pilot and two US Navy pilots. Fearful that the Americans would be killed during any raid, CIA officials decided to attempt to bribe the guards into releasing the Americans. It didn't work. It alerted the communists that the Americans in their prison camp had been identified. They immediately moved the American prisoners to another prison camp. The CIA lost track of them.

Late in 1966, Blackjack became concerned when a team of three Montagnard warriors watching the Ho Chi Minh Trail failed to report. He sent a squad of fifteen Montagnard to find the watch team. When they returned, the squad leader reported that the watch team was gone from the position they had been assigned. Blackjack and the village chief wanted to find their missing warriors. They sent more teams out to locate them.

One of the teams searching near the Ho Chi Minh Trail captured a Pathet Lao defector and brought him to the village. With a Montagnard warrior armed with his long knife threatening to cut the prisoner's balls off, it didn't take long to get the location of the three missing warriors. They had been captured and were being held in a prison camp near the Laotian village of Ban Naden. The interrogator also discovered that an Air America employee was being held at the same location along with forty captives. According to the defector, forty Pathet Lao guards protected the prison camp. After compiling the information, the CIA believed that the three American pilots and the Montagnard warriors were being held at the same prison camp. There was no way to know for sure without going there and checking it out for themselves.

The CIA began making plans for a heliborne assault to free the prisoners. The problem, of course, was how not to kill the prisoners in the crossfire. After reviewing their options, the CIA planners decided that a quiet ground operation using a small elite force would produce better results and hopefully spare the prisoners' lives.

Because of the potential publicity windfall that would be created if the mission was successful, the CIA did not want any Americans involved in the operation. Technically, the Americans were not supposed to have any military forces in Laos. The CIA planners selected Sergeant Te, a Lao Theung soldier that was raised near Ban Naden, to lead the mission.

An ex-paratrooper, Te was considered the best road watch team leader. The CIA gave Te a free hand to pick his team for the rescue. The team spent two weeks training under tight security. Only Te and his radioman knew the raid's destination. Everyone else was kept in the dark for security reasons. The defector would accompany the team.

On January 5, 1967, the ten men of Team Cobra flew in an Air America Sikorsky H-34 to a landing site two days march to Ban Naden. Even though the team members were in top shape physically, it was a hard slog through dense mountain jungle and crossing multiple fast-moving streams. The triple-canopy jungle and the mountain fog kept the team from being seen as they approached their target.

On January 7, 1967, Team Cobra used a creek bed for cover as it edged toward the camp for observation. When the camp became visible, the team saw a pair of caves at the base of a 400-yard cliff face. The entrances to the caves were five yards across. They could see about twenty prisoners behind a set of bamboo bars in each cave. There were two bamboo huts in front of the cave entrances. They could also see holding cells burrowed in the ground, but they could not see if there were prisoners held in them.

After radioing their base, Cobra Team attacked the camp at 4 AM. The team sniper unit took out one of the guards as the rest of the team advanced killing two more guards.

Seeing their comrades fall and an unknown force charging the camp, the surviving guards broke and disappeared into the surrounding jungle. Te used bolt cutters to sever the chains holding the bamboo bars in place at the cave entrances. After cutting open the sunken cells, Te was surprised to find a total of eighty-two freed prisoners, far more than he had planned. There were no Americans, but they did find Blackjack's three warriors. The team's exit strategy was a heli lift, but the additional prisoners would overload the aircraft waiting at their extraction point.

An urgent radio call was relayed through an aircraft circling overhead. The team needed twice as many helicopters as originally arranged. The problem was not the availability of helicopters, but the availability of pilots. Since both crew members on the Choctaws were qualified pilots, Air America commanders waived the requirement for co-pilots and doubled the number of pilots available. As Te was arranging for more aircraft, some of the released prisoners that lived in the area disappeared into the jungle as they headed for their villages. The load was lightened to fifty-three escaped prisoners needing rescue.

Te knew that the guards that had abandoned their post would be returning with reinforcements. Cobra Team and the escaped prisoners headed for the first extraction point. Many of the prisoners were weak from torture, too little food, and dehydration. They had to be helped by Te's men which meant that many of the team members couldn't protect the group as it traveled through the jungle. If a firefight broke out, Cobra Team would be at a severe disadvantage.

After a half day of rough traveling with too many rest stops, it became obvious to Te that they would never reach either of the planned extraction sites in time. It was just too far for the sick prisoners. The sun was setting, and it would be dark soon. Studying a map, Te decided that the only alternative landing zone was the middle of the Ho Chi Minh Trail. After calling headquarters to change the landing site, the group altered their course and headed for the infamous trail. Te's rear guard spotted a large unit of Pathet Lao coming up fast behind their group. Te stopped for a brief moment to order his rear guard to slow down the pursuers and to radio for air support.

Cobra Team and the prisoners were lucky. A flight of F-4E Phantom IIs had been escorting a flight of bombers in Northern Vietnam and was now returning to their base in Ubon, Thailand. They were only a few dozen miles away and had a full load of ammunition, including 640 20 mm rounds for the M61A1 Vulcan cannon that each aircraft carried in its nose.

Te ran back to his rear guard and warned them to get out of the way. He popped colored smoke and tossed the canister toward the enemy to mark their position for the Phantoms. Having engaged their afterburners, the Phantoms arrived within a minute and unleashed hell on the column of Pathet Lao chasing the escaped prisoners. When the Phantoms finally left, Royal Lao Air Force T-28s entered the area. They strafed and bombed the Pathet Lao who decided they had had enough and broke off their pursuit of the prisoners.

With the threat of attack gone, Te guided his team and the prisoners to an open clearing on the Ho Chi Minh Trail. The Choctaws swooped in and landed. The prisoners and the team were loaded up in the helicopters. The helicopters took off just as the sun set behind the mountains.

The Ban Naden raid was the only successful rescue of Allied prisoners during the Vietnam War. When the CIA debriefed some of the prisoners, they decided to change their focus on the Ho Chi Minh Trail. Instead of just watching and counting the traffic on the trail, the CIA teams began laying ambushes and called in air strikes on targets of opportunity. The teams became much more aggressive. An official account of the raid was never released to the public or media. The raid was classified and used as a case study by the CIA to train their officers.

January 10, 1967 – US Congress, Washington DC, USA

Another year had passed, and President Johnson once again stood before the US Congress and the American people to give his State of the Union address. And once again, the Cold War and the Vietnam War were at the heart of his speech. In part, he said, "...we, the American people and our allies, will and are going to see Vietnam through to an honorable peace.

We will support all appropriate initiatives by the United Nations, and others, which can bring the several parties together for unconditional discussions of peace--anywhere, any time. And we will continue to take every possible initiative ourselves to constantly probe for peace.

Until such efforts succeed, or until the infiltration ceases, or until the conflict subsides, I think the course of wisdom for this country is that we just must firmly pursue our present course. We will stand firm in Vietnam.

I think you know that our fighting men there tonight bear the heaviest burden of all. With their lives, they serve their Nation. We must give them nothing less than our full support--and we have given them that-nothing less than the determination that Americans have always given their fighting men. Whatever our sacrifice here, even if it is more than five dollars a month, it is small compared to their own.

How long it will take I cannot prophesy. I only know that the will of the American people, I think, is tonight being tested.

…let us also count not only our burdens but our blessings--for they are many. And let us give thanks to the One who governs us all.

Let us draw encouragement from the signs of hope--for they, too, are many.

Let us remember that we have been tested before and America has never been found wanting."

No Boy Scout

Saigon, South Vietnam

Lucien Conein was a contradiction… a very useful contradiction. Originally an anti-tank rifle gunner in the French Army, Conein had fled to Southern France when the Nazis overran the French lines and occupied northern France in World War II. It was in the south that he met Mathieu Franchini, a Corsican mob boss working to undermine the Nazis through covert actions. They worked together and became trusted friends.

Conein knew better than to betray Franchini. Corsicans had very long memories and were very patient and violent when it came to revenge. Conein eventually left France for the United States and became an American citizen. He joined the OSS and led a team of saboteurs in Europe and later a team of commandos in Indochina near the end of the war. His superiors found that Conein's talents were best used in paramilitary operations, not espionage or counterintelligence. Conein liked fighting and was surprisingly gifted at planning missions.

Years later when both Franchini and Conein lived in Saigon, Conein was recruited by the CIA and Franchini was put in charge of the Corsican mob's business interests in Indochina. Franchini became Conein's connection to the underworld. The CIA and MACV recognized that Conein's Corsican connection put him in a very unusual and powerful position. Controlling much of the opium trade, the Corsican mobsters were known for having a huge network of spies and smugglers throughout Indochina. Conein made sure that Franchini and the Corsicans were compensated whenever they were asked for information or to carry out a distasteful task.

But Conein was not without his issues. Most American officers either loved him or hated him. There was no in-between with Lucien Conein. He was a belligerent alcoholic and a womanizer with a flair for exaggeration and emotional volatility. He was also thought well on his feet when things did not go as planned. He was often the go-to guy when a mission seemed like it had little chance of success. Conein always found a way to accomplish the impossible. He wasn't afraid to bend the rules, when necessary, which was much of the time. He was a smartass and spoke his mind even with his superiors. He was especially good at sabotage which he had learned firsthand from the Corsicans.

By 1967, Conein was looking for a way out of the CIA. He was forty-seven years old. He had served his country for decades and felt it was time to serve himself and his family. He was a true patriot and let his superiors at the CIA know that he would be leaving soon so they had time to adjust without him. In the meantime, he began shoring up his business connections and planning for the future.

Conein was not involved in the harvesting or

manufacture of opium and its byproduct heroin. Owning and selling the narcotics would put him in competition with the Corsican mob and he was far too smart to fall into that quagmire. Franchini was a friend and protected Conein, but friendship only went so far when money was involved. Conein's talents were in the transportation of raw materials in Southeast Asia and the final product to various markets around the world.

Sitting in a booth at the back of a Corsican restaurant in Saigon's old quarter, Lucien Conein and Mathieu Franchini were in a heated discussion. Not an argument. It wasn't wise to argue with Corsican mobsters. A heavy drinker, Conein was on his third glass of Mitro, a traditional Corsican liqueur, and it didn't look like he was slowing down. "I can't do it, Mathieu. No growing, harvesting, or manufacturing of opium. It's where I draw the line," said Conein.

"And I am not asking you to cross that line. I just want you to talk to the village chief and see if you can convince him to grow more of the poppies. Like an emissary… a go-between as you say," said Franchini. "We are in a spot, Lucien. And we need your help. Our customers are clamoring for more heroin. If we don't get more product into our markets, our competitors will. Then we will have a turf war and that's bad for business."

"I understand, but you got the wrong guy. I hardly even know the chief. I met him once when I first set up the deal. That was years ago, and I haven't seen him since. He has no reason to trust me."

"You have helped his people buy medicine and weapons to protect their families, have you not?"

"Well, yeah… but that's just business."

"Important business. All you would be asking is for his village to make even more money. How can that be bad?"

"Mathieu, you don't know the Montagnard. Money only motivates them so far."

"So, find something they want, and we will trade for it. I know you can do this, Lucien. You have a talent for convincing people."

"Well, I admit I do."

"I know you can't take a cut without violating your ethics, but perhaps there is another way we can compensate you."

"Like what?"

"You could increase your transport fee. Say… three hundred US dollars per pound."

"Seven hundred seems more appropriate."

"Seven hundred is robbery."

"You're right. I shouldn't have brought it up. I just wanted to help you if I could. I apologize, my friend."

"There was no harm in asking. What about five hundred?"

"As I say, I'd like to help… but I have costs too. More product means more risk. Bribes are expensive."

"Of course, of course. Maybe six hundred would be fairer?"

"As you are my dear friend, I accept. But I can't make any promises. I'll talk with the chief and we'll see what happens. But I get my additional transport fee no matter what, yes?"

"You are an asshole, Lucien."

"I think we both know that is true."

"You promise to do your best?"

"Absolutely."

"Then we have a deal," said Franchini shaking

Conein's hand.

Mountains - Laos

Flying over a dense jungle canopy flowing down a mountainside, a Pilatus PC-6 Porter banked toward its final destination – a newly built landing strip in a clearing which were few and far between.

Coyle sat in the pilot's seat with Conein sitting next to him. After the mid-air hijacking that had occurred the year before, Conein had arranged for Coyle's Porter to be modified with two underwing pylons each holding a M260 Rocket Pod. Each pod held seven Hydra-70 rockets designed for air-to-ground support. However, Coyle wanted the rockets to discourage mid-air pirates wanting to steal the opium he carried for Conein. In reality, the 2.75-inch Hydra rockets would not have been very effective against another aircraft because they were unguided, but they made Coyle feel better and they were lightweight, so they didn't diminish the aircraft's load capacity by much.

Conein didn't like flying in the small plane that seemed to creep along just a few yards above the jungle canopy. There was no armor to protect the occupants or the engine from ground fire and crashing in the Laotian mountains was not his idea of fun. But the Porter had a strong design meant to withstand landing on uneven terrain. In addition, the aircraft could carry a lot of cargo for its size. "When we get there, just keep your mouth shut and let me do the talking," said Conein.

"Fine by me," said Coyle. "I thought you stayed out of this kind of thing?"

"I do… normally. I am doing a friend a favor. If it

works out, I will be doubling your loads."

"That's not a good idea. It's hard enough to take off from the side of a mountain as it is."

"Stop your whining. Your compensation will be adjusted for the larger loads."

"You keep forgetting… I ain't doing it for the money."

"I am well aware of why you do it. If I say you fly larger loads then you fly larger loads."

"Blackjack ain't gonna like it. The Montagnard are going to have to cut out a larger runway each time. He's got enough problems keeping them in the fight against the Pathet Lao and NVA as it is."

"Let me worry about that."

"I always do. I'm just the pilot."

"Everybody wants something. I just need to figure out what that is and I own them."

"Interesting view of life."

"Don't be a smartass. I'm not in the mood. How are the new rocket pods working out?"

"Fine, I guess. I've never needed to use them."

"Do you think you can hit the broadside of a barn with those things?"

"A barn… yes. An aircraft moving at 300 miles per hour? That I am not so sure. But if it happens, I promise you I will give the old college try."

"You'd better. If you lose another load of opium, I won't be able to help you. General Pao is not the forgiving type and he's been on edge lately."

"Why do you suppose that is?"

"He doesn't know who he can trust. That's the problem with being a general in Laos… everyone wants your job and the money that goes with it."

"You think another general might kill him?"

"If given the opportunity… absolutely. It's why he keeps his own army around him. And while his men are protecting him, they are not fighting the Pathet Lao. He's already lost the Plain of Jars. It's only a matter of time until they attack his headquarters."

"What happens if they overrun it?"

"Then I'm out of business. His heroin manufacturing facilities are at his headquarters. No heroin, no smuggling."

"That wouldn't be the worst thing."

"It would be for me. I've got plans and they require money."

"You could go home to the United States and finish raising your family."

"I've tried that before. I was bored beyond my wits. I admit it… I am addicted to the action."

"I know the feeling, but still… it would be nice not having people shooting at you all the time."

"Like I said… boring."

A few minutes later, Coyle spotted the new landing strip in a clearing a few miles from the Montagnard village. It was short, only 100 feet, and narrow, barely enough for his wings. Coyle only need fifty feet to land the plane, but taking off was a different matter. The plane would need to clear the top of the jungle canopy surrounding the airfield. Not an easy task with many of the trees over eighty feet tall.

Once he cleared the jungle canopy, he dropped the plane like a rock, then leveled it out at the last second. The wheels hit hard stressing the struts to capacity. The plane slowed quickly as the landing strip was cut and cleared on an uphill slope. He stopped at the end of the landing strip and whipped the plane around for downhill takeoff. Two Montagnard carrying large rocks appeared from the jungle and ran toward the plane. They placed the rocks in front of the wheels to keep the aircraft from rolling. Coyle was always nervous when the Montagnard got anywhere near the plane's spinning prop. But the warriors knew what they were doing. Blackjack had taught them. Coyle shut down the engine.

As Coyle and Conein emerged from the aircraft, Blackjack, the SOG team, and more Montagnard warriors appeared from the jungle. The warriors moved to unload the cargo, mostly ammunition and some boxes of medical supplies, from the aircraft. When they were done, they would load the plane with bags of opium for the second leg of the journey to General Pao's headquarters. The third leg would be bringing the payment for the opium to the Montagnard village, then home to Vietnam. "How's it hanging, Coyle?" said Blackjack shaking his hand.

"Best I can expect, I suppose," said Coyle.

Blackjack turned to Conein but didn't offer him a handshake and said, "What brings you to the mountains, Lou?"

"I'm here to talk with the chief," said Conein.

"About what?"

"None of your damned business."

"I think it is my damned business."

"I set you and your boys up, Blackjack."

"And we are mighty grateful, but that was a long time ago. We've built trust with these people. I don't want to see that fucked up."

"I'm not going to fuck anything up. He'll be happy. You'll see. I'm gonna need you to translate."

"Then I suggest you tell me what this is about."

"Fine. I need the village to double the opium harvest as soon as possible."

"Lou, that's crazy. They would need to cut more fields out of the jungle. There is no more level land within miles from the village."

"I don't care about the logistics. I just want it done and I am willing to pay for it."

"They don't care about money."

"Bullshit. How are they gonna buy their medicine and farm tools?"

"That's just it. They are making enough money the way things are right now. They don't need more."

"If they don't double the harvest, we'll cut them off and find someone who will."

"You're gonna threaten them?"

"If I need to."

"That's not going to go over too well. They don't like threats."

"Blackjack, just take me to the old man and let me worry about the negotiating strategy."

"Okay. Have it your way, Lou."

Blackjack took the lead followed by Conein and Coyle. They disappeared into the jungle.

Montagnard Village, Laos

Conein talked with the village chief through Blackjack. It did not go as planned. The chief was angry and threatening to remove Conein's head with his long knife. Conein didn't panic or even flinch when the blade came close. Blackjack tried to cool down the chief. He wasn't helping. "I think you should leave, Lou."

"I ain't going anywhere until we have a deal."

"He's really angry. I told you threats don't work with him."

"Okay. You were right about that. But everyone wants something. If you want me gone, you'd better figure out what he wants."

Blackjack nodded and turned back to the chief. They had a short conversation that made the chief stop and think for a long moment, then... said something that surprised Blackjack who turned back to Conein and said, "You were right. He does want something."

"Okay. Spit it out. What is it?"

"He wants a car."

"A car? What's he gonna do with a car? There're no roads."

"I imagine he'll sit in it and let his people admire him."

"That's the stupidest thing I've ever heard."

"Do you want me to tell him he said something stupid?"

"No. What kind of car?"

"I don't think it matters much as long as it's American, shiny, and red. He likes red."

"How the hell am I supposed to get a car into the middle of the mountain jungle? Jesus. It's gotta be fifty miles to the closest road."

"More like a hundred," said Blackjack.

"It's a pickle that's for sure," said Coyle. "A Chinook with an underbelly sling might work."

"Yeah. Alright. Tell him he's got a deal."

Blackjack turned to the chief and told him what Conein had said. The chief smiled.

Two weeks later, a red 1965 Ford Mustang glided over the jungle canopy. It was carried by a sling attached to the underbelly of a twin-rotor Boeing CH-47 Chinook. With its 26,000-pound external load capacity, the Chinook had no problem transporting the pony car.

As the helicopter passed over the Ho Chi Minh Trail, dozens of NVA soldiers opened fire with their rifles from below. Most shot at the red car floating overhead and thought it was great fun, something to distract them from the monotonous trek across Laos. Bullets pierced the gas tank, muffler, and oil pan. Fortunately, the Chinook's aircrew had enough forethought to empty the gas tank to prevent a fire or explosion. The idea of carrying a flaming car underneath their aircraft was not something they wished to witness although it would make a great story for their grandchildren if they survived.

After another half hour the red Mustang was slowly lowered into the center of the Montagnard village as Conein and Blackjack watched. "She's a beauty. Where did you find her?" said Blackjack.

"In the Philippines. A warlord had bought himself a nice vehicle collection. I traded him for a Panard Armored car," said Conein.

"Sounds fair."

"He seemed to think so."

Blackjack noticed the bullet holes in the undercarriage and said, "Do you see those?"

"The bullet holes?" said Conein.

"Yeah. I mean… I don't think the chief will care. He doesn't know what a car is supposed to look like from underneath and there is no place to drive it, but still…"

"Best we don't draw attention to the flaws in his new toy."

"I agree."

The red Mustang gently touched down in an area the chief had made by removing a rice storage hut. The suspension bounced for a moment, then the car settled to stop, still and glorious. The SOG team detached the sling, gave the pilot an okay signal, and the helicopter flew off disappearing over a nearby ridge.

With a big grin on his face, the chief climbed into the driver's seat and honked the horn. The villagers gathered around. They had never seen something so fine-looking. The chief's wives fought over who got to sit in the passenger seat. The chief ended the argument by allowing his oldest son the honor. The wives piled into the backseat. The chief had no idea how to start the car which was a good thing because the gas tank and oil pan were empty. It didn't matter. He was satisfied with the vehicle that brought him great honor among the hill tribes. No other chief had a red car.

Conein let the chief play with his new toy for an hour then had Blackjack remind him that he needed to keep his half of the bargain and have his villagers clear another field to grow more poppies. The chief wasn't happy being interrupted but grunted orders to his people. They grabbed their tools and headed into the jungle followed by Conein and the SOG team. Conein wanted to make sure that the field was cut and cleared properly. His reputation with the Corsicans was riding on the expanded opium harvest.

The chief and his family stayed in the Mustang. His son found the cigarette lighter in the console and pushed it. Moments later it popped outward. The boy removed it and showed his father the glowing coil. The chief was proud until the boy touched the red-hot coil and burned the tip of his finger dropping the lighter onto the passenger seat and burning a hole into the leather. He whacked the boy on the head and told him to get out which reignited the fight among the wives on who got to sit in the passenger seat.

Pershing

Armor was the great force equalizer in most modern conflicts, but not in Vietnam. At least not in the countryside. Tanks were almost useless during the monsoon season when the roads and trails turned to a grayish sludge, and the rice paddies filled to the brim turning the entire countryside into a series of muddy square ponds surrounded by soggy dikes.

Beyond its mobility drawbacks, armor protected soldiers and reduced casualties. It also helped win battles. The armor commanders did their best to keep their units moving, so the enemy could not hunt them down with their recoilless rifles and Type 51 Chinese bazookas. Movement meant survival during battle, especially for armor.

In Vietnam, tanks like the M48 Patton were mostly used in urban environments where they could fight or protect on solid ground. But fighting in a city was not the best use of tanks. With a 90 mm cannon as its main armament and a speed of thirty mph, the Patton fought better at a distance than close up.

In the countryside, most commanders preferred using M113s which could cross shallow rivers and wouldn't get bogged down in rice paddies. Its main armament, the M2 Browning machine gun tore through the jungle and most huts like they were paper. It also could transport fifteen soldiers to the battlefield in relative safety. It wasn't a tank, but it was more effective in most cases.

A World War II combat veteran that was awarded the Distinguished Service Cross for valor, General William Rosson was the commanding general of I Field Force, a corps-level command with its base in Nha Trang. Under the authority of MACV, I Field Force was responsible for twelve provinces in Vietnam's Central Highlands. He was also in charge of Operation Pershing designed to hunt down and wipe out the NVA 3rd Division (aka the Yellow Star Division) and take control of Bong Son Plain and the An Lao Valley.

Much of the terrain in the Bong Son and An Lao was flat and could make good use of armor. But as his troops would move more towards the mountains, Rosson was concerned with snipers and ambushes. He asked Westmoreland for tanks to protect his troops and bulldozers to collapse any enemy bunkers they might encounter. M113 with shielded gun turrets would keep his troops and their field commanders protected against snipers. Using the M113 more like a light tank rather than just a troop transport vehicle, the ARVN had redesigned their "tracks" with multiple gun turrets. The US commanders liked the idea so much that they ordered all their M113s to be modified following the South Vietnamese design. The gas engines in the armor transports had also been replaced with more fuel-efficient and fire-resistant diesel engines. The engineer companies would provide and operate the bulldozers Rosson had requested but would need to be transported to battle by Sikorsky CH-54 helicopters.

The armor would slow the operation, but Rosson

figured it was worth it. Besides, he had 1st Cavalry and their helicopters if he needed to jump ahead and surround the enemy once encountered. Tanks and helicopters were a mean combination when dealing with the NVA and Viet Cong. Westmoreland gave him 1st Battalion, a mechanized battalion from the 50th Infantry Regiment. In addition to the mechanized battalion, Rosson had the 1st Cavalry Division, the 3rd Brigade, 25th Infantry Division, the Army of the Republic of Vietnam (ARVN) 22nd Division, and the South Korean Capital Division all taking part in the operation.

The 1967 Tet Holiday ceasefire had not yet ended when Operation Pershing began. Rosson reasoned that the NVA and Viet Cong had not kept to the conditions of the ceasefire in the area and the allied task force was entitled to a leeway of nineteen hours before the ceasefire officially ended. The North Vietnamese would launch a complaint with the U.N. but by the time it was filed it would be too late and the operation would be underway.

The operation kicked off at 11 am on 11 February with waves of helicopters flying north. Surprised by the aerial assault, many enemy soldiers were caught fleeing from their hamlets without their weapons. As they attempted to escape into the jungle, American gunships hovering overhead cut them down. The Americans were intent on eliminating as many enemy soldiers as possible before the real conflicts began. No mercy was shown, and none was expected in return. Many VC and NVA hid until dark before trying to escape into the jungle. Patience saved their lives.

Cavalrymen from the 2nd Brigade leaped from their transport helicopters and searched the hamlets looking for enemy soldiers and collaborators. The allied troops were making few friends of the civilian villagers who were rounded up and interrogated at gunpoint.

Carried by CH-54s, bulldozers were unloaded on the Bong Son Plain. Guided by the allied troops that had engaged the enemy, the bulldozers collapsed tunnels, bunkers, and huts often crushing the enemy inside with their heavy metal treads. With the operators protected from gunfire by the thick steel blades and enclosed armored-plated cabs, the bulldozers were an unstoppable force that the enemy had not counted on and was unprepared to defend against.

Some of the enemy soldiers captured and interrogated indicated that there were large numbers of their comrades hiding nearby as they waited to do battle with the Allied troops. 2nd Brigade continued the search but made no heavy contact. The Allied forces were slowed down by throngs of civilians fleeing the area.

The Viet Cong in the area covered the withdrawal of the NVA soldiers which also slowed the Allied advance. Fifty NVA were killed on the first day of Operation Pershing, but as the search continued the following days the enemy body count decreased dramatically. Well-hidden bobby traps and mines along the trails going to and from the hamlets accounted for a high number of Allied casualties. Within a week, the Americans were losing one soldier killed for every enemy soldier killed. It was not a kill ratio Rosson found acceptable. Operation Pershing had been designed as a lightning strike deep in the enemy's territory but was quickly turning into another drawn-out sweep with little results.

As the second week of the operation commenced, a rifle company from Smith's 1st Brigade encountered the NVA 9th Battalion from the 22nd Regiment entrenched in the fortified hamlet of Tuy An. The sun was setting when the battle began. It made it difficult for the company and reinforcing units to encircle the enemy or even determine its size. Artillery pounded the enemy positions as darkness descended. Around midnight the gunfire ceased, and the Americans lost contact with the enemy.

In the morning, the Americans entered the hamlet and found six enemy bodies in the rubble. The hamlet was destroyed. The allies did discover a few documents left behind that included sketches of the Landing Zone English and the Lai Giang bridge. The results of the battle were far from glorious. Nine days later, Smith's brigade tangled with a company from the NVA 9th Battalion and killed another nineteen enemy soldiers. Throughout February, the enemy continued to be elusive and there was little fighting.

At the beginning of March, two air cavalry helicopters were on patrol north of Tra O Marsh, twelve miles southeast of LZ English. One of the pilots spotted a man disappearing into a foxhole just outside of Hoa Tan hamlet. While one helicopter hovered in an overwatch position, the other landed and the door gunner jumped out in hopes of capturing the man for questioning. Heavy rifle fire erupted from a nearby hedgerow. The helicopter hovering above returned fire. An enemy bullet pierced the landed helicopter's hydraulic system. Leaving the door gunner behind, the pilot was able to get the damaged helicopter into the air but only for a short time. It was forced to land again

800 yards away surrounded by sand dunes. The second helicopter kept the enemy away from the stranded door gunner as the co-pilot radioed for help. Lieutenant Colonel Pumphrey, the commander of the 1st Squadron, 9th Cavalry, ordered reinforcements to save the abandoned door gunner.

Gunships arrived on site and opened fire on the enemy position. A rifle team in one of the helicopters landed and rescued the door gunner. While the gunships kept the enemy pinned, the rifle team investigated the hamlet and was met with heavy gunfire. More reinforcements were called in and five allied rifle companies surrounded the hamlet as fighter-bombers, gunships, and artillery kept the enemy pinned down. Darkness once again descended on the battlefield forcing the aircraft back to their bases. The artillery barrage continued through the night as the five rifle companies kept a close watch on the hamlet.

When morning arrived, the Americans entered the hamlet of Hoa Tan and only found one enemy soldier which they quickly captured. The rest had either fled during the night or had been killed. The prisoner revealed that the headquarters of the 9th Battalion, 18th Regiment along with two rifle companies had been stationed in the hamlet but were able to escape in the darkness. Seven Americans along with 82 NVA soldiers had been killed during the brief battle.

Throughout March, there were several skirmishes between the Americans and the NVA and Viet Cong. But Rosson's main target of the NVA 22nd Regiment remained elusive. The enemy commanders refused to engage with the Americans. The only reason Rosson could find to explain the NVA commander's shyness was that the Americans had struck the area with such swiftness that they had scattered the NVA units. The communist units had not yet reformed and were therefore understrength. Rosson thought his enemy counterpart to be a coward waiting for the conditions to be perfect before accepting battle. But Rosson had to admit avoiding battle was an effective strategy that tied up a major part of two US Divisions searching for an enemy that refused to be found. It wasn't until the end of the rainy season that the Viet Cong and NVA began offensive operations against the Americans and even those were slow to start.

During April, the American 3rd Brigade swept through the An Lao Valley in hopes of tracking down the headquarters of the NVA 3rd Division. And again, aside from a few short skirmishes that produced anemic body counts, the results of the sweep were negative. Rosson was frustrated as hell but there was little he could do except to continue the search someplace else in the hopes that eventually one of his units would stumble upon the main force of Viet Cong and NVA. He hated fighting that way, assault by blindman's bluff. With the majority of his battalions being shifted away to support other divisions that had come in contact with the enemy, Rosson should have been more careful in what he was asking for… even though they were still in hiding, the NVA and Viet Cong forces were on the rise with the replacement troops filling in the gaps. Colonel Thu, the new 3rd Division commander was preparing for battle.

Thu set his troops in motion sending the 22nd Regiment to resume its attacks north of the Lai Giang River, while the 2nd Regiment advanced south of the river and the 18th Regiment deployed to carry out operations against the South Koreans. During the long rainy season, Thu had been conserving his troops and resources so he could hit the allies with powerful punches from multiple directions overwhelming the enemy's artillery and air power. Not even the Americans could be in all places all the time. Something had to give, and Thu was prepared to exploit any breach in the Allied defenses. His troops were anxious to make the Americans bleed.

As the Americans entered the Song Re Valley in Quang Ngai Province, fifteen miles west of Ba To, they encountered a narrow valley with highly cultivated rice paddies and pens with well-fed livestock. What made the Americans feel uneasy was that there were no people to attend the rice paddies or livestock. Something or someone had driven them off, perhaps warning them that there would be a fierce battle in their valley. Whatever happened, the farmers had left in a hurry leaving their livestock behind.

The Americans advanced cautiously through the valley, each battalion leapfrogging over the other battalions. With each movement, they redeployed their firebases and set them up before advancing again. It was slow going... cautious going...

For two days the Americans did not find the enemy, but they felt they were being watched at a distance and stayed prepared for anything. Just as the American commanders were about to declare the search another failure, a cavalry company conducted an air assault on three small hills called Landing Zone Pat, eleven miles from Gia Vuc. As the last of six helicopters unloaded their troops and lifted off the landing zone, the enemy opened fire with heavy machine guns. Enemy bullets ripped through the metal panels and windows of all the helicopters. Three of the choppers crashed, while the other three escaped the barrage and flew back to Gia Vuc.

On the ground, the NVA and VC swarmed the company attacking it from all sides. Caught midway up one of the hills, the isolated American soldiers formed a defensive perimeter as their commander, Captain Raymond Bluhm radioed for artillery and air strikes.

Knowing there wasn't much time until the American aircraft would attack, the enemy troops pounded the American company with everything they had taking a heavy toll. They had been right and shortly after Bluhm's radio call, artillery shells rained down on the enemy positions taking their toll and keeping the NVA and VC pinned down, unable to continue their attack on the Americans. There was little doubt in anyone's mind that the company of Americans would have faced extinction had it not been for the very accurate artillery barrages.

Four hours later, the firefight ended with the communists vanishing. The Americans had suffered eleven killed and twenty-seven wounded. Only a few enemy bodies and no wounded were found. The battle had been brief but fierce.

Although the Allied forces continued to sweep through the enemy territory, they found nothing. The enemy had once again gone into hiding and the Americans knew little more about the enemy's position than when they had started their sweep. After having been encouraged by the ambush of LZ Pat, General Rosson had once again been disappointed.

Intelligence indicated that the NVA were planning to attack 1st Cavalry Division logistic installations before the approaching South Vietnamese presidential elections. The Americans assumed that the NVA would attack LZ English which was the largest logistical air base south of the Bong Son Plain and just north of Lai Giang. Instead, the communist forces chose to attack the American division's forward command post on LZ Two Bits, a few miles south of LZ English.

Just before midnight on August 22nd, the Americans guarding the perimeter of LZ Two Bits detected enemy movement and suspected they were about to be attacked. To trick the communists into revealing their positions, the commander of the defense force ordered a Mad Minute, where the soldiers would fire every weapon they had for one minute even if they didn't have a target in their sights. It worked.

The communist units responded to the random Allied gunfire with a fifteen-minute barrage of recoilless rifles, mortar fire, and heavy machine guns. The Americans quickly learned what they were facing and called in artillery strikes and gunships. Once again, the communists broke off their attack and disappeared into the surrounding countryside.

On September 14th, an understrength 3rd Brigade finally found the headquarters of the NVA 22nd Regiment in a narrow draw at the mouth of the An Lao Valley, eleven miles northwest of LZ English. Unfortunately for Rosson, the headquarters had been quickly abandoned. No NVA or VC were killed or captured. The American forces did find a large stockpile of crew-served weapons and ammunition, plus a long-range radio and code books. But it was a shallow consolation prize.

Because it had only been planned to destroy an enemy division, Operation Pershing had become a sideshow as MACV stripped away more and more of Rosson's battalion to fight elsewhere. Unwilling to give up, Rosson continued his search for the NVA 3rd Division which had become his white whale. In mid-November, Rosson finally found his nemesis.

Analyzing intercepted radio transmissions, Army intelligence reported that the 22nd Regiment was preparing to move from Quang Ngai Province to the Bong Son Plain. Rosson sent multiple units to locate the regiment as it moved back into the Bong Son Plain.

Just after midnight on December 6th, the 22nd Regiment sent one of its battalions to attack LZ Tom, an ARVN landing zone seven miles north of LZ English. A US radio research unit incepted transmissions from the battalion commander and 22nd Regiment headquarters. The US radio research unit was able to pinpoint the headquarters location to Dai Dong, a village southeast of LZ Tom. The village had four hamlets. A reconnaissance helicopter spotted a long radio antenna protruding from a bunker near Hamlet Dai Dong #2.

An American Blue Team from 1st Battalion, 9th Cavalry Division was hele-lifted into the area and landed in a field west of the hamlet. The rifle reconnaissance team immediately came under heavy fire from the hamlet and was pinned down. A second Blue Team was flown in. They too came under heavy fire and were pinned down. Somebody was serious about keeping the Americans away from that hamlet.

At 6 PM, the 1st Battalion, 8th Cavalry Regiment landed near the hamlet and linked up with 1st Battalion, 50th Infantry Regiment which had arrived in M113 armored vehicles. Together, the two battalions were able to rescue the two Blue Teams and encircle the hamlet with a tight perimeter. Darkness descended and they dug in for the night.

The next morning, more troops from the 8th Cavalry Regiment arrived, along with ARVN 40th Regiment, 22nd Division. As the new troops moved into place around the perimeter, the hamlet was hit with aerial rockets and artillery. The allied troops waited as aircraft and artillery softened up the enemy troops within the hamlet with a relentless bombardment.

At 2 PM, the 8th Regiment assaulted the communists using flamethrower APCs to clear out trenches and fortified firing positions. The allies broke through the communists' defensive line but were unable to advance deeper into the hamlet as enemy machine gun and recoilless rifle fire intensified. The Allied forces took their time and kept their siege ring intact. Their commanders' most important objective was to not let the communists escape. As the fighting continued, darkness again descended, and everyone dug in for the night as tracer rounds crisscrossed overhead.

The next morning, the Allies pumped CS gas into the enemy positions. The potent tear gas drove many of the NVA and VC from their trench and out into the open where they were gunned down by Hueys hoovering above the hamlet. With most of the communists wounded or dead, the ARVN 50th Regiment began a sweep of the area destroying any remaining enemy positions. Once the sweep was completed, the ARVN troops withdrew to LZ English which was still believed to be an NVA target for attack in the coming days.

At 5 AM the following day, the ARVN 3rd and 4th

Battalions of the 40th Regiment came under attack from the 8th Battalion, 22nd Regiment near Highway 1 and LZ Tom. Gunships and artillery helped repel the attack. But the ARVN were not eager to let the communists flee. They carried out a series of counterattacks and pursued the NVA and VC as they tried to break contact. It was the ARVN that had the communists by the belt and they wouldn't let go without a fight.

Allied intelligence received reports of villagers fleeing Truong Lam #2 Hamlet. The American 1st Battalion, 12th Cavalry Regiment joined ARVN 5th Regiment as they investigated the report and searched Truong Lam. At 10:55 AM, the 1st Battalion, 12th Regiment came under heavy enemy fire from Truong Lam #1 Hamlet. US 12th Cavalry was quick to assist in attacking the hamlet's flanks. The combined allied forces made three assaults on the hamlet but were unable to break through the enemy's defenses. They backed off to incircle the hamlet and once again let the artillery and gunships soften up the enemy positions. As darkness approached the gunships left the area, but the artillery barrage continued throughout the night.

The next morning, US 12th Cavalry assaulted Truong Lam #2 with only sporadic resistance. US 2nd Battalion, 8th Cavalry set up blocking positions and ambushed multiple communist units as they tried to escape to the south.

The ARVN 40th Regiment was relieved by the South Vietnamese 3rd and 4th Marine Battalions. The combined allied forces began sweeps of the area. In the late morning, the Allies engaged the communists once again and quickly overran their positions. From that point, contact between the Allies and communists broke off except for a few small skirmishes. General Rosson was determined to keep the pressure on the 3rd Division now that he had found one of its main elements.

Three days later, the 1st Battalion, 12th Cavalry once again located 22nd Regiment. An intense firefight broke out. The Americans backed off to a blocking position and called in artillery and aerial strikes. During the day, the ARVN 40th Regiment and elements of the US 8th Cavalry arrived to reinforce US 12th Cavalry. Outnumbered and being pounded by Allied artillery and gunships, the communists broke out of the hamlet and retreated into the countryside with Allied gunships, cavalry, and infantry elements chasing after them. The allies were relentless causing as many enemy causalities as possible. As the sun set, the communists broke off contact with the Allies and escaped.

Three days later, the 9th Cavalry once again located the 22nd Regiment near the village of An Nghiep. Aerial reconnaissance located a long antenna emerging from a large bunker complex. Elements of the US 8th Cavalry were flown in to reinforce the 9th Cavalry. Together, the two Cavalry units supported by artillery and aircraft attacked the communist bunker complex. As the battle intensified, more allied troops were flown in to establish blocking positions. Throughout the night, the artillery continued its attack on the communist bunker.

The next morning, the Americans swept through the village of An Nghiep meeting no resistance. When they approached the bunker complex there was no enemy gunfire, only twisted and torn bodies. The bunker complex had been completely destroyed by the American artillery.

The Americans had lost fifty-eight killed and 250 wounded while the ARVN had thirty killed and seventy-one wounded. The communist forces had 650 killed and thirty-one captured. Operation Pershing was finally considered a success with a total of 5,401 North Vietnamese and VC killed against 882 Allied troops killed and twenty-two missing. The NVA 3rd Division was considered combat ineffective. After almost a year of searching, General Rosson and the allies had finally caught their white whale.

Fall

February 21, 1967 – Street Without Joy, South Vietnam

Born in Austria to Jewish parents, Bernard Fall moved with his family to France after Austria was annexed by Nazi Germany. When France fell to the Nazis in 1940, Fall's father joined the French Resistance. His father was captured, tortured, and killed by the Gestapo. His mother was deported, and he never heard from her again.

Two years later at the age of sixteen, Fall followed his father's example and joined the French Resistance. The teenager fought the Germans in the Alps. When France was liberated in 1944, Fall joined the French Army until the war ended. He was awarded the French Liberation Medal. After the war, Fall worked as an analyst for the Nuremberg War Crimes Tribunal and helped investigate Krupp Industries, a 400-year-old German dynasty known for its steel, artillery, ammunition, and other armaments.

Fall studied at the University of Paris, then attended the University of Munich. After completing his undergraduate studies, Fall was awarded a Fulbright Scholarship and earned his Ph.D. at Syracuse

University in the United States. Fall continued his postgraduate studies at Johns Hopkins School for Advanced International Studies where one of his professors suggested he study Indochina because of his French background.

Unwilling to study Indochina from afar, Fall traveled to Vietnam where the First Indochina War was being fought between the French Union forces and the Viet Minh. Because he had French citizenship, Fall was allowed to accompany French soldiers and pilots into enemy territory. After observing the French and the Viet Minh fighting for over a year, Fall correctly predicted that the French would eventually lose the war. When the French garrison at Dien Bien Phu was overrun by the Viet Minh, Fall blamed the defeat on the Americans saying that the United States did not properly support the French during the war.

After returning to the United States, he taught international relations at Howard University. But his fascination with Southeast Asia didn't end. Receiving several grants from various organizations, he traveled back to the region five times to study developments in the rise of communism. In 1962, Fall was invited to interview Ho Chi Minh in Hanoi. He accepted the offer willingly. During the interview, Ho Chi Minh suggested that communism would prevail in South Vietnam in about a decade. He was off by three years.

What made Fall special was that he was a political scientist that had once been a soldier. He spoke the language of soldiers and shared the soldiers' lives on the frontline. He slogged through the rice paddies and jungles of Vietnam with the French, American, and ARVN units. He combined his academic analysis of the Indochina and Vietnam Wars with the soldier's perspective on the battlefield. He also spoke with intelligence to political leaders and generals. He wrote eight books on the Indochina and Vietnam Wars and spoke at hundreds of lectures while he was back in the United States or traveling around the world. Fall was considered the most prominent Western authority on Southeast Asia.

Fall supported America's military presence in South Vietnam and Laos. He believed that the Americans could save Vietnam from falling into communism. But he was also an outspoken critic of South Vietnam's government, especially under President Diem's American-backed regime. He criticized the tactics used by the American military in Vietnam.

As the war escalated, Fall became increasingly pessimistic. He saw that the American military was not learning from the French mistakes and that history would most likely repeat itself once again. Finally, in 1964, Fall predicted that America would lose to the Viet Cong and North Vietnamese. Fall's research was invaluable to many American military officials and diplomats. Fall's dire prediction about the war caught the attention of the Federal Bureau of Investigation which started monitoring his activities both at home and abroad.

It was hard to argue with Fall's conclusion because his writing was well-documented with accurate and comprehensive data. In Colin Powell's 1995 autobiography, *My American Journey*, he wrote:

"I recently reread Bernard Fall's book on Vietnam, *Street Without Joy*. Fall makes painfully clear that we had almost no understanding of what we had gotten ourselves into. I cannot help thinking that if President Kennedy or President Johnson had spent a quiet weekend at Camp David reading that perceptive book, they would have returned to the White House Monday morning and immediately started to figure out a way to extricate ourselves from the quicksand of Vietnam."

By 1967, Fall was suffering from retroperitoneal fibrosis which resulted in the loss of a kidney and severe back pain. As he departed on his final trip to Vietnam, his wife, Dorothy, saw that his condition had created a sense of fatalism within Fall. She was understandably worried that he was returning to the battlefields of Vietnam in such a state. But Fall was not to be deterred from his quest to understand the war.

Once in Vietnam, he joined the 1st Battalion, 9th Marines on Operation Chinook II in the Street Without Joy, Thua Thien Province. Distracted by a Marine photographer that had been assigned to him, Fall stepped on a "Bouncing Betty" mine. The mine was launched three feet in the air and exploded blowing off Fall's left leg and most of his right. His wounds were fatal, and he died shortly after the explosion as Marine Corpsmen tried to save his life. The photographer with him was also killed. The tape recorder he was using at the moment of his death recorded his last words, "We've reached one of our phase lines after the firefight and it smells bad—meaning it's a little bit suspicious... Could be an amb—"

(Note: Bernard Fall's book *Hell in a Very Small Place* inspired this author to write The Airmen Series. Thank you, Bernard.)

Second Battle of Bau Bang

March 19, 1967 – Ap Bau Bang, South Vietnam

The First Battle of Bau Bang took place in November 1965 and was the first major American battle in the Vietnam War using armored vehicles. Two Viet Cong regiments overran an American defensive position protected by M113s. The Americans were able to drive back the VC and regain control of their position. Both sides claimed victory. In March 1967, the Viet Cong and NVA were ready for round two…

The commander of Troop A, 5th Cavalry Regiment was Captain Raoul Alcala, a West Point graduate. Although the young captain had been commanding armored units for five years, he didn't have much battle experience beyond a few skirmishes. But then again, few armor commanders had battle experience in Vietnam. If significant armor, especially tanks, was part of any force the VC or NVA were planning to attack, their plans quickly changed once the armor was discovered. Having little armor of their own, the communists in Vietnam had little experience fighting armor and avoided it like the plague. Based on after-battle results, it was a wise move.

With 129 men, six M48 tanks, three 4.2 mortar carriers, and twenty M113 armored personnel carriers, Alcala's unit was deployed within Fire Support Base 20 in Tay Ninh Province to the west of Saigon. FSB 20 was one mile outside the village of Ap Bau Bang west of Route 13. It was surrounded by mostly flat terrain which made it ideal for armor. The area was also known for being a Viet Cong stronghold. Alcala's mission was to defend B Battery of the 7th Battalion, 9th Artillery Regiment under the command of Captain Duane Marion. Upon arrival, the armored vehicles positioned themselves along the perimeter like a circular wagon train defense, each vehicle capable of supporting its neighboring vehicles. The Americans were expecting an attack.

An abandoned railway ran twenty yards to the east and parallel to Route 13. There was a rubber plantation to the south of the base and wooded areas to the north and west. Both Alcala and Marion suspected the Viet Cong would launch their attacks from the plantation or wooded areas since they were the only nearby cover. It was an obvious assault plan that played to the Americans' advantage since the VC would need to advance in the open while under bombardment of an overabundance of artillery.

Alcala sent his 2nd platoon to lay out an ambush on a frequently used trail by the VC. The position of the ambush was one mile north of the fire support base.

The perimeter of the firebase was manned by 1st Platoon commanded by First Lieutenant Roger Festa to the west and 3rd Platoon to the east commanded by Second Lieutenant Hiram Wolfe.

At 10:50 PM, the Viet Cong began probing attacks using fifteen belled cattle driven northeast of the fire support base perimeter to distract the Americans as the Viet Cong moved into position.

Ten minutes later, the Viet Cong opened fire with a wheel-mounted .50-caliber machine gun positioned to the northeast and using the railway embankment for cover.

One of the American tanks turned its turret-mounted searchlight on the machine gun, aimed, and fired its cannon. After just a few shots, the enemy machine gun was destroyed, and the enemy gun crew was killed.

A lull in fighting followed the brief first engagement. The tank of 2nd Lt. Wolfe conducted reconnaissance by fire in the woods to the east. The idea was to get the enemy to return fire and reveal their position and strength. After a few minutes, the tank ceased fire with no results. The enemy was disciplined and didn't fire back at the tank. The Americans reverted to infrared devices to find the enemy. That tactic didn't work well either. The Americans just had to wait until the enemy attacked. It didn't take long…

Just past midnight, the Viet Cong resumed their attack using mortars, rifle grenades, rockets, and recoilless rifles. The Americans returned fire wherever they saw a mortar or muzzle flash. Tracer rounds and rockets streaked across the night sky. Illumination rounds from the American mortars lit up the area surrounding the fire base in an eerie yellow-green.

To the west, 1st Lt. Festa's M113 was hit by a VC recoilless rifle round and his sergeant was wounded. Smoke filled the vehicle. The Americans on the ground protected the soldiers inside their damaged vehicle as they continued to fight using the .50-caliber machine gun on the shielded gun turret. Together, they kept the VC from overrunning their position, driving them back to cover.

Alcala requested more artillery support to destroy the VC's mortar positions which had been located in an abandoned village one mile west of the FSB. The enemy mortars had been located by radar from Lai Khe and confirmed by aerial observation. The American officer commanding the artillery battery thought the airborne artillery observers were more accurate than the radar operators after having seen the mortar tube flashes. He adjusted his howitzer fire accordingly.

If the VC had time, they dug shallow foxholes next to their mortar positions which they would use during heavy enemy artillery attacks. The temporary foxholes were far from perfect, but they did protect a crew from being wiped out by counterfire. When the bombardment concluded, the VC mortar fire had decreased but was still active.

Two more M113s were hit destroying the vehicles and wounding several Americans. Two tanks from the 3rd Platoon were hit but not heavily damaged. Since most of the battle was being carried out at a distance, it was difficult for the Americans to gauge what effect their tanks and artillery were having on the enemy. Regardless, they kept up their counterfire hoping to take out the enemy's mortars which were ripping up the Fire Support Base and wounding the Americans.

A short time after the anti-tank fire and mortar attack began, the VC commenced their ground assault. The main enemy effort came from the south and southeast from Viet Cong that had been hidden in the rubber plantation. The enemy's main assault was accompanied by another ground assault from the north. The surviving enemy mortars covered the Viet Cong advance toward the firebase perimeter.

Realizing that the main attack had begun, Alcala

ordered 1st and 3rd platoons to return to the firebase. Moments later he recalled 2nd Platoon from its ambush position to also return to the FSB perimeter. When his superiors radioed to get an update, Alcala responded that he was confident that with all his forces concentrated within the perimeter, his men and armor could repel the enemy assaults but asked that reinforcements be ready on short notice if needed. His commanders agreed.

As 3rd Platoon returned to the firebase, Wolfe spotted movement in the darkness. He called in a request for a large flare from a 4.2-inch mortar. When the flare illuminated the area, the Americans saw a large number of VC crossing Route 13 east to west. Wolfe's platoon fired on the VC, and they dove for cover. A short time later an AC-47 Spooky gunship and a team of helicopter gunships arrived to aid Wolfe's platoon. The aircraft opened fire on the enemy keeping them pinned and unable to advance or retreat while Wolfe's platoon kept pounding their position.

The Viet Cong broke through the southwestern perimeter and swarmed over some of the M113s that were buttoned up like mini fortresses. The VC tried to force grenades into the firing portholes but to no avail. The crew and troops inside were safe. A nearby modified M113 with a cannon fired canister rounds at M113s under siege. The canister rounds did not pierce the M113s armor but cleared off the VC. Suffering high losses, the enemy quickly retreated.

As the enemy retreated, a VC heavy mortar round scored a direct hit on one of the APCs killing one crew member and wounding several others. The armored vehicle was destroyed. A short time later, Wolfe's APC took a second hit from an RPG-2 anti-tank rocket wounding the entire crew including Wolfe. They evacuated the smoking track which was out of the fight for the duration.

As 2nd Platoon reentered the firebase perimeter, they were hit by enemy recoilless rifles and grenades. Several Americans were wounded, but none were killed. The survivors took up covered positions inside the perimeter and joined the battle, pouring gunfire and tossing grenades at the VC wave trying to overrun the compound.

Moving along Route 13 as they returned to the fire support base, the armored vehicles of Troop C of 3rd Platoon came under heavy enemy fire. Before entering the firebase perimeter, Alcala ordered the troop to sweep west in front of the rubber plantation defenders, firing on the enemy hidden in the trees. Once they completed their initial pass, the vehicles turned and fired again as they sped past the defensive line. They entered the FSB perimeter to the southwest and took up positions between Troop A's vehicles. The fire base's perimeter was gaining much need firepower as each platoon returned. In fact, it was getting crowded. At 2:20 AM, Alcala ordered a counterattack which he used to expand the firebase's perimeter by forty yards on all sides.

A team of VC tried to remove the .50-caliber machine gun from one of the burning M113s. Seeing the raiders' silhouettes, the Americans opened fire and killed all of them. Still, another VC team stormed the foxholes where many of the American wounded had hidden after their APC had been destroyed. The Americans fought back. Seeing their comrades in trouble, a nearby APC joined the fight forcing the VC to retreat and saving the wounded Americans. Under the protection of the APC, the wounded were evacuated back into the perimeter.

At 3 AM, the VC attacked the southern perimeter once again. The VC stopped twenty yards from the perimeter and took up firing positions. Behind them, an unarmed group of VC carrying ropes with hooks recovered their fallen from the battlefield.

The Americans showed no mercy and poured on gunfire killing whoever they could. Gunships and air strikes from fighters attacked from the darkness above. The Americans had not begun this fight, but once it started, they had no intention of letting the Viet Cong retreat without severe punishment. That battle on the southern perimeter continued for four hours with the VC taking heavy losses.

The American armored vehicles were using up huge amounts of ammunition throughout the night. Each APC and tank had to be completely resupplied with ammunition two to three times during the battle. Expended brass casings were scattered everywhere around the firebase. And still, the Viet Cong continued their assault.

At 3:30 AM, the gunfire eased. The Americans used the seventy-five-minute lull to evacuate their wounded and resupply the units around the perimeter.

At 4:50 AM, the VC massed on the south and southeastern side of the base. Ten minutes later, they attacked in force. The enemy human wave was met with artillery, cluster bombs, napalm, and 500-pound bombs. That final assault ended a short time later with the Viet Cong retreating from the battlefield and disappearing into the surrounding trees.

During the battle, the Americans claimed to have killed 227 Viet Cong and captured 3. There were also extensive blood trails leaving the battlefield which meant that the VC had carried away many more of their dead and wounded. The Americans reported that they had lost three killed and sixty-three wounded. They had also expended 3,000 rounds of artillery and twenty-nine tons of ordnance. The Viet Cong claimed they had killed over 400 Americans and destroyed sixty-three armored vehicles. As usual, the truth from both sides was somewhere in between.

Following the battle, General Hay send a letter translated into Vietnamese to the 9th Division commander. The letter was duplicated into leaflets and dropped by aircraft in a Viet Cong-controlled area. It read:

"This is to advise you that during the battle of Ap Bau Bang on 20 March the Regimental Commander of Q763 (273d Regiment) and his Battalion Commanders disgraced themselves by performing in an un-soldierly manner. During this battle with elements of this Division and attached units, your officers failed to accomplish their mission and left the battlefield covered with dead and wounded from their units. We have buried your dead and taken care of your wounded from this battle."

The Offer

Chau Doc, South Vietnam

The names of suspected communists that need to be captured and aggressively interrogated were piling up on Granier's desk. He and his team were victims of their success. The CIA and South Vietnamese Intelligence wanted more than Granier could deliver. He and his team did their best, but it just wasn't enough. Something had to be done…

Granier and his team had tracked Liem Van Duy, a local government official suspected of being a communist recruiter to Chau Doc, a small city in An Giang province. An Giang bordered Cambodia and was also part of the Mekong Delta region. The Hau Giang and Tien Giang branches of the Mekong River wove their way through the province facilitating NVA covert weapon shipments deep into South Vietnam. For once, the communists had more weapons than fighters. They needed more recruits and Liem was determined to find them.

Like many of the communist leaders, Liem felt the revolution was gaining momentum. He wanted the war to end so he could return to his normal life. The communist leaders had told Liem and the other recruiters that their efforts were crucial for the final victory. Lien reasoned that this was true and put in countless hours making it a reality.

Liem had gone to a meeting room in the back of a restaurant filled with eager recruits that were the fruits of his labor. Forty-two new soldiers were to be trained before joining the Viet Cong forces in the area. In addition to recruiting, Liem was responsible for orienting the recruits and informing them of the road ahead.

At the end of the meeting, Liem stayed to answer individual questions from the recruits. He was tired but realized the importance of starting these young warriors off on the right foot. He wanted them to understand that their leaders cared deeply about their well-being. They needed the confidence to fight the ARVN and the Americans. It was his job to help them find that confidence early on in their new careers as soldiers of the revolution.

Outside the restaurant, Granier and his team waited for Liem to appear. They wouldn't grab him right away. There were too many people around the restaurant. They would follow him until he was alone, then execute a snatch-and-grab.

Granier climbed up to the pitched roof of a building overlooking the back of the restaurant. Some of the roof tiles were shaky and loose. He didn't like it, but the location gave him an excellent view of where he thought Liem would exit. He lay on the opposite side of the roof's crest and used his binoculars to survey the area around the restaurant.

There were a surprising number of young men congregating in small groups in the back of the restaurant. He didn't like that either. There were only six members of his team including himself. While they were well armed with the latest weapons, their mission was not to engage the enemy in a firefight. Stealth was their shield, not firepower. A mission was considered successful only if the subject was apprehended and no shots were fired. That wasn't always possible. The young men did not seem to be armed but he could never tell for sure.

Four team members were stationed with Granier near the back, while only two covered the front. Each team member had a small radio that allowed them to communicate with the others. Once Liem emerged, they would move as a unit to keep him encircled until they could isolate and capture him.

They waited another twenty minutes until Liem appeared in the back doorway. The young men gathered around him like he was a movie star. He moved through the crowd answering their questions and accepting their praise. For most of the recruits joining the communist revolution was the most exciting thing that had done in their lives.

Granier radioed the two team members in front to move to the back through an alley on the side of the restaurant. They were to stay in the alley until Liem moved away from the restaurant. He also ordered two of the team members in the back of the restaurant to relocate to a position forward of where he thought Liem would eventually exit the area. Granier wanted to keep Liem boxed in on all sides if possible. Liem was a high-value target, and Granier couldn't allow him to escape. The final two team members were the sniper unit that would remain in place and provide overwatch for the team.

When Liem finally pushed his way through the crowd of young men they followed him down the street. "Shit," said Granier, watching.

Liem turned and asked the young men to go back to the restaurant where their new instructor would meet them. The mob of young men complied and Liem was left alone.

Satisfied that Liem was heading in the right direction, Granier climbed down off the roof. One of the loose tiles dislodged and started sliding down the roof. Granier used his boot to stop it which worked for a moment, but then the tile broke in two, and one of the pieces slide down the steep roof. The piece of tile fell over the edge of the roof and crashed onto the ground below. Granier cursed himself.

Liem slowed but didn't stop when he heard the tile smash on the ground. It could have been a cat walking on the roof or… it could have been something else. He was unsure and cautious as he continued down the street. He turned into an alley.

Granier used hand signals to instruct the two advanced team members to stay put, while he joined the two members that had been stationed at the front of the restaurant.

Together they turned into the alley. Liem was nowhere in sight. The alley was long and Granier didn't think Liem would have had enough time to reach the end, even if he had run. That meant he was either hidden in the alley or he had entered the two buildings on either side of the alley through a doorway. Granier pulled out his pistol and chambered a round. The two team members followed suit pulling out their own pistols and chambering rounds. As they moved down the alley two kept watch while Granier checked the doors to the buildings to see if they were locked. They were. Of course, Liem could have had a key to any of the doors. Granier was betting that he didn't and was still hiding someplace nearby. The three moved deeper into the alley.

Liem sprung from his hiding place from behind a dumpster and opened fire with a small caliber pistol he had retrieved from his jacket pocket. Granier's instincts kicked in and he pivoted behind an iron fire escape. A bullet from Liem's pistol zinged past him and hit one of the team members. He went down. Granier leaned out from behind the fire escape and fired twice. Both bullets found their mark in Liem's chest and throat. He collapsed. Blood flowed. The other team member tended to the wounded team member while Granier moved toward Liem writhing on the ground. As Granier stood over Liem he saw that both his bullets had caused fatal wounds – one in the heart and the other cutting through an artery in Liem's throat. There was nothing Granier could do to save him. Liem had lost too much blood. A minute later, Liem stopped moving as the last of his blood was pumped out of his wounds and his heart finally stopped beating. "Dammit," said Granier.

Granier moved back to check on his wounded team member. He had caught a bullet in his shoulder. Granier was still concerned and wanted to get him to a hospital as soon as possible. Small caliber bullets had a bad habit of bouncing off bones and changing trajectory inside the body, slicing through vital organs. He turned the wounded team member over hoping to see an exit wound. There was none. Not a good sign. Granier's radio turned to static for a moment, then "Boss, we got a problem."

"What's up?" said Granier.

"That group of young men heard what I am guessing is your gunfire and is heading your way. There are a lot of them. Do you want us to stop 'em?"

"No. Everyone avoid gunfire if possible. We've got one wounded that we need to take to a hospital. We'll meet you at the rendezvous point once we're done."

Granier removed his shirt and used it as a compress to slow the bleeding. He helped the wounded team member to his feet. They moved up the alley leaving Liem's body.

When they reached the entrance to the alley, Granier saw a mob of young men moving toward the alley. There wasn't much time. He looked around and saw a tricycle taxi up the street. He motioned the driver to pick them up. The driver, watching the approaching mob, was hesitant. Granier pulled out a wad of money and held it up as if he would give it to the driver. The driver started the engine and raced to pick up the three passengers. The mob saw the tricycle and began to run toward the alley. It was going to be close. While the two team members boarded the tricycle, Granier stood his ground with the mob only two dozen feet away. He fired five rounds over the heads of the mob. They scattered. Granier jumped in the back of the tricycle and the driver sped off.

May 1, 1967 - Saigon, South Vietnam

Granier hated being summoned to the American embassy, especially by Bill, his CIA handler. It was never good news when Bill showed up in South Vietnam. Granier imagined that Bill had read his report on the botched mission and was there to read him the riot act. Liem would have been a valuable source of information had they been able to interrogate him. His death was a setback.

Entering the embassy, Granier was escorted to a conference room where Bill waited along with Robert Komer, the new head of the Civil Operations and Revolutionary Development Support program known as "CORDS." US Ambassador Henry Cabot Lodge Jr. had given Komer the nickname "Blowtorch Bob" because of his brisk management style. Komer cut to the chase no matter who he offended. Granier wasted no time and said, "It couldn't be helped. Liem shot one of my men. I had no choice but to take him down. Maybe I could have shot him once rather than twice, but it's hard to know what is going to happen in a situation like that. I don't think it would have mattered. Both wounds were lethal. It was instinct. It's what I have been trained to do."

"This isn't about that, Granier. Would you like some coffee?" said Bill.

"Coffee?"

"You do know what coffee is?" said Komer.

"Rene Granier, this Robert Komer. He's your new boss," said Bill.

"Where are you going?" said Granier.

"Back to Langley where I belong. Once I get the ball rolling, I am done. Director Komer will take it from here. But before I go, I want you to head up a new project called, 'The Phoenix program'. It's an expansion of what you have been doing."

Granier considered the offer for a moment, then said, "No."

"What do you mean 'No', Officer Granier," said Komer cutting in.

"It means I won't do it."

Komer turned to Bill and said, "You said he would play ball."

"Sometimes he needs a little convincing," said Bill.

"Not this time. I'm out. And if you force me to do it, I'll resign."

"Then good riddance," said Komer. "I only want patriots on my team."

Granier expression sharpened. "Hang on," said Bill. "Granier is our best operative. We need him."

"Not if he's a coward."

"Granier is far from being a coward."

"Okay. He is not a coward. He's a pussy."

"Jesus," said Bill.

"It's okay, Bill. It's good to know what my new boss thinks."

"Granier, please don't kill him."

"In his dreams," said Komer.

"I'm not going to kill him, Bill. I just met the man," said Granier.

"Good. Well, that's a good start," said Bill. "If you don't want to head the Phoenix program, then maybe you would consider training the officers entering the program."

"I would consider that," said Granier, his eyes locked with Komer. "That is if Blowtorch Bob doesn't mind having a pussy heading up his training program."

"I think that would be fine. Those that can't do, teach, right?" said Komer.

Granier laughed and said, "Right, Boss."

Granier hated to admit it, but he liked Komer's straightforward manner. At least there was no bullshit between them.

Washington DC, USA

Sitting in his White House office staring out the window, McNamara was between a rock and a hard place. He was still Secretary of Defense even though he had concluded that America would not win the war. The problem was that he was loyal to President Johnson, who along with most of his advisors still believed the war could be won. It was McNamara's job to prosecute the war even though he no longer believed it was the right path for the country. He wanted it to stop and to bring the US troops back home. But that wasn't the hand he had been dealt. He couldn't just slam on the brakes and end it. He had to figure a way out that would not damage America's reputation and international relationships, especially with those countries participating in NATO. America needed to keep its allies onboard with the agreements they had made. An exit from Vietnam would seem to many leaders that America was abandoning the Southeast Asian country just because things got tough. They would question whether the United States would come to their aid when needed and required by the treaty they had signed. And even if the Americans came, would they stay until the enemy was defeated? With the USSR at Europe's doorstep, NATO was far more important to America than Vietnam.

What McNamara needed was to find a way to force the North Vietnamese to the negotiating table and strike a deal. He was less worried about the Viet Cong. They would collapse if North Vietnam pulled their support. The North Vietnamese were the key to peace. His original plan was to bomb them to the peace table. That didn't work. The North Vietnamese infrastructure was crude, often made from wood instead of concrete. In a country filled with forests, this made building material readily available. The North Vietnamese had an ant army of volunteers that would repair the damage caused by the American bombers, most of the time within hours or a few days from the destruction. But most of all, the people were patriotic and believed in their leaders. That was something McNamara had not counted in his calculations. It didn't help that South Vietnam's leaders were often despised by their own people and corrupt.

The generals and admirals in the Pentagon had not come up with an effective strategy to defeat the North Vietnamese and Viet Cong. Even now, the new strategies that they were proposing were mostly rehashed ideas that required more US soldiers and resources. McNamara often felt like the Pentagon was throwing mud against the wall and seeing what sticks. Not an effective way to run a war.

McNamara's expensive IBM computers didn't help either. Over his years in office, he had collected warehouses of data from military personnel in the field. Technicians inputted the data and programs into the thinking machines through punch cards stored in long plastic trays. These were the devices that were supposed to give McNamara the answers he sought. The programs were complex and one bent card or hanging chad shut down the blinking lights on the computer's control panels until the problem could be rectified. He and his team spent much of their time tweaking the programs and adding even more data points to come up with the answer to how to win the war. But the answer remained elusive.

There was still much they didn't know about their

enemy, things that couldn't be quantified. He missed his days as the president of Ford Motor Company where the questions were easier, and the answers were more beneficial. He knew the American consumer, but the North Vietnamese were an enigma.

Nothing kept McNamara from trying new ideas. Maybe he was wrong. Maybe the war could be won if he just came up with the right strategy. He so wanted to be wrong, just this once. While his heart wanted to win, his mind told him victory was highly improbable if not impossible. He trusted his mind.

Several years earlier, the Pentagon had come up with various plans to build a defensive line on the northern border of South Vietnam and the southeast border of Laos. The border barriers would prevent communist infiltration into the south and starve the Viet Cong into submission. The schemes had been rejected because they required a large number of military personnel to be permanently deployed along the line to defend and repair the barriers. They would also force the North Vietnamese to deploy their forces deeper into Laos to keep the Ho Chi Minh trail functioning. The North Vietnamese might even extend much of the trail into Cambodia to skirt the defensive line. None of that was good and the plans were abandoned.

But the situation had become more difficult, and McNamara was more open to out-of-the-box ideas, perhaps he was even desperate. If the defensive line worked, even partially, it could force the North Vietnamese to the negotiating table, and he could end the damned war without destroying America's reputation. At least it was something he hadn't tried yet.

McNamara met several times with Carl Kaysen, a former Kennedy National Security Council staff member. Kaysen had submitted a proposal that had originally caught McNamara's eye and McNamara was resurrecting the idea. Kaysen proposed to build an electronic barrier to hinder the North Vietnamese that stretched from the eastern coastline to the western border. If the North Vietnamese sappers cut the electrified wire on any segment of the barrier, the Allied troops would know because of the drop in voltage for that segment. The allied troops patrolling near the breached barrier segment would be alerted and cut off the enemy's infiltration.

McNamara embraced the idea and assigned John McNaughton and a group of scientists in Cambridge, Massachusetts to help Kaysen flesh out the proposal into a working plan.

Once created and approved by McNamara, the plan was submitted to the Joint Chiefs of Staff for comments. And as he suspected, the JCS disliked the plan. They still felt it would take a large number of soldiers to guard the barrier and there would be a number of problems constructing the fence in certain places along the border. JCS suggested that the construction of the barrier would take up to four years to complete.

In addition, McNamara approved a summer study program in Cambridge for a group of forty-seven scientists and academics in the Jason Advisory Group which would refine the electronic barrier concept. The Jason group met at Dana Hall in Wellesley, Massachusetts under high-security conditions for one week. Once finished with their discussions, the group generated a report for McNamara's review. The report noted that the bombing campaign against North Vietnam had been a complete failure and had not produced any measurable results that the bombing was having any significant effect on Hanoi's ability to support military operations in the South. McNamara had already come to that conclusion, but the finding stung, nonetheless.

The report had more constructive advice when it suggested a two-defensive barrier system to slow the NVA infiltration of troops and supplies. One barrier would be stretched along the southern side of the demilitarized zone from the coast to the western border. Fortified outposts would send out patrols to protect the barrier. The second barrier would be electrified and run along the Laotian border with Khe Sanh being the southern anchor point. Aircraft patrols, high-tech acoustic sensors, heat-detecting sensors, and strategically placed minefields would be used to detect and counter any enemy attempts to breach the barrier. The second barrier would also require a small number of permanently deployed ground troops.

But the part of the Jason Group's report that was most encouraging to McNamara was that the construction of both barriers could be finished within one year if the needed resources were retained. If it worked, it would most likely press Hanoi into negotiations. With a little luck, the Americans could end the war and withdraw.

McNamara went back to JCS and presented the Jason Group report. Although most of the Joint Chiefs were still against the plan, General Wheeler, the chairman of the JCS was for the plan. When distributed to CINPAC and MACV, both Admiral Sharp and General Westmoreland were against it saying it would be impractical to construct and maintain.

McNamara knew that it was much easier to criticize a controversial project than to support it. But the way he saw it, the barrier system was the best idea among a lot of bad ideas. At least it was a new approach. It could work. Despite strong resistance, McNamara ordered the proposal to be implemented. Lieutenant General Alfred Starbird, director of the Defense Communications Agency, was appointed to implement the project.

If the defensive barrier system was a failure, President Johnson always had the option of asking for McNamara's resignation as Secretary of Defense. In a way, it would be a blessing. McNamara had chosen to stay inside a system that he knew was badly flawed and try to change it for the better. Running was easy. Staying was hard. While history has shown that McNamara had many flaws, lack of courage was not one of them. With a $1.5 billion construction budget, the barrier also required a $740 million annual operating budget. It was not a cheap project. Although the code name for the project was The Practice Nine, the defensive barrier system was nicknamed The McNamara Line and the Great Wall of Vietnam.

When the project code name The Practice Nine was leaked to the press, the name changed to Illinois City, then to Project Dye Marker, then to Muscle Shoals, and finally to Igloo White.

As construction began in 1967, USMC engineers in the 3rd Marine Division were ordered to bulldoze a strip of land nine miles long and 500 yards wide from Gio Linh to Con Thien. Hundreds of farms and entire villages were displaced to build The Trace, the nickname the Marines had given the strip of land.

Three fortified bases were built along the trace – Alpha 2, Alpha 3, and Alpha 4. 7,578 Marines were deployed to protect the defensive barrier. An additional 4,080 American troops were deployed for air-support interdiction efforts.

When almost finished at the end of 1967, the northern defensive barrier was forty-seven miles long. The defenses included radar, motion and acoustic surveillance, trip mines, gravel mines (dropped by air), and mile-long segments of barbed-wire entanglements.

The western barrier stretched from Khe Sanh through the special forces camp at Lang Vei. This barrier seemed more effective at cutting off enemy reinforcements and supplies. It certainly antagonized the communists trying to support their troops already deployed in the south. Many analysts believed that it was the creation of the Western barrier that triggered the North Vietnamese siege of Khe Sanh and the destruction of the special forces camp at Lang Vei.

Although he continued to support The System as he called it, McNamara would never see the construction of his namesake completed. He would resign in 1968 shortly after the Tet Offensive. Without the Secretary of Defense's support, all construction of the McNamara line ceased and many of the strongholds that had already been built were abandoned to free up static forces for a mobile defensive strategy. The McNamara Line had become another Maginot Line. Believing they had new modern ideas and technology; American leaders had failed to learn from history.

Will of the Jungle Spirits

A constant drizzle from the clouds clinging to the mountain range made every step along the steep slope a potential disaster. Even the Montagnard that lived in the mountains struggled to keep their footing. The thick jungle canopy squeezed out the light making it difficult to see the vine-covered ground.

The SOG team and their Montagnard warriors were deep in the mountains close to the North Vietnamese border. They had been on a roll with five enemy convoys destroyed since the start of the year. Loses had been light for the warriors. The tribal leaders wondered if their streak would hold. For many of the Montagnard, it was up to the spirits that lived in the jungle. They sacrificed animals to appease the spirits before each mission. Some of the tribesmen believed in the Christian god and prayed for success in slaughtering their enemy.

Blackjack knew he was pushing their luck when he decided to go after a convoy loaded with mortar shells. It was a big prize and he wanted it the moment he was informed of its existence by CIA intelligence. He promised himself he would let his warriors rest and spend time with their families after the mission. Of course, that's what he thought during the last mission. He knew the Montagnard didn't mind the extra mission. They liked killing communists and seemed tireless in their hunt for the enemy. If successful, the warriors would pilfer some of the mortar shells and use them for booby-traps along the Ho Chi Minh Trail to kill even more communists. But the warriors had been fighting for months with only one or two-day breaks in between missions to resupply and eat the roasted pigs that Blackjack provided after each success. Even the SOG team members were getting worn down and needed a week of rest. Fatigue caused everyone to lose focus and in the mountain jungle that could be deadly.

Intelligence had discovered the mortar shells shipment during an interrogation of a captured truck driver. The North Vietnamese convoy would be using a rarely used alternate road near the border. The road, only used for the most important cargo, would shorten the delivery time of the much-needed ammunition. It was the enemy's version of a secret highway and was kept clear of the usual traffic that clogged the Ho Chi Minh Trail.

As usual, the Montagnard scouts led the way through the mountains keeping off the trails to avoid the enemy's booby-traps and outposts. It took longer and was more grueling, but it was safer.

After almost a week of hiking through the jungle, the task force was approaching their target – a bridge that spanned a deep gorge. It was an obvious chokepoint. If the team could destroy one truck on the bridge, the other trucks would be blocked from crossing and easy targets. The bridge was bombed almost weekly which was why the North Vietnamese truck drivers didn't use the road very often. Work crews would rebuild the bridge during the day. In this case, the workers would time their completion of repairs with the arrival of the convoy carrying the mortar shells. Blackjack and his warriors would need to arrive well ahead of the convoy to set up their ambush. They would not be able to blow up the bridge because the workers would be able to spot them placing their explosives. Instead, they would simply set up firing positions above the bridge and paralleling the road. They had carried with them one 60 mm mortar and a recoilless rifle plus ammunition. Neither was strong enough to take out the bridge but would have an easy time taking out the trucks if they were trapped on the road. He did not want to destroy the trucks' cargo which he planned to pilfer, but he would need to disable some of the trucks to keep the convoy from escaping. A recoilless rifle round could put a hole in a truck engine without a big explosion.

Blackjack suspected that the North Vietnamese would have extra security guarding the convoy because of its value. As usual, his SOG team would focus on taking out the enemy officers and sergeants while the Montagnard focused on the convoy. It was a simple plan that required surprise and aggression.

The SOG team members and the Montagnard were taking longer breaks than usual. It was a sure sign of fatigue. Even with a tight schedule, there wasn't much Blackjack could do about it. He would gently encourage the Montagnard to get up and move along, but he couldn't order them. They only took orders from their chief. As for his men, they were professionals and well understood the timetable. They would fight off their fatigue with the "go pills" allotted to them before each mission. Popping one in his mouth every couple of hours, Blackjack felt like he was living off the things. Everyone on the team knew they could get addicted, but sometimes a mission's objectives outweighed the personal risks. Blackjack knew how to monitor his team members and deal with any addiction problem they encountered, including himself.

As the sun began to set, one of the scouts returned and reported to the chief who in turn reported to Blackjack. They had arrived. Blackjack ordered another rest stop as he went forward with the scout, the Montagnard chief, and his team members to get a look at the bridge before it got too dark to see at a distance.

Crawling up the crest of a range, they looked down at the gorge and the bridge. There was no sign of the convoy. It might have already passed but unlikely if the intelligence he had been given was correct. Veteran commanders rarely trusted intelligence completely and prepared for the worst-case scenario. They could see that the North Vietnamese work crew was still working on the bridge. That was a good sign. No need to work on a bridge if the convoy had already passed. The American reconnaissance planes would soon spot the repaired bridge and their bombers would soon follow to destroy it once again. It was an endless cycle.

"We'll wait until dark before proceeding. We'll need to set up our firing positions quickly once we arrive. I figure we've got three, maybe four hours before the first truck arrives," said Blackjack.

Blackjack knew there was no need to tell his team what to do. All were veteran fighters that had executed dozens of similar operations. Still, he wasn't taking any chances and pointed out the positions where he wanted everyone to set up. The mortar crew would fire parachute flares to illuminate the convoy, then switch to high-explosive, anti-personnel rounds. They were to avoid hitting the back of the trucks when possible.

As darkness fell on the jungle, the SOG and the Montagnard moved silently down the mountain toward the road and bridge. What they didn't see was that they were being watched by the scouts of an elite enemy unit waiting in an ambush.

Knowing that the Americans would recognize the bridge as a chokepoint and the best location to ambush the convoy, the North Vietnamese had set up machine gun firing positions above where they suspected that the Americans and the Montagnard would set up their firing positions. The NVA positions were well camouflaged and the soldiers that occupied them were motionless. The elite NVA ambush force outnumbered the SOG and Montagnard five to one. The elite Brigade commander knew he and his men would only get one chance at destroying the troublesome SOG and their tribesmen. Sometimes overkill was what was needed to ensure nobody escaped.

On their way down the mountain slope, the unsuspecting SOG and Montagnard hiked past the camouflaged NVA firing positions. The highly disciplined NVA team held their fire. There was no need to risk their lives until all the NVA forces had arrived and were in a position to wipe out the Montagnard and SOG.

Checking to make sure nothing was amiss, Blackjack motioned for the SOG and the Montagnard to take up their positions. There were enemy guard posts with machine guns on both sides of the bridge. A Montagnard squad had been sent to the opposite side of the bridge to take out the guards and the machine gun, then attack as a flanking force from across the bridge.

Like most of the SOG and Montagnard battles, Blackjack thought the fight would be over quickly. Once the drivers and their guards realized the bridge was blocked and there was no way to turn the trucks around on the narrow mountain road, they would flee into the jungle and the battle would be over. Overlooking the road, Blackjack's ambush team waited. Above them, the enemy ambush team waited.

Peering through his binoculars, Blackjack watched the repair crew pack up their tools and supplies. The repairs were finished. The crew of fifty workers hiked down the road passing Blackjack and his men hidden in the thick foliage. When the crew disappeared down the road, the chief ordered his scouts toward the area where the convoy would appear.

It took another hour and a half for the first sounds of a truck engine to pierce the silence. Blackjack and his men tensed. The show was about to begin, when… a rock rolled down from above Blackjack's position and stopped in the middle of the road. Blackjack jerked around. He saw nothing. He could hear the trucks approaching. One of the Montagnard scouts returned and reported that twenty-six trucks were coming up the road. A very nice prize.

Not easily spooked, Blackjack used his binoculars to survey the area above his positions. He saw nothing amiss. But there was that rock. Why? A voice in his mind was screaming that it was an ambush and to pull his men out before it was too late. The first headlights appeared. The prize was close. He turned to the chief and asked him to send the scout up the slope behind them. The scout crawled up the slope, keeping as low as possible.

Blackjack refocused his attention on the convoy as the first truck passed his position and approached the entrance to the bridge. Just before it reached the entrance, a parachute flare was launched from the Montagnard's 60mm mortar. The flare illuminated what was about to become the battlefield.

Blackjack signaled for a hidden Montagnard machine gun to open fire. The gunner had been given strict instructions to only hit the cab and engine, not the cargo bed where the mortar rounds would be stored. Two short machine gun bursts left the driver dead and the truck's engine compartment smoking. Disabled, the truck rolled to a stop as did the trucks that followed it.

Blackjack ordered the rest of the assault force to open fire. Just as he thought, it was a turkey shoot with drivers and their guards abandoning their truck cabs and fleeing into the jungle on the opposite side of the road.

Two Montagnard teams assaulted the guard posts and took out the machine guns with well-thrown grenades. Blackjack's plan was working like a charm. He ordered a fire team led by one of SOG members to examine the cargo area of the first truck to confirm that the mortar shells were indeed inside.

When the SOG team member opened the back flap of the truck, his eyes went wide when he saw the barrel of a machine gun pointed directly at him. A moment later, his head disappeared in a red explosion. The Montagnard with him was also mowed down and fell dead on the road.

Spotting the hidden enemy forces on the hillside, the scout above Blackjack's position shouted a warning until he too was cut down by a hail of rifle fire. The enemy's machine guns opened up on Blackjack's firing position paralleling the road. Unable to turn their machine guns in time, a dozen Montagnard warriors were shredded by streams of bullets. The Montagnard chief rose to rally his men and was cut down by enemy fire. He fell dead.

A hundred enemy soldiers sprang from the back of the trucks and emerged from the jungle on the opposite side of the road, opening fire on the Montagnard. More warriors were hit and fell into the tangle of vegetation. Blackjack and his two remaining SOG team members couldn't believe what was happening. They were fighting a lethal two-front battle against an overwhelming enemy force. Their instincts took over as they returned fire and sought cover that protected them from an enemy attack from all sides. There was none.

The Montagnard were fighting back as best they could, but it was a hopeless situation. They were surrounded and outnumbered. Blackjack signaled the survivors to follow him as he looked for a way out. Surrender was not an option for the Montagnard who would certainly be killed once unarmed. The NVA offered no mercy to savages. Many had lost comrades to the Montagnard's long knives.

Blackjack looked down the road at the line of trucks and enemy troops advancing toward them. He looked up the slope at the machine guns, some reloading to continue the slaughter. He looked to the opposite side of the road and saw more troops firing from the edge of the road. Finally, he saw the bridge with his warriors on the other side. It was the only way out, but he knew his men would be sitting ducks once they began crossing without cover. The parachute flare fell through the jungle canopy, and everything went dark once again.

Fighting as he retreated, he made his way toward the bridge entrance stepping over the bodies of dead warriors. His men followed, also fighting as they carried their wounded comrades. Many tossed grenades at the enemy driving them to cover. Hundreds of muzzle blasts and tracer rounds strobed through the darkness blinding everyone. The night was the only thing saving Blackjack and his men from being completely wiped out. Then, the enemy's mortars launched their own flares and the battlefield was once again illuminated making the SOG and Montagnard easy targets.

As they reached the bridge, Blackjack told the Montagnard and his SOG to run without firing their weapons. They were in the open without good cover. The faster they crossed the bridge, the more of his men would be saved. Below the din of gunfire, Blackjack heard the familiar thumbs and flashes of light of mortars being launched from the mountainside. A few moments later, explosions on the bridge deck blocked their retreat. Knowing that stopping meant certain death, Blackjack waved his men on into the mortar explosions. Many would die, but some would survive. It was the only way. Covering their retreat with his submachine gun, Blackjack was the last to cross as the enemy closed in on the bridge. He too stopped firing his weapon and ran. His eyes stung from the smoke and dust in the air. Halfway across, a mortar landed behind him and launched shrapnel into both his legs. He fell on the bridge's deck. Watching Blackjack fall, the surviving Montagnard that could still fight and the

SOG ran back onto the bridge to save him.

The enemy fought their way toward the wounded American. Suffering from incredible pain, Blackjack crawled toward his men and freedom. It was too little too late. The enemy soldiers reached him first and took him captive, grabbing his arms and dragging him back across the bridge. Afraid of hitting Blackjack, the Montagnard and SOG stopped firing their weapons and retreated across the far side of the bridge. Once across, the Montagnard and SOG took up firing positions and opened fire on enemy troops attempting to cross the bridge and chase after them. The Montagnard and SOG's revenge was sweet but short-lived as the enemy retreated to the opposite side where they found cover. It was a stalemate with the bridge as no man's land. The battle was over for the moment. Leaving a few men to defend the bridge until the others with the wounded escaped, the Montagnard and SOG retreated further down the road.

Corporal Singer, the SOG heavy weapon expert, and Specialist Butler, the team's engineer and explosives expert, sat next to each other catching their breath and watching the road for the enemy as the surviving Montagnard tended to their wounded. "We need to get off this road and back into the bush," said Singer.

"Yeah. So, we head back to the village?" said Butler.

"No. Too long a trek. Too many of the wounded will die. Besides, that's what the NVA will expect us to do. They'll hunt us down if we go that way."

"So, what do you suggest?"

Singer pulled out his map and flashlight with a red lens. After a few moments to access their position, he said, "Lima Site 85 near Phou Pha Thi."

"You wanna head North?" said Butler.

"The NVA will never suspect we would go north with our wounded. It'll be safer. There's an airstrip there. We can fly the wounded to a field hospital."

"What about Blackjack?"

"He's gone. We have no way of finding him. He always knew being captured was a possibility. He wouldn't want us to risk more lives going after him."

"I don't care what he wants or doesn't want. I'm not leaving him to be tortured by those bastards."

"How do you plan to find him?"

"I don't know. But there has to be a way."

"Well, it's a long hike to Phou Pha Thi. You'll have plenty of time to think about it."

Butler, Singer, and the Montagnard chopped their way through the thick vegetation as they climbed another mountain slope heading north. Singer stopped to study the map he carried in his front pocket. Butler stopped beside him and said, "I think I've got it."

"Got what?" said Singer.

"A way to find Blackjack."

"How's that?"

"He was pretty badly wounded on the bridge, right?"

"Yeah. It looked like he took shrapnel in both his legs."

"So, they've got to get him to a doctor that can remove the shrapnel before they transport him back to Hanoi. Otherwise, he'll die of infection or bleed out."

"I suppose."

"So, we nab a couple of NVA and find out where their closest medical facility is located along the trail."

"That might work. But we probably don't have

much time before they move him again. We'd have to haul ass and get real lucky."

"Okay. But there's a chance it might work. We owe it to Blackjack to at least try."

"I agree. We should try once we drop off the wounded."

Hacking their way out of the jungle, Butler and Singer saw Lima Site 85 on top of a steep mountain called Phou Pha Thi. Below, was an airfield used for supplies and to bring in replacements. In the distance sat a village housing the Hmong secret army that protected the Lima site.

In 1966, the United States Ambassador to Laos William Sullivan approved a plan by the USAF to construct a TACAN site atop Phou Pha Thi which would guide US bomber aircraft to their targets in North Vietnam. In 1967, under the code name Heavy Green, the facility was upgraded with the all-weather TSQ-81 radar bombing control system, which could direct and control attacking jet fighters and bombers to their targets and provide them with precise bomb release points. When the new system became operational, American bomber accuracy skyrocketed.

It was the closest Lima site to the Ho Chi Minh Trail and was responsible for directing fifty-five percent of American bombing missions to their targets in Laos and North Vietnam. The equipment at the site was highly classified. Concerned that if the site was overrun by the NVA or Pathet Lao, the Soviets and Chinese would be offered the equipment for reverse engineering purposes, the CIA had decided to rig every piece of equipment on Lima Site 85 with explosives. If the operators ever felt their equipment might be in danger of being captured by the enemy, they had strict instructions to destroy it completely. Just like a US embassy, all code books, computer tapes, and classified documents would be burned in a portable incinerator. Revealing the operation of any of the classified equipment on the site even under torture would be considered treason. Personnel at the site was constantly rotated so that no one would become fatigued and forget their duty. Security was serious business at Lima Site 85.

The CIA had constructed a 2,300-foot airfield in the valley below the site. Personnel working at the site were supplied by weekly flights of the 20th Special Operations Squadron, based at Udorn RTAFB in northeastern Thailand operating under the code name Operation Pony Express.

The CIA and the USAF had gone to great lengths to keep the site a secret. Always on the lookout for the enemy, the soldiers guarding the site were not pleased to see the Montagnard and SOG stumbling out of the jungle. They had heard about the ambush and hoped the North Vietnamese had not followed them. Upon seeing the badly wounded Montagnard, nothing was said, and medical help was immediately offered.

Having done their best to get the Montagnard to safety, Butler and Singer were now free to pursue the search for Blackjack. Luck was with them. The CIA officers stationed at the Lima site had been interrogating three NVA soldiers that had been captured several days earlier. With a little extra encouragement from a pair of pliers, the NVA revealed the location of the closest supply depot to the bridge with medical facilities. As Butler and Singer suspected the NVA knew nothing about the location of the captured American. It was too soon after the ambush.

"It's a crapshoot if he's there," said Butler.

"Even if he is, he won't be there long. They're gonna want to get him to Hanoi as soon as possible," said Singer.

"We need to get there fast."

"I might have an idea how to get there. Let's find a radio."

Late in the afternoon, Coyle, in his modified Pilatus PC-6 Porter, a single-engine STOL utility aircraft armed with under-the-wing two rocket pods, touched down on Lima site's airstrip. Butler and Singer were waiting as he taxied to a stop and got out. "Thanks for coming, Coyle," said Singer.

"Blackjack's a friend. I'll do what I can," said Coyle shaking their hands.

"I won't lie. There's a lot of risk in what we're asking."

"Well, I should hope so. Otherwise, any pilot could do it."

"But you're not any pilot?" said Butler.

"You tell me."

"You'll do," said Singer with a grin.

"I need to refuel before we take off. I've got a fuel bladder in the cargo hull that'll give us the range we need. It's gonna be a bit cramped and weight is gonna be an issue."

"What do you mean?"

"I can only take one of you."

Butler and Singer exchanged glances. "It should be me. I should go," said Butler.

"No. We don't need to blow shit up. I'm the heavy weapons guy. I'll go," said Singer.

"I think it should be Butler," said Coyle. "We may need to blow some shit up as a diversion. Besides, you can't bring anything heavier than a submachine gun anyway. I already took out my M60 and the rockets in the pods to lighten the load. But we still need as much fuel as we can carry."

"I'll get my stuff while you refuel," said Butler moving off like the decision had been made.

"Singer, why don't you grab a map and show me where you think the NVA might be holding Blackjack?" said Coyle.

"I can do that. But I just want you to know… I'm a better shot than Butler."

"I imagine you are, but I don't think that's gonna matter too much if we get in a firefight. We'll be heavily outnumbered and outgunned."

"Right. So, don't get caught."

"I don't plan on it."

Coyle and Singer pulled the fuel trailer over to the aircraft and began filling the fuel tank and bladder. Singer pulled out his map and showed Coyle where the NVA prisoners had indicated the location of the medical facility.

"I borrowed some aerial recon photos of the area around the supply depot from our CIA friends.

I found this rock quarry that the NVA built to supply gravel for the road. I thought it might be a good place to land," said Singer.

"Maybe," said Coyle studying the photos. "I suppose that's better than landing on the actual road."

"Finding Blackjack… It's a real shot in the dark," said Singer.

"No. I think there is good logic behind the location of where they might be keeping him, but I'll admit…

timing is gonna be everything."

"Yeah, timing…"

"All we can do is our best. The rest is in God's hands. We just have to accept it, one way or the other."

Wearing camouflage paint on their faces, Butler and Coyle flew over the mountains shrouded in jungle. Butler was the navigator and kept on the lookout for landmarks to identify their current location. They were getting close. "We don't have much daylight left. Can you land in the dark?" said Butler.

"I can land. It's just a matter of whether we'll crash when I do it," said Coyle.

"That doesn't sound very promising."

"It ain't."

Coyle studied the CIA recon photos comparing them to the ground below. "There," he said pointing. "That's where I'll put her down… next to that pile of gravel. The medical facility should be a mile or two up the road from the entrance to the quarry."

"That's not much room."

"Nope. But I don't need a lot."

Coyle dove down toward the quarry. The shadows were long making it more difficult to determine the size of things."

Moments later, Coyle steered the aircraft toward the gravel pile as he descended, then landed. The aircraft rolled fifty feet and came to a stop a couple of feet in front of the gravel pile. "Nice landing," said Butler.

"You're damned right it was," said Coyle as he reeved the engine and turned the plane around for takeoff. He shut off the engine and they climbed out with their weapons – two submachine guns and one grenade each. Butler also had a rucksack with a small amount of explosives. "Daylight's running. We gotta move," said Coyle.

As they left the quarry they stuck to the up-slope side of the road covered with jungle. It would provide good camouflage if they were at risk of being spotted. They made good time and came to the entrance of the truck park where there was an NVA guard post. Coyle and Butler moved deeper into the jungle and approached the site through the heavy foliage.

When they reached the edge of the truck park, they could hear the voices of the North Vietnamese drivers getting their trucks ready to move as the night approached. They would waste little time once darkness fell and the threat of being spotted by American reconnaissance planes was minimized. Thirty minutes earlier, they had heard the sound of an engine of a small plane and wondered if it was looking for their convoy or truck park. The sound of aircraft always made the truck drivers jittery.

Butler pointed to a building that he thought might be the medical facility. Coyle nodded his agreement with Butler's assessment. They moved toward the building using the jungle as cover.

Positioned under the roof, there was an empty fuel drum with the top removed filled with crutches and several upright stretchers leaned against the wall. Butler and Coyle nodded to each other. They had found the right place where Blackjack might be.

While the rest of the truck park seemed to be coming to life, Coyle and Butler stole into the building through a side door.

Inside the building, they checked each room for signs of Blackjack. There were none. A doctor with a chart came around the corner. Coyle and Butler raised their weapons. The doctor dropped the chart and raised his hands. "The American... where is he?" said Butler.

The doctor shook his head as if he didn't understand. Coyle tried the same question in French. The doctor responded. Coyle looked disappointed and said, "Blackjack's gone. He left this morning in a truck headed for Hanoi."

"Shit," said Butler.

Coyle asked the doctor more questions in French and got a response. "What'd he say?" said Butler.

"I asked him what road he would take to Hanoi. He said he didn't know, but there was only one pass in the area leading into North Vietnam. It's about six hours away by truck."

"What are you thinking, Coyle?"

"That I gonna have to land in the dark on a road that I've seen."

"Can you do that?"

"I hope so. I wonder if they have any flares stored someplace in the supply depot?"

"I'll find 'em if they do."

"You do that. I'm gonna continue my conversation with the good doctor and see what I can find out."

Butler moved back out the side door as Coyle continued interrogating the doctor as to Blackjack's condition. The hot shrapnel from the mortar round had cauterized his wounds and stopped the bleeding. It probably saved his life. But the doctor had to remove the shrapnel to prevent further infection and the bleeding had begun again as Blackjack's cauterized flesh was torn open. The doctor had done what he could to save Blackjack's legs, but he wasn't sure if he would make it to Hanoi if the bleeding didn't stop or if infection set into the wounds. It was a long journey to the capital and the roads were rough.

It was pitch dark as the Porter flew over the mountains. Butler watched the road below hoping to see the headlights of the truck carrying Blackjack. "Even if you see a truck, we have no way of knowing that Blackjack is inside," said Coyle.

"I realize that, but it gives me something to do," said Butler.

"Suit yourself."

"Any idea how we are going to spot the truck once we land?"

"Not really. The doctor said that the truck was not part of a convoy, so that will help a little. He also said there were three soldiers and an officer guarding Blackjack."

"I imagine he's a pretty big prize."

"Let's hope so. They'll want to keep him alive at all costs to receive their bonuses."

"Bonuses?"

"Bonuses. Bounties. The leaders in the politburo pay common soldiers and low-level officers for the capture of Americans. But their prisoners have to be alive to collect the reward."

Coyle grabbed the map sitting in the door pocket. He used a red lens flashlight to study the map. "We're coming up on the border."

"How far in are we gonna go?"

"I don't know. We need to find a place to land close to the road."

"How about the road itself?"

"It's too windy. We need a straight runway."

"And how are we gonna find that in the dark."

"Study the map. Look for a building or something that might have an access road like the quarry," said Coyle handing Butler the map.

Butler poured over the map and said, "It's not very detailed."

"I'm not sure there is a lot out here. It doesn't have to be perfect, just relatively flat and straight. Without rocks or fallen trees would be nice too."

Ten minutes later, Butler showed Coyle a point on the map and said, "There's a reservoir with a dam not too far from the road. We might be able to land on the top of the dam. It should be flat."

"Not bad. It could work if there are no big rocks or ruts."

"And how do we find out?"

"We'll drop the flares you found. But to be honest, it's gonna be hard to see no matter what we do. We just gotta land and take our chances. If it doesn't go well and we end up crashing, we need to get away from the aircraft as quickly as possible."

"Got it."

"Slip into the cargo area and open the side door. When you light the flare make damned sure nothing burning falls on the deck next to the fuel bladder."

"Okay. How many flares should I light?"

"All of them except one. We are only gonna get one chance at landing. Might as well light up the area as much as possible."

"What's the reserve flare for?"

"The truck if we find it."

As Coyle continued flying, Butler grabbed five flares, leaving one on in his rucksack, and climbed into the cargo area. He opened the side door and it locked in place. "I found the dam. I'm going in. Get the flares ready. We can make multiple passes if needed," said Coyle.

Butler got the flares ready to ignite. He situated himself between the open door and the fuel bladder for extra protection against a stray spark. "It looks pretty good," said Coyle studying the dam and the top of the embankment. "Drop the flares on my mark."

"I'm ready."

"Mark."

Butler lit the first flare. The light blinded both he and Coyle. He dropped the burning rod out the door without seeing where it would land.

The flare landed on one end of the embankment. "Good. Drop another. Mark."

Butler repeated the process and dropped another flare.

The flare landed in the middle of the embankment. Then another flare was dropped at the end of the embankment. Coyle turned the aircraft and made another pass. Butler dropped the last two flares. Coyle turned the aircraft one more time and flew as low as he dared surveying the top of the embankment, searching for obstructions that might take out the landing gear and cause the aircraft to crash. There was nothing that he could see, but he couldn't see everything. The grass on the top of the embankment could have been hiding some large rocks. "Alright. Get back up here and strap in. We're gonna land."

Butler obeyed. Coyle pulled his seat harness tight. Butler followed his example. Coyle completed the final turn and nosed the aircraft down.

The Porter's wheels touched down on the grassy embankment. Coyle let the aircraft straighten for a moment, then hit the brakes. The aircraft rolled to a stop without incident.

Butler sighed with relief. "Ditto," said Coyle loosening his harness. They climbed out of the aircraft, again taking their weapons and Butler's rucksack, and headed for the road in the distance.

After waiting two hours and watching a large convoy pass their position heading in the opposite direction, Coyle and Butler, hidden along the side of the road, spotted a pair of truck headlights coming down off a mountain. "Is that it?" said Butler.

"Your guess is as good as mine," said Coyle. "The timing is right given the distance the truck had to travel, but this truly a shot in the dark."

"Well, let's get lucky… for Blackjack."

They chambered rounds in the submachine guns and Coyle said, "I'm gonna move up the road a bit in case we're right and the guards in the back come out to fight. When the truck gets fifty feet away, light the flare and toss it in the middle of the road. If the drive doesn't stop, kill him."

"The truck will crash. What about Blackjack?" said Butler.

"He'll just have to take his chances. It's better than being imprisoned and tortured."

Coyle moved up the road in the direction of the approaching truck headlights. He moved into the long grass and knelt to conceal himself among the blades.

As the truck approached, Butler lit and tossed the flare in the middle of the road. The truck didn't slow. Butler readied himself and aimed at the driver's side windshield. He had little doubt the driver could not see the flare. He had signed his own death warrant, thought Butler. Nothing would stop Butler while there was still a chance of finding and freeing Blackjack. It was the unspoken promise between warriors. Butler heard the engine groan as the truck accelerated. When the truck closed to twenty-five feet, Butler opened fire. A burst of ten bullets shattered the front windshield on the driver's and passenger's side. The truck slowed, then its wheels rolled up the side of an embankment and the truck slowly tipped over on its side and skidded to a stop.

Butler moved up quickly and checked the truck cab. The driver and the officer sitting next to him were riddled with bullets. Very dead.

Coyle came running behind the truck, his weapon fixed on the closed flap on the cargo bed. Butler moved back to join him and signaled with two fingers the men he had killed. Coyle nodded, then called out, "Blackjack, it's Coyle. Keep your head down."

There was no response and Coyle wasn't expecting one. Coyle and Butler didn't toward the back of the truck. Instead, they waited for the guards in the back to make the first move. A minute passed, then two… nothing. "Go grab that flare before it burns out," Coyle said.

Butler obeyed and returned with the flare still burning. "Toss it up on the canvas."

Butler tossed the flare up on the truck bed canvas. It caught fire. The North Vietnamese smeared their truck canvases in grease to waterproof them. The flames spread quickly. "If Blackjack is in there, we've got to get him out," said Butler.

"Wait…" said Coyle.

As the entire side of the truck was engulfed in flames, the back flap opened, and the three guards leaped out opening fire in all directions, their vision blinded by the fire against the darkness. Butler and Coyle aimed and returned fire. It was over in two seconds. The NVA guards fell dead on the pavement. Butler rushed forward toward the flames and jumped into the back. Coyle checked the guards to ensure that they were indeed dead. They were.

A moment later, Butler emerged dragging Blackjack. He was alive and in pain. "Hang in there, Boss. We'll get you outta here," said Butler.

"You're an idiot for coming after me," said Blackjack. "But thanks."

Blackjack saw Coyle, "You don't happen to have a bottle of Jack Daniels on you?"

"Nope," said Coyle. "Don't be a pussy, Blackjack. You're just gonna have to gut it out."

Blackjack laughed, then groaned in pain. "Gentlemen, we gotta move before the truck's gas tank explodes and lights up the sky," said Coyle.

Taking up the rear-guard position, Coyle stayed back for a minute to ensure that they weren't being followed. Satisfied, he moved up beside Butler and slipped his arm around Blackjack to help Butler carry him. A moment later, the truck's fuel tank exploded sending an orange ball of flame into the night sky. The NVA would be coming soon to investigate.

When they got back to the plane, Coyle decoupled the fuel bladder and rolled it out the side door onto the embankment. "Aren't we gonna need that?" said Butler.

"No. It's mostly empty and we need to shed weight. We got a short runway," said Coyle as they loaded Blackjack in the back of the aircraft. Butler climbed in with him and used the plane's first aid kit to tend to his wounds as best he could. "I'll be back in a minute," said Coyle.

Coyle turned on his red-filter flashlight and walked to the top of the embankment searching for obstructions. Even with time running short before the NVA arrived, it seemed foolish to come all this way and crash on takeoff. He found a half-buried log in the middle of the embankment. It was a miracle they hadn't hit it on landing. He used his KA-Bar to pry the log out of the ground and tossed it over the side of the embankment. He filled in the hole the log had left with small rocks and soil. It wasn't a great fix, but it would do. He continued his inspection and found nothing of note before returning the aircraft.

Five minutes later, the Porter's engine whined under the strain as Coyle released the brake. Gaining momentum, the aircraft rolled swiftly across the top of the embankment, then lifted into the air. Coyle saw the burning truck below and multiple headlights from approaching enemy vehicles in the distance. He was right – they had left just in time.

It was getting light out as dawn approached. He banked his plane and headed south instead of west. He would cross the North Vietnamese border into the south by flying low through a valley. He had gone that way before and hadn't had a problem. He wanted to get Blackjack to a military hospital with experienced surgeons as soon as possible. With a bit more luck they could save Blackjack's legs.

They crossed the border just before dawn. They were safe on the South Vietnamese side of the border. Blackjack was alive and grateful.

After stopping to refuel, Coyle flew to Pleiku where he knew the USAF had top-notch doctors to tend to Blackjack's wounds. Blackjack was strong and lucky. Most men would have lost their legs from infection. It took three hours of surgery to ensure that all of the mortar shrapnel in Blackjack had been removed. The doctors watched him over the next few days, and he recovered quickly. The doctors had a hard time convincing him not to leave the hospital and return to Laos. The enemy had killed one of his SOG team members and he wanted payback.

The one time he did try to leave the hospital, he lasted almost ten seconds on his feet before he started feeling woozy and had to sit down on the floor. A cute nurse scolded him, then helped him back to his room and tucked him in bed. A little later, the nurse returned with a stack of the latest novels from the hospital library. Blackjack loved spy novels. He chose two and decided it wasn't a bad idea to catch up on his reading. The cute nurse was a factor in his decision too.

Miniguns & Boxcars

Coyle returned the USAF reconnaissance photos that he had borrowed from Lima Site 85. While in the intelligence facility, he examined the latest reports of enemy movements. It seemed the Viet Cong were overly active, especially near the village where Nguyet and her daughter were living. His best friend McGoon had made him responsible for Nguyet and Chau after he died. Although he had been unable to Chau, Coyle felt obliged to watch out for Nguyet and her ten-year-old girl, who could very well be McGoon's daughter.

While there were no reports of impending attacks, Coyle would keep an eye on things. He wished he had pushed harder for Nguyet and her daughter to relocate to one of the large cities where there was an overabundance of ARVN troops protecting the population. Nguyet did not want to raise her daughter in a big city where the temptation of easy money could lure a young woman down a dishonorable path. Because her daughter was so unusually large and white-skinned, she felt she was safer in a village and would learn how to farm, an honorable profession. Coyle couldn't argue against it, or maybe he didn't want to.

But now, things were different. The war was accelerating and enemy attacks, especially against unfortified villages, were on the rise. He considered flying back out to the village and insisting that they relocate. He had spent enough time with Nguyet that he knew she could be quite stubborn in a very nice way. Like a willow tree, she would bend but not snap. Coyle decided to put the visit off until he could figure out a good argument that would convince Nguyet.

While he thought, Coyle resumed his duties with the CIA flying the most difficult missions that only he had the experience to make a success. He also continued training pilots and gun crews to fly the AC-47 gunship, an aircraft he knew like the back of his hand. After all, he had helped develop the fixed-wing ground assault plane. He had been flying the beast longer than anyone.

The demand for "Spooky" gunships all around South Vietnam was extremely high. They were victims of their success. Firebase commanders had seen what the gunships did to even the odds when they were outnumbered. The invisible gunships with their streams of red tracer rounds frightened the Viet Cong who thought they were dragons. One broadside from the gunships could break up an enemy human wave assault and send the VC fleeing back into the jungle.

The biggest problem in creating more fixed-wing gunships was the miniguns. There weren't enough to go around. Each gunship required three miniguns.

Plus, American ground forces also wanted the 7.62 mm miniguns to protect allied convoys using modified gun trucks. With names like "Snoopy, Eve of Destruction", and "The Undertaker" painted on the armor-plated sides, the gun truck crews and commanders all wanted miniguns to be mounted in the truck's cargo area. Even a VC human wave assault on a 200-truck convoy had little hope of success when the gun trucks' miniguns let loose firing up to 6,000 rounds per minute. The gun truck program was so successful that MACV wanted one gun truck for every ten transport trucks in a convoy, especially in hot spots like the "Devil's Hairpin" in An Khe Pass and "Ambush Alley" below Mang Yang Pass where enemy ambushes on convoys occurred almost daily.

General Electric, the minigun manufacturer, was cranking out the weapons at full capacity and was given top priority for raw materials from the war department. But nothing seemed to satisfy the need for the high-speed Gatling guns as more and more commanders found uses for them.

The second problem with the fixed-wing gunships was the wear and tear on the C-47 Dakotas many of which had airframes that were already twenty-five years old. Each minigun produced 600 lbs. of recoil when it fired. Firing a broadside of three miniguns for an extended period put extreme stress on the gun mounts which were attached to the airframe. The aircraft maintenance crews kept a close watch for structural cracks in the airframes.

To make matters worse, GE kept coming up with innovative options like an auto-reloading device that added significant weight to the entire system. The more weight that was added, the less ammunition the aircraft could carry. During a firefight, the miniguns used ammunition like a whale eats fish. It was massive and never-ending. During the middle of a battle, the gunship was frequently forced to land and reload because of its limited cargo weight capacity.

Like an idiot, Coyle had suggested that the USAF and CIA look into using the C-119 Boxcar instead of the C-47 Dakota as the weapon's aerial platform. The

USAF had already completed Project Gunship II with the development of the AC-130 gunship which had a much larger cargo weight capacity than the AC-47. But the C-130 was still in use as a transport aircraft and was in short supply.

Like the C-47, there were a lot of retired C-119s floating around and parts were easy to find. But unlike the C-47, the C-119 had more powerful engines and was more stable in flight. It could handle double the cargo weight which meant more ammunition onboard. The C-119s also had a lot more room in their cargo holds which meant more weapon and ammunition capacity. Coyle thought the C-119's robust airframe might be able to handle the vibration of a 20mm canon which could be useful in destroying fortified enemy bunkers. The C-119 had one more advantage – a rear loading ramp. While ammunition and supplies needed to be lifted and loaded through a side door on the C-47, the C-119 had a rear ramp that allowed carts of ammunition and supplies to be rolled into the aircraft. The re-arming time was drastically reduced and if the crew was in the middle of a firefight, time was everything.

The USAF was so impressed with Coyle's understanding of the C-119 Boxcar and the current AC-47 Spooky, they asked him to oversee the development of the new weapon platform. He tried to back out, saying his plate was full, which it was, but the CIA, who also wanted him to oversee the project said that they could free up his time by removing some of his workload. Coyle had little choice but to accept.

The project was called Project Gunship III and the aircraft took on the call sign "Creep" during initial development. Later the aircraft's call sign would change to "Shadow" which was much more dignified and to the USAF's liking.

Coyle put in long hours during the initial development. He and the engineers under his supervision decided on four GAU-2 miniguns for Shadow. Why not? It could take the extra weight and more guns made it more lethal. Call sign "Stinger," the AC-119K variant was to be used on the Ho Chi Minh Trail. To take out vehicles from a long distance, Coyle and the engineers added two M61 Vulcan 20mm six-barreled Gatling cannons. Both versions of the new AC-119 gunships had sixty Mk 24 flares in LAU-74/A flare launchers. Visor Nocturno night vision and an AVQ-8 Xenon light were also included on both planes. The AC-119 was a substantial upgrade of the AC-47. Coyle was exhausted but proud of his creation.

Returning to his quarters well past midnight, Coyle saw a note on the door. It was from his son Scott stationed at Camp Holloway just two miles away from Pleiku. He wanted to meet Coyle when he had some free time. Free time? *That's a laugh*, thought Coyle. But this was his son and he would do anything for him including pissing off the USAF and the CIA.

Scott entered the Pleiku officer's club with a box of orange Nehi under his arm. Coyle was already seated at a table and had a beer sitting in front of him. "Why do I think this conversation might involve a favor?" said Coyle seeing the box of his favorite soda.

"Because you're very intuitive," said Scott.

Coyle laughed as Scott set the box down on the table. Coyle rose and hugged his son. Hugging was still awkward for them both, but they were working on it.

They sat. "So, what's up?" said Coyle.

"No, chitchat?" said Scott.

"If you want chitchat, we chitchat."

"Nah. It's probably better we get straight to it."

"Sounds serious."

"I need your advice… and help."

"Okay. Shoot."

"The Army wants me to re-enlist for another tour."

"Of course, they do. You're a good pilot."

"Well, I'm thinking about not re-enlisting."

"Oh, well… That's probably a smart move. You could make a lot more money flying privately back in the States. I'm gonna miss you… and the orange Nehi."

Scott moved closer and lowered his voice, "No. I don't think you understand. I want to join the CIA."

Coyle was a bit taken aback and said, "Why?"

"Because you guys make a difference. I want that. Lately, it seems like we fly out, hunt for the bad guys, and come home emptyhanded."

"Well, at least you're not getting shot at."

"That's thing… I never know what's gonna happen or when. If I am gonna risk my life, I want it to mean something. I want it to count."

"I can understand that. But I think you may be overestimating what we do. I spend a lot of time on wild-goose chases just like you. It's part of the job."

"I know, but your missions seem a lot more focused. You have clear objectives, and when you achieve them, they make a difference."

"Not always."

"Okay, but far more than mine."

"Yeah, that's probably true."

"So, will you help me?"

"Help you how?"

"Talk to your superiors. Recommend me as a potential recruit."

"Yeah, sure. But first… Why not go back to the States, get a plum flying job, settle down, and have a family? It could be a very rewarding life."

"Like you did?"

"I was different, Scott. I saw things… I did things… It was difficult to go back with all that stuff rolling around in my head. I needed time to figure it out."

"I feel the same way. I'm not ready to go back. Not yet."

Coyle nodded. He knew that Scott had similar experiences to himself.

"I think you could be a great asset to the company. I just wanna make sure you know what you are getting yourself into. It's not the same as being in the military."

"I know. That's why I like the idea. You guys are a lot more autonomous. You do what is necessary without the need for orders."

"We still receive orders. But you're right. Once we're given a mission, it's up to us to find a way to achieve its objectives. They give us a long leash, but it's still a leash."

"It sounds better than the military."

"If you join, you may be asked to do some things that you might find distasteful… or even unethical."

"I am aware of that. I'm a patriot and I want to protect my country. If I need to bend the rules, I'll do it."

"It's not just bending the rules. You could be asked to assassinate targets."

"That's no different than hunting Viet Cong with air-to-ground rockets."

"It is different, especially if you need to get up close."

"Do you think they may ask me to do that?"

"Realistically, probably not. You're a pilot. But it could happen. I just want you to be prepared for it."

"I appreciate that. But it's something I have thought about and I am willing to accept such an assignment if need be."

"Okay, but know this… When you're in the military, you're protected somewhat by international laws. If you join the company, you become a civilian and that protection goes away."

"I don't see the Viet Cong or the NVA giving any credence to international law when it comes to the treatment of military prisoners. Everyone gets tortured during interrogation."

"Well, they're willing to spend a lot more effort interrogating a civilian intelligence officer than a military one."

"I'm willing to take that risk."

"If you are captured by the enemy in a place where you are not supposed to be like Laos, the United States government will most likely deny that you even exist. There will be no cavalry arriving. You'll be on your own."

"I know that, and again, I am willing to accept the risk."

"Look, there is a lot more to it than just those things I mentioned. When is your current enlistment up?"

"Middle of next month."

"Okay, so you've got a bit of time. Use it to consider your options and the risks. We can talk again."

"I'm not going to change my mind, Dad."

The word "Dad" struck Coyle like a thunderbolt.

He was a dad and would do anything to protect his children. But it was strange to hear Scott, a grown man, call him Dad. Two years ago, Coyle didn't even know he had a son or a daughter. Now, he was a dad and carried all the responsibility that went with the title. If he was being honest with himself, he was scared to death that Scott might be seriously wounded or even killed. He couldn't breathe when he thought about the possibility of his children getting hurt or dying. But he was also proud as hell that his boy wanted to follow in his footsteps. Scott was courageous and a patriot that was willing to lay down his life for his country. That was more than most fathers had a right to expect of their children. Still, he wanted to protect his son if possible… "I'll make you a deal," said Coyle. "You take one more week to consider all the possibilities before making your final decision. After that, if you still want to join the company, I'll talk to some people I know about accepting you as a recruit."

"One week?"

"One week."

"I can do that."

"Great. Now let's see if this dive has some ice for my orange Nehi."

Saigon, South Vietnam

Accompanying another AP journalist, Ken Brand, Karen took photos of a Vietnamese man that claimed he was kidnapped by a group of NVA soldiers led by an American in plain clothes. Taken to a covert interrogation site, the American advisor observed and advised the interrogator on methods of torture while he was trying to extract information from his detainee.

The man said that he didn't know anything and therefore couldn't offer any information that might make his interrogator stop torturing him. It seemed like the information was secondary to the instruction the American was giving the interrogator.

Taking off his shirt and pants, the man revealed burn marks resembling cigarette burns, but more severe. Karen was repulsed by the gore but didn't turn away. The man showed his genitals and demanded that Karen take photos of his painful wounds. He wanted evidence of what they had done to him. He broke down weeping as he relived the experience in his mind.

Karen knew that no newspaper or magazine would purchase photos that included a man's genitals, but she took the photos anyway to document the event. Whoever tortured the man was a sadist and needed to be brought to justice.

As they left the interview, Karen asked, "Have you ever seen anything like that before?'

"I hate to admit it but yeah. This is Vietnam and we're at war. It happens," said Brand.

"And we do nothing about it?"

"We do our jobs and report it, but if I am being honest there is little chance the story gets published."

"Why?"

"I don't know. An invisible hand stops it or maybe readers just don't care to hear about such things."

"But it happened. You saw the burn marks."

"I did. But that doesn't mean the man was telling the truth. He could be VC or at least a communist supporter. Maybe even a recruiter. Whoever captured him must have had a reason. They don't just pick random people off the street."

"Even if they had a reason, that is no way to treat another human being."

"Have you seen what the Viet Cong do to the villagers that stand in their way?"

"Two wrongs don't make a right."

"No, they don't. But I don't think it's smart to bring a knife to a gunfight. We have to be just as tough and devious as the VC if we're going to win."

"So, that's it? It's okay to torture people to win the war?"

"Well, yeah. If it's necessary."

"And who gets to decide that… if it's necessary?"

"I don't know. I sure as hell wouldn't want to be that guy. Can you imagine the guilt he must feel?"

"What if I could get photos of an actual torture session? Would that make a difference?"

"Don't be stupid, Karen. Nobody gets that close. And if they do, they don't live to tell about it."

"But would it make a difference?'

"I don't know. I doubt it would be published by a major newspaper, but if given to the right people I suppose some congressmen might look into it."

"That's something at least."

"Karen, you're a great photographer, and the photos you have been taking make a difference in exposing this war for what it really is. There is no need to risk your life beyond what you are already doing."

"Yeah, I know… but still…"

"No buts, Karen. You don't want to be digging around whoever is behind this. They've already shown that they are willing to break the rules. You don't poke a tiger."

Riding in the back of a truck with Brand, Karen

considered her options. Although she had probably met many CIA officers and didn't know it, she only knew two CIA officers for sure – her father Tom Coyle and the mysterious sniper Granier. There was little chance Granier would divulge any information since it was difficult to get him to talk about anything let alone his job. Her father was a different nut to be cracked. She didn't know how much she could use their new relationship with Coyle to wiggle out information and she wondered if it was even ethical. She figured it didn't hurt to ask. He could always say no.

Pleiku Air Base, South Vietnam

With the overhead fan spinning at top speed and blowing papers off his desk and onto the floor, Coyle sat in his office going over a new list of candidates for his gunship training program. The CIA only had three covert gunships which were mainly used in Laos to interdict enemy convoys on the Ho Chi Minh Trail. He wondered why the CIA wanted so many gunship teams. He concluded that they were preparing the expand the program. The more the better, he thought. The gunships had proven their effectiveness and were now in high demand. The under-development AC-119 would be even more effective once it was officially accepted into the fleet. The main problem with building gunships was the supply of miniguns. GE had a long waiting list for the weapons, and it was getting longer by the day. With a firing rate of 3,000-6,000 rounds per minute, the days of enemy human wave attacks would be numbered as more of the miniguns arrived in Vietnam.

There was a light knock at the door. Coyle turned

to see his son Scott poking his head through the open door. "Got a minute?" said Scott.

"For you, I've got two minutes," said Coyle.

"Well, it's not just me…"

As Scott opened the door wider, Coyle saw Karen standing in the hallway. Coyle grinned. It had been a long time since he had seen his daughter. "Well, if it isn't the mountain coming to see Mohammad," said Coyle.

"I was in the neighborhood," said Karen walking into the office and giving her father a somewhat awkward hug.

"I insisted that she drop by and say hello," said Scott.

Coyle didn't mind. He would take what he could get when it came to his newly found children. "Come on in and take a load off your feet," said Coyle realizing that he only had two chairs in his office and he was sitting in one. The office was a mess with stacks of reports filling up every empty space that wasn't the floor. He cleared the extra chair by setting the stack of reports on his desk and offered it to Karen. He grabbed his desk chair and whirled it around for Scott. He sat on the edge of the desk. "So, Karen… what brings you to our neck of the woods?" Coyle asked .

"Enemy activity. I hear it's on the rise around Pleiku and Dak To. AP was hoping to get some more battlefield photos," said Karen.

"Kinda dangerous work, don't you think?"

"And flying aircraft isn't?"

"Yeah, but it's different."

"Because?"

"Don't fall for it," said Scott. "She'll have your liver for breakfast."

"It's different because you're my daughter," said Coyle avoiding a Chauvinistic comment.

"Nice save," said Scott.

"Scott's your son, but I don't see you giving him a lecture on safety," said Karen.

"Oh, so close," said Scott.

"Believe me, I've tried," said Coyle. "He is just as stubborn as you."

"It's a twin thing," said Karen as his eyes wandered around the room at the stacks of folders marked "Confidential" and "Secret." "That's quite a collection of folders you've got."

"Yeah, I really need to take some of those back to secured storage."

"Don't do it on my account. I'm sure it's fascinating reading."

"Don't even think about it. Never gonna happen."

"Really. Makes me ask… what are you guys hiding?"

"Everything. That's the point. Covert stays covert."

"Okay. So how about helping find a unit to embed with? You must know someone."

"You want me to help you go in harm's way?"

"You did it before."

"That was different. You were just starting out and needed a hand. Sides, I stacked the deck and made sure you weren't in too much danger."

"And that was probably a good idea. I didn't know anything when I first arrived. But now things are different."

"Well, yeah… I gotta admit. You know your way around a battlefield. But it's still dangerous. The enemy is very active and overly aggressive at the moment."

"Perfect. That's what I'm looking for."

"I don't think you understand—"

"Look, sis, if you want to imbed with a unit, I know an officer that owes me a favor," said Scott cutting in.

"Scott, why are you helping her?"

"Because she's gonna do it anyway. That's the way she is. At least this way, I can have the company commander watch over her. My guys and I saved his unit's ass a few months back."

"Alright. I guess there is nothing I can do about it if you both have made up your minds," said Coyle.

"One more thing before we leave… That discussion we had last week."

"Yeah."

"I'm still in."

"Okay. I'll see what I can do."

"What are you guys talking about?" said Karen.

"Father and son stuff. You wouldn't understand."

Karen slugged her brother in the arm like when they were kids. "Now, is that any way to treat your brother?" said Coyle.

"That's exactly how to treat him when he's a smartass," said Karen. "It puts him in his place."

Central Highlands, South Vietnam

A telescopic view of a street vendor pushing a hand cart stacked with coconuts. The crosshairs of the scope followed the vendor through the village. When a customer bought a coconut, the vendor would use a machete to cut off the top of the coconut which allowed the customer to drink the juice and scoop out the white meat inside the shell. The only customers the pushcart had were the Viet Cong soldiers that were occupying the village. Everyone else was hiding in their huts or outside the village tending to their fields or collecting wood for the evening's rice-cooking fires. The villagers wanted to stay away from the Viet Cong as much as possible. The VC felt entitled to whatever they wanted. They may have been dedicated communists, but they were also human and had needs and desires. Most of the time they couldn't tell the difference between the two and just took what they fancied in the name of the revolution. Looting was a common occurrence during wartime, and so was rape. The best way to avoid trouble was simply to stay out of sight.

The Viet Cong had overrun the village late yesterday. Strangely, neither the ARVN nor the Americans had attempted to take it back. That suited the Viet Cong just fine. While the village was not a five-star resort, it was far better than sleeping in the jungle. They had been marching south for almost a week and needed rest.

It was Granier who was watching the coconut vendor through his sniper scope. He had no intention of killing the man. He was Granier's operative. It was also Granier that had kept the ARVN and US Marines from retaking the village. He was looking for evidence that the VC had a spy in the village. He wanted the spy and the information he knew. He just had to find him… or her. He had to be certain.

There was a group of ten Phoenix trainees with Granier. They too were watching through binoculars and unmounted scopes. Granier would quietly instruct them as the surveillance continued. For a prize like an enemy intelligence operative, it was sometimes worth spending several days observing before springing the trap. Observation would occasionally reveal others in the spy network. In this case, Granier's undercover operative was flushing out the prey.

As the vendor pushed his cart he glanced at the open doorways and windows hoping to catch sight of the target – a well-respected village elder turned into an enemy spy. Approaching the center of the village, the vendor saw his target through a window in the village's meeting hall. The spy was talking and laughing with the Viet Cong commander and a political officer. It was the evidence that Granier had wanted. The spy looked out through the window and saw the coconut vendor studying him. The spy turned to the Viet Cong and motioned angrily toward the vendor.

Granier was watching through a window on the opposite side of the building and saw the enemy spy jump up and point to the vendor as if accusing him. Granier had all of the evidence he felt he needed to seal the fate of the enemy spy.

Knowing that his cover had been blown, the vendor abandoned his coconuts mid-sale to a customer. He ran up the main road and turned down a narrow alley. The VC commander ran out of the meeting hall and ordered his men to track down the vendor. The soldiers ran after the vendor.

Granier could see through his scope that the vendor was in trouble and said, "Shit."

He turned to his radioman and said, "Our guy's cover is blown. Radio HQ and tell them to attack the village now."

The vendor emerged from the alley and ran across a rice field toward Granier. "You, idiot. Don't lead them to us," said Granier.

It was too late. Granier leveled his rifle and aimed at the alley. When the first VC soldier emerged,

Granier took him out with a single shot to the head. Three more soldiers emerged from the alley and fired at the fleeing vendor halfway across the field.

Granier fired again and again taking out two more VC. His aim was deadly but aiming took time. He watched as the vendor climbed the embankment of the field's surrounding dike and was hit in the back with a bullet. He fell backward into the muddy water. He was dead. Granier cursed and took out the third VC soldier as retribution. More soldiers poured out of the alley and headed across the field toward Granier's position. "Everyone, retreat to the rendezvous point. If I'm not there in four minutes, head back to the airfield," said Granier to his trainees.

"What about you?" said one of the trainees.

"I'll be dead. Now go!"

The trainees moved out as Granier continued to take out the approaching VC which were now over a dozen and moving fast. They were elite troops and did not break off their attack even as their comrades fell from Granier's bullets. He was outnumbered and outgunned. The closer they came to his position, the more accurate their fire. Enemy bullets were churning up the dirt in front of him. It wouldn't take long until one of them found its mark. But Granier wouldn't leave. He had to buy time for the trainees to escape. They were his responsibility. He remained in control as he fired. He would not be distracted even though he might soon be dead.

When the enemy troops got within fifty feet, Granier knew he was in deep trouble. He heard the familiar whooshing sound of a UH-1C helicopter blades cutting the air as it approached. Moments later, fourteen 2.75-inch Mk4 Folding-Fin Aerial Rockets were launched from the gunship, flew across the sky, and exploded in the rice field full of VC soldiers chasing Granier. Most of the VC that were smart enough to dive into the muddy water were saved, while the others that continued the chase were shredded with shrapnel from the rockets. It didn't matter.

A second UH-1C paralleling the first, flew to one side of the field and the door gunner opened up with his swivel-mounted M60. The enemy was caught in the open and there was nothing they could do about it except return fire. It didn't help. They were cut down as several more gunships swooped in and had their turn at the enemy. It was an impressive display of air-to-ground support.

Granier didn't move. He didn't want to risk being mistaken for the enemy. He waited until the team of helicopters peeled off and headed toward the village where a remaining company of VC were firing their weapons at the enemy aircraft. Before getting up, Granier looked out at the rice field. There was no movement. The muddy water had turned into a nauseating reddish-brown.

Granier rose and backed into the surrounding jungle. He was safe. He wanted to go back to the village and capture the enemy operative that had ordered the coconut vendor killed but that was no longer Granier's job. One of the main changes from the Keyman Project to the Phoenix Program was that the hunters were no longer responsible for capturing their targets. The AVRV and US military had the assignment. Part of the reason was to divert attention away from the operation. The targets would be captured during what looked like normal operations. Since the enemy didn't suspect the capture of the target as the main objective of the enemy mission, it was thought that the target had been caught up in a normal sweep during and after the assault. This allowed some of the prisoners to be turned into double agents without the VC or NVA suspecting anything. Granier would catch up with the enemy spy once he was captured and turned over to the Phoenix interrogation team.

The Phoenix operators were far too valuable to waste on military missions that could be handled by regular forces. The information they extracted from their prisoners saved the lives of tens of thousands of Allied soldiers and civilians. The Viet Cong and NVA's network of spies was finally being revealed and systematically dismantled one spy at a time.

Kon Tum Province, South Vietnam

As Scott had expected, the company commander was grateful and willingly agreed to allow Karen to imbed with his unit. Scott flew her out and dropped her off in a jungle clearing. The company commander was waiting and promised Scott he'd watch over her.

As Karen had expected, the company had come in heavy contact several times in the last week and was now heading for a village that had been taken over by the Viet Cong. The village was a few miles north of Dak To, a strategically important rural district in the Central Highlands. She carried extra film canisters and planned on using them.

When they arrived at the edge of the jungle just outside the village, the company stopped and took up defensive positions using the trees as camouflage. "Why are we stopping?" said Karen.

"We're waiting for a signal to advance," said the

commander.

"A signal from who?"

"There's an operative inside the village. He's scouting it out. He'll let us know when to advance."

"Scouting it out?"

"That, and he's locating someone."

"Who?"

"Karen, I'd love to tell you, but I have my orders. That part of the mission is covert."

"Okay. I understand. I was just asking."

"Hang tight. It shouldn't be long before we move again. After that, things might get a little hairy."

"Good to know."

Karen knew better than to move around too much. She could give away their position as easily as a fidgeting recruit. She watched quietly among the foliage in the shadows of the jungle canopy. A familiar voice crackled on the radio identifying himself as Witch Six. She couldn't pin the voice down, but she was sure she had heard it before. Witch Six said, "I have eyes on target in the northeast section of the village. The enemy is twenty-eight souls with one light machine gun set up in a hutch in the southwest corner of the village. You are authorized to advance and engage. No artillery or air support at this time. Direct fire weapons only. Once the target is captured and clear of the village, you are all weapons-free."

The commander acknowledged the message and ordered his company to move out. Karen held back until the majority of the company had left the jungle. She knew that advancing without artillery or air support was dangerous. She was sure it was a snatch-and-grab operation. "This guy must be really important," she said to a passing sergeant.

"What guy?" said the sergeant.

"Nevermind," said Karen.

As the Americans closed within two hundred yards, the enemy machine gun opened fire. The company fell to the ground and disappeared in the long grass denying the machine gunner a clear target. The rest of the way would be on their bellies. The company commander ordered his men to fix their bayonets. With bullets whizzing overhead, Karen snapped photos of several soldiers putting their bayonets on the end of their rifle barrels. Two light machine gun teams set up positions on both sides of the company's line of advance. Karen belly-crawled over to the closest machine gun team and snapped several more photos. This was what the AP wanted and there was plenty of it.

A bazooka team moved up to the front of the company. They crawled as far as they dared toward the machine gun that was spraying bullets across their lines. Karen was right behind them crawling in their path of smashed grass. The loader slipped a missile into the back of the bazooka and tapped the gunner on the helmet signaling that the weapon was ready to fire. The gunner aimed through the long grass and fired. Karen snapped a photo of the rocket leaving the bazooka with a trail of exhaust out the back of the tube. The missile flew across the open ground and hit the hut where the machine gun was located. Exhilarated, Karen snapped another photo. It didn't get any better than this for a war photojournalist. The explosion ripped apart the hut killing the machine gunner and his loader. Another photo was snapped as a ball of flame ascended into the sky above the remains of the burning hut.

With the enemy machine gun out of the battle, the

Americans had the advantage. The company commander ordered his men to charge. The faster they could enter the village; the more American lives would be saved. Several wounded Americans dropped as the Viet Cong kept up a steady barrage of gunfire with their rifles. The Americans returned fire as they ran. The American light machine guns laid down suppressing fire on the enemy positions within the village forcing them to put their heads down. As the Americans overran the Viet Cong lines and entered the village, the conflict reverted to hand-to-hand combat. Rifle bayonets slashed and stabbed. The Viet Cong used their rifles as clubs. Keeping her distance at the edge of the village and hiding behind a tree trunk, Karen was terrified at the violence but continued to snap her photos. It was a bloody battle with casualties on both sides. But it was the Americans that prevailed.

As the surviving Viet Cong fled, the American company commander took a team and advanced through the village to the target's position. Karen followed at a distance and reloaded her camera. The target was identified and apprehended by the American soldiers. Karen snapped several photos. "You shouldn't do that," said the commander.

"Is it some kind of secret?" said Karen taking another photo.

"You could say that," said a deep voice moving up behind Karen.

She turned to see Granier flanked by two of his Phoenix recruits walking toward her. "You?" said Karen snapping Granier's photo. "You're Witch Six?"

"I'm gonna need that film," said Granier.

"Like hell."

Granier motioned to his two recruits. They grabbed

Karen and wrestled away her camera. "Goddammit. That's my property," said Karen. "I'm just doing my job."

"And I'm just doing mine," said Granier as one of the recruits handed him the camera. Granier opened the camera's back and ripped out the film from the canister exposing it to sunlight.

"You fucker," said Karen.

Granier closed the camera, handed it back to her, and said, "Covert means covert. What are you doing here anyway, Karen?"

"Trying to find who is behind all of this."

Frustrated, Granier turned to the company commander and said, "Why did you let a reporter imbed with your unit? You knew the mission parameters."

"I owed her brother a favor. It was a mistake," said the commander knowing he was in hot water.

"It was. A big one. You keep her away from my men."

"Yes, sir."

"Too late. I know who you are," said Karen.

"Then I guess I'll have to shoot you," said Granier.

Karen tensed, unsure if he was serious. Granier chuckled, "Gets 'em every time."

"Prick!"

"Bitch."

As Granier walked away, Karen tried to reload her camera, but the company commander reached out placing his hand over the camera, and said, "That's enough for today, Karen."

Frustrated, Karen cursed. She watched as Granier and his recruits took custody of the target in handcuffs from the soldiers and left the village. "Where is he taking him?" said Karen.

"I don't know, and I don't care as long as it's away from me and my men," said the commander.

"Kind of a chicken shit attitude."

"Maybe. But those boys play by their own rules. You best steer clear."

"They don't scare me."

"They should."

Silent No More

Senator Robert F. Kennedy and President Lyndon B. Johnson despised one another. Even though Johnson had asked Kennedy to stay on as Attorney General after his brother's assassination, Kennedy was reluctant. Johnson wanted stability. Kennedy wanted Johnson to carry out his dead brother's strategy on Vietnam and the Cold War. The only thing the two could agree on was Civil Rights and the elimination of poverty, especially among minorities.

While in Johnson's White House cabinet, Kennedy was a team player and did not voice his opinion against Johnson's policies even when they conflicted with his own and those of his brother. He continued to work on the things that he cared about. All the while, he let the things that he could not support slide unless directly ordered by the president to take action.

When Johnson moved up to president, the vice-president position became open. There was talk among Johnson's advisors and political allies about making Kennedy vice president. Kennedy was unsure that he wanted to be involved with Johnson any more than he already had. He and those that counseled him felt he needed to develop his own power base if he was to advance his political career. Johnson could not stand the thought that he needed Robert Kennedy to win an election, even if he did have the sympathy vote. The president tried to squash the idea before it gained momentum. But there were powerful forces that supported Kennedy and wanted him to eventually take his brother's place at the pinnacle of the American political system.

Kennedy was asked to introduce the film *A Thousand Days* about his late brother during the 1964 democratic party convention. When he was introduced, the crowd of delegates, elected officials, and party bosses applauded like thunder and became tearful. It took twenty-two minutes before the audience would let him speak. He was emotionally moved by the sentiments of so many people that loved his brother. He struggled to keep from breaking down as he talked about JFK's vision for the party and the nation. He recited a quote from Shakespeare's Romeo and Juliet that Jacqueline Kennedy had given him before his tribute:

When [he] shall die
Take him and cut him out in little stars,
And he will make the face of heaven so fine
That all the world will be in love with night
And pay no worship to the garish sun.

The death of his brother affected him deeply. It seemed like RFK had appointed himself the custodian of his brother's dream and strategy. But as time went on, Robert Kennedy's reliance on the government declined and the memory of his brother's dream faded. He charted his own course. He sought his own conclusions on where the nation should head and what he needed to do to ensure it reached a safe harbor. That was especially true when it came to the war in Vietnam.

Kennedy had seen his brother waffle back and forth about Vietnam and committing troops. Robert never thought sending combat troops was a good idea but kept his opinion between the two brothers and said little publicly about the war. The same was now true with Johnson. He only offered his opinion when asked and never in public. It was probably for the best. Johnson did not value Kennedy's opinion beyond his position as the nation's attorney general and even then, Johnson was suspect of any counsel that came from Kennedy. The president acknowledged that Robert Kennedy knew the law and was good at his job. But he also knew that Kennedy had higher political aspirations and therefore considered his advice tainted. Johnson thought that Kennedy might purposely ambush him or embarrass him in public to advance his own career. That was not Robert Kennedy's style, but Johnson was paranoid nonetheless.

Kennedy stayed in Johnson's cabinet for nine months after his brother's death. That was enough. He asked Johnson to make him ambassador to South Vietnam and the president declined. So, Kennedy decided to run for the US Senate seat representing New York. The Kennedys were well known in New York and RFK was well-liked by Democrats. Surprisingly, Johnson gave Kennedy his support figuring that by making Kenney a senator it would satisfy him for a time and keep him away from the White House. Kennedy won the senate seat.

Because of his brother's reputation, Kennedy was far more powerful than the average senator. He was also a good orator when it came to supporting bills and many senators went out of their way to hear him speak on the senate floor. But Kennedy had gone from the president's advisor to one of a hundred senators. He felt it was a step down in power and became frustrated with collaborative lawmaking. Although he was generally well-liked in the senate, his blunt fashion of discourse made him unpopular with some of the senators.

As he began his tenure in the senate, Senator Kennedy kept his disagreements with President Johnson private and did not speak against the president's policies in Vietnam. It wasn't easy.

In January of 1967, Kennedy began a ten-day tour of Europe where he discussed the Vietnam War with many of its diplomats and leaders, including the British Prime Minister Harold Wilson who was adamantly against the war. There were many European leaders with the same opinion.

When he returned to the States, the press confronted him by asking him if his conversations abroad had undermined President Johnson's foreign policy. Kennedy assured everyone that was not his intention and that he respected Johnson's right to control foreign policy. There was only one president as the framers of the Constitution had intended.

But by April 1967, Kennedy felt he could no longer stay silent while so many lives were on the line. He began publicly advocating a stop to the bombing of North Vietnam. It was well known that the bombing missions had been ineffective at drawing the North Vietnamese leaders to the negotiating table. While Kennedy understood the need to subdue the enemy, he didn't feel the killing of innocent civilians, especially women, and children, was improving America's standing in the world community and was morally repugnant. It was senseless to continue with the failed strategy.

Even so, Kennedy did not want to be labeled anti-war and was displeased when protestors chanted his name at their rallies. He did not agree with the arguments of Oregon's Senator Wayne Morse, who opposed the war in Vietnam calling it "unconstitutional." Like many senators, Kennedy wanted negotiated peace, not surrender.

Kennedy argued hard with the White House to do more to secure the release of American prisoners from the North Vietnamese and Viet Cong. During a meeting with Philip Heymann, the State Department's Bureau of Security and Consular Affairs, Kennedy tried to convince Heymann that more could be done to secure the POWs' release. Heymann responded that the administration believed the "consequences of sitting down with the Viet Cong" mattered more than the prisoners they were holding captive. Kennedy was dumbfounded.

Shortly thereafter, Kennedy released a statement criticizing Johnson's bombing of Haiphong Harbor. But he avoided criticizing Johnson's entire strategy for Vietnam or any other of the president's foreign policies. While Kennedy had contempt for Johnson, he did not want to be in open rebellion against his president. Public criticism of the president seemed unpatriotic, especially in a time of war.

During an appearance on *Face The Nation*, Kennedy suggested that the Johnson administration had deviated from his brother's strategy and policies for Vietnam. He also said that the idea that Americans were fighting in Vietnam to end communism was immoral. Whether he liked it or not, Kennedy was becoming one of the nation's top leaders criticizing the Vietnam War and the South Vietnam government. In one of his brochures, Kennedy stated that he did not support a simple withdrawal of American forces or the surrender of South Vietnam. He favored a change of course in action and strategy that would bring about an honorable peace. Kennedy was walking a tightrope that could very easily smack him in the face.

April 4, 1967 – The Riverside Church, New York, NY

It was well known that Martin Luther King was against the Vietnam War but avoided publicly discussing his feelings about the war for fear of confusing the Social Rights issues that were his main focus. Many critics claimed he was a coward and by keeping his own counsel he was condoning the war. King was a man of principle and didn't care what others thought as long as he believed he was doing the right thing. But there was little doubt this one issue stirred up conflicts and doubts within the civil rights leader. He had been inspired by Muhammad Ali's outspokenness when it came to the war, even when Ali was forced to surrender his heavyweight title belt for his stand against the war.

It was in the spring of 1967 when King broke his silence and spoke about the Vietnam War during an outdoor event in front of his church in New York. The crowd was a sea of black and brown faces salted with a few white faces. They were his people. His followers. He felt they were owed the truth about the way he saw the Vietnam War since many of their kin were fighting in that war too far.

After a prayer and hymn from the choir, King rose and spoke strongly against America's role in the war. He argued that the U.S. was in Vietnam "to occupy it as an American colony" and called the U.S. government "the greatest purveyor of violence in the world today." He connected the war with economic injustice and argued that the country required serious moral change. He said, "A true revolution of values will soon look uneasily on the glaring contrast of poverty and wealth. With righteous indignation, it will look across the seas and see individual capitalists of the West investing huge sums of money in Asia, Africa, and South America, only to take the profits out with no concern for the social betterment of the countries…"

King also opposed the Vietnam War because it took money and resources away from social welfare programs at home. The United States President and Congress were spending more and more on the military and less and less on anti-poverty programs in America. He said, "A nation that continues year after year to spend more money on military defense than on programs of social uplift is approaching spiritual death."

He further stated that North Vietnam "did not begin to send in any large number of supplies or men until American forces had arrived in the tens of thousands" and accused the U.S. military of having killed a million Vietnamese, "mostly children."

King also criticized American opposition to North Vietnam's land reforms which brought about the starvation of millions.

It didn't take long for King's critics to lay the preacher low. King's opposition to the war cost him substantial support among white allies, including union leaders, major newspaper publishers, the evangelical minister Billy Graham, and even President Johnson who had been a fan of King's social reform policies. King felt persecuted for telling the truth and said, "The press is being stacked up against me."

King went on to complain of what he called a double standard that applauded his nonviolence at home but deplored it when applied "toward little brown Vietnamese children."

Life magazine called his speech "demagogic slander that sounded like a script for Radio Hanoi."

The Washington Post wrote that King had "diminished his usefulness to his cause, his country, his people."

King's "Beyond Vietnam" speech was an evolution of his political advocacy. From that point, he began to speak of the need for fundamental changes in the nation's political and economic life. He continued to express his opposition to the war and his desire for a redistribution of resources to correct racial and economic injustice. He was still guarded in public when referring to political and economic theories for fear of being labeled a communist by his critics. But in private he discussed his support of democratic socialism. King had read Marx while studying at Morehouse. While he rejected traditional capitalism, he rejected communism because it denied religion and endorsed totalitarianism. Growing impatient with the slow turning wheels of social equality, King wanted to see the world change and he wanted that change to occur sooner rather than later.

King said that America was on the wrong side of a world revolution and needed to rethink its priorities. It should embrace and support the shirtless and barefoot people in the world instead of suppressing their attempts at revolution. He said that true compassion is more than flinging a coin to a beggar. We must see that the edifice that produces beggars needs restructuring.

King often sounded like a communist, but he wasn't. He was a socialist fighting for equality. But the Beyond Vietnam speech had already done irrefutable damage. Within a year, King would be killed by an assassin's bullet, but his heritage would not be silenced. He had created the long-lasting idea of change. His followers would see that his dream was not forgotten.

April 15, 1967 – New York, New York USA

The day before the Spring Mobilization to End the War anti-war demonstration, a young protestor created a banner – Vietnam Veterans Against The War. On the day of the demonstration in New York, twenty Vietnam War veterans spotted and gathered under the impromptu banner. Although 400,000 protestors took part in the march, everyone realized that this small group was special… and powerful. They had been there and knew what had happened during the war. They were not pacifists like most of the protestors. They were anti-Vietnam War. Their military experience in Southeast Asia gave them credence and authority. When they spoke, people listened, even people that did not agree with the protesters.

The march attracted hundreds of thousands of people, including Dr. Benjamin Spock, Tom Hayden, Martin Luther King Jr., Harry Belafonte, and James Bevel. It started in Central Park where the protestors gathered and moved through the streets of New York to the United Nations complex. During the march, protestors stopped along the way to burn their draft cards in spur-of-the-moment baby bond fires. Many of the anti-Vietnam War veterans spoke and the massive crowd hushed to listen.

After the protests, six of the veterans got together and formed an official organization called, "Vietnam Veterans Against The War" (VVAW). While most of the other Vietnam War veteran groups did not recognize or support the VVAW, their members could not deny that these men and women had served and sacrificed for their country. The VVAW would grow to over 30,000 members as more disgruntled veterans returned home and Americans changed their opinions about the continuation of the Vietnam War. They wanted it stopped.

Several VVAW members moved on to prominent positions in government and society. Bobby Muller co-founded the Vietnam Veterans of America in 1978. In 1982, John Kerry was elected as Lt. Governor of Massachusetts and went on to become a US Senator and US Secretary of State. Ron Kovic wrote his autobiography, Born on the Fourth of July which was adapted as a movie by Oliver Stone and won several Academy Awards.

April 28, 1967 - Houston, Texas USA

Muhamad Ali was a fighter like no other in and out of the ring. On February 25, 1964, Cassius Marcellus Clay Jr. won boxing's Heavyweight Championship from Sonny Liston by Technical Knockout when Liston failed to return to the center of the ring at the beginning of the seventh round. Liston had enough of

Clay's stinging punch combinations. Clay ran to the edge of the ring where the press was located and shouted, "Eat your words! I am the greatest! I shook up the world. I am the prettiest thing that ever lived."

Changing his name to Muhammad Ali a short time later, Ali was known worldwide for his boxing talent, but it was his political stands that would truly shake the world. In 1962, Ali registered for conscription in the United States military on his eighteenth birthday and was immediately listed as 1-A meaning he could be drafted into the military. In 1964, Ali failed the U.S. Armed Forces qualifying test because of his writing and spelling skills which were substandard because of dyslexia. He was reclassified Class 1-Y which meant he could only serve in the military in times of national emergency. In 1965, Ali was again reclassified 1-A when the army lowered its standards to allow more conscription for the Vietnam War. Ali could once again be drafted and inducted into the U.S. military.

When notified that his status had changed, Ali announced that he would not serve in the army because he considered himself a conscientious objector. Ali, who had converted to Islam a year earlier, said, "War is against the teachings of the Qur'an. I'm not trying to dodge the draft. We are not supposed to take part in no wars unless declared by Allah or The Messenger. We don't take part in Christian wars or wars of any unbelievers. We are not to be the aggressor, but we will defend ourselves if attacked. Man, I ain't got no quarrel with them, Viet Cong. Why should they ask me to put on a uniform and go ten thousand miles from home and drop bombs and bullets on brown people in Vietnam while so-called Negro people in Louisville are treated like dogs and denied simple human rights?"

Ali's protest did not sit well with the white establishment. Powerful forces began to align themselves against him.

On April 28, 1967, Ali appeared in Houston for his scheduled induction into the U.S. Military. When his name was called to step forward, he stood still defiant. His name was called two more times and he didn't move. An officer warned him that he was committing a felony punishable by five years in prison and a fine of $10,000. He called Ali's name once more and still, Ali refused to budge. The government had had enough, and he was arrested. The news traveled around the world like wildfire.

Later that same day, the New York State Athletic Commission suspended his boxing license and stripped him of his World Heavyweight Champion title. Other boxing commissions around the country quickly followed suit. Ali would not be allowed to professionally box in the United States for the next three years. He was twenty-five years old and in the prime of his life. Pound-for-pound, Ali was considered one of the best fighters in the world.

When Ali refused his induction, he became the most hated man in America. He received many death threats. Those that supported him were also threatened. Kareem Abdul-Jabbar said, "I remember the teachers at my high school didn't like Ali because he was so anti-establishment and he kind of thumbed his nose at authority and got away with it. The fact that he was proud to be a black man and that he had so much talent ... made some people think that he was dangerous. But for those very reasons, I enjoyed him."

Ali's example inspired many black Americans and anti-war protestors. Because of Ali, more and more celebrities and columnists began to speak out against the war. William Rhoden, The New York Times columnist, wrote, "Ali's actions changed my standard of what constituted an athlete's greatness. Possessing a killer jump shot or the ability to stop on a dime was no longer enough. What were you doing for the liberation of your people? What were you doing to help your country live up to the covenant of its founding principles?"

At Ali's trial on June 20, 1967, it only took the jury twenty-one minutes of deliberation to find him guilty of violating Selective Service laws. He became a felon. He appealed. The Court of Appeals upheld his conviction. He didn't stop fighting. He submitted his case to the U.S. Supreme Court in hopes of reversing the decision. Ali was allowed to remain free until his case was heard in the Supreme Court. It took four years.

While waiting for the Supreme Court to rule on his case, Ali became a popular speaker at colleges and universities throughout the United States. During one of his speeches in front of a roaring crowd of students, Ali said, "My enemy is the white people, not Viet Cong or Chinese or Japanese. You my opposer when I want freedom. You my opposer when I want justice. You my opposer when I want equality. You won't even stand up for me in America for my religious beliefs— and you want me to go somewhere and fight, but you won't even stand up for me here at home?"

On June 28, 1971, the U.S. Supreme Court in Clay vs. United States overturned Ali's conviction by a unanimous decision. The court did not address the merits of Ali's claims. Instead, he was freed by a technicality. The Court held that the appeal board had given no reason for denial of a conscientious objector exemption for Ali and it was therefore impossible to determine which of the three basic tests for conscientious objector status were used by the appeal board. Like a dog trapped in a kennel, the court had wiggled its way under the fence and Ali's conviction was reversed. It wasn't pretty, but Ali was free. In speaking of the cost on Ali's career for his refusal to be drafted, his trainer Angelo Dundee said, "One thing must be taken into account when talking about Ali: He was robbed of his best years, his prime years."

Civil rights figures believed that Ali had an energizing effect on the freedom movement as a whole. It was probably Al Sharpton who best defined what Ali had done when he spoke of his bravery at a time when there was still widespread support for the Vietnam War. Sharpton said, "For the heavyweight champion of the world, who had achieved the highest level of athletic celebrity, to put all of that on the line— the money, the ability to get endorsements—to sacrifice all of that for a cause, gave a whole sense of legitimacy to the movement and the causes with young people that nothing else could have done. Even those who were assassinated, certainly lost their lives, but they didn't voluntarily do that. He knew he was going to jail and did it anyway. That's another level of leadership and sacrifice."

Bob Arum, Ali's promoter for much of his career, did not support Ali's choice at the time he refused to be drafted. However, in 2016 Arum said, "When I look back at his life, and I was blessed to call him a friend and spent a lot of time with him, it's hard for me to talk about his exploits in boxing because as great as they were they paled in comparison to the impact that he had on the world. ... He did what he thought was right. And it turned out he was right, and I was wrong."

Hanoi, North Vietnam

Deep in the politburo, Le Duan sat at the head of the conference table listening to his generals as they laid out their plans for the upcoming offensive in South Vietnam. "And what about the Americans?" said Le.

"We are, of course, concerned. But we have made preparations to distract the Americans before and during the offensive, especially in the beginning," said Tran Van Tra, deputy commander of the communist military.

"I fear you will need more than a distraction."

"We believe we can lure and engage an entire American Corps in the northernmost reaches of South Vietnam. The roads in that region are poor and the Americans will not be able to relocate easily. It will be at least a week before they can reach any large city or air base."

"The success of the campaign hinges on the temperament of the people. If they feel that the South Vietnamese military cannot protect them from our armies, they will join the revolution if for no other reason than to survive."

"And we will make sure that happens."

"The Americans don't need roads to return to the large population centers. They have helicopters and aircraft."

"Which is why we plan to attack all the air bases in the region and destroy their helicopters and transport aircraft just before the campaign begins. They will not have time to replace their losses. We will ensure they are indeed crippled and unable to return to the cities."

"Timing will be vital. We must prevent the Americans from returning before the revolution can obtain the required momentum. Failure would be terrifying to consider."

"I fail to see the need for your grand campaign," said General Giap, the strategist that conquered the French and was now North Vietnam's minister of defense. "You are already planning to assault Khe Sanh. Khe Sanh is a fortress-like Dien Bien Phu. It is a lynchpin for both the South Vietnamese and the Americans. Destroy Khe Sanh and you win the war."

"I doubt it's that simple, General," said Le.

"But it is that simple once you understand the logistics."

"Enlighten us."

"Khe Sanh with its artillery and airfield is the anchor that supports the outposts in the region. The outposts prevent us from bringing supplies and ammunition in from the trail in Laos. Once Khe Sanh falls, we will control the entire area. Supplies, ammunition, and weapons will pour into the South and the Americans will be powerless to stop us. Without Khe Sanh to protect its western flank Pleiku will easily fall within weeks along with the rest of the Central Highlands. Hue will fall within two months, then Da Nang with its huge air base. The people will know that the Americans do not have the power to stop us. In fact, I doubt the Americans will stick around for the final defeat of Saigon. Their president and his generals will not want to lose face. Khe Sanh is the key to everything. Khe Sanh is Dien Bien Phu."

"I will be overjoyed if Khe Sanh falls as you say. But

I am not willing to risk all as you did at Dien Bien Phu. The Americans are not the French. They are far more powerful and have unlimited resources. I doubt they will just pull up stakes and go home. We must defeat them in battle. Our time has come."

Kadena Air Base, Okinawa, Japan

When the U-2 Francis Gary Powers was flying was shot down over the Soviet Union while on a reconnaissance mission, the US Air Force realized that they had a big problem. The U-2 was too slow and vulnerable to avoid new missile technology and advances in radar. Recognizing the shortfall, but still needing the intel, the CIA contracted with Lockheed's Skunk Works to build twelve A-12 spy planes that were undetectable to radar and could outfly an anti-aircraft missile.

Developed under the code name Operation Oxcart, the aircraft was based on the designs of Clarence "Kelly" Johnson and used the code name "Archangel" for the aircraft while under development. Like the U-2 which it was designed to replace, the A-12 only had one seat designated for the pilot. Its final variations used two Pratt & Whitney J58-1 turbojet engines with afterburners. The engines cranked out 32,500-foot pounds of thrust when the afterburners were engaged reaching a maximum speed of Mach 3.35.

On April 25, 1962, the A-12 first flew at Groom Lake, Nevada. The CIA was not disappointed. Its radar signature was ninety percent lower than the U-2 and it flew at an altitude of 85,000 feet. SAM missiles were faster but needed to use all of their fuel just to catch up with the A-12, then with no fuel to maneuver, they were pretty much harmless. The A-12 was also faster than any Soviet interceptor, including the Mikoyan-Gurevich MiG-25.

The CIA used specially trained USAF pilots for the A-12. They were the best of the best. The aircraft was first introduced into active service in 1967 and was stationed at Beale Air Force Base in Yuba, California. Later it would also fly out of US Kadena Air Base, Okinawa, Japan for missions in the Pacific and Asia, including Vietnam.

Satellites were becoming more advanced in their ability to record high-resolution photography. Many believed that satellites would make all covert reconnaissance aircraft obsolete within a few years. But while flying at a much higher and therefore out-of-reach altitude, satellites had two major disadvantages – they circled the earth in predictable patterns and timetables that the enemy could detect and avoid. The second disadvantage was that if they needed to be retasked and change their orbit for any reason, they were required to use their limited fuel to make the change and were therefore limited in their location flexibility. Reconnaissance aircraft like the A-12 could fly wherever and whenever they were needed.

While the USAF ordered and flew three YA-12 as super-sonic interceptors, the CIA ordered and flew another ten high-altitude reconnaissance aircraft (A-12s) and reconnaissance drone carriers (M-21s).

Originally designed to replace the U-2 on its missions over the Soviet Union and Cuba, the A-12 never was used in those areas. After a U-2 was shot down in May 1960, the CIA decided to only use satellites to collect intel over the Soviet Union. That left the U-2s to fly over Cuba and it was determined that there were enough to perform the task. The director of the CIA ordered the A-12s to be deployed for use in Asia. The first A-12 arrived at Kadena Air Base on Okinawa on May 22, 1967. A few days later, two more arrived, and shortly thereafter the unit was declared operational. The unit operated under the code name Operation Black Shield. The pilots immediately began overflights of suspected SAM sites to identify their locations.

The CIA flew multiple missions over North Vietnam during the Vietnam War, including gathering intel on the location of POWs for potential rescue missions. Although several crashed because of mechanical failures, no A-12 was ever shot down by the enemy. They flew too high and too fast. But the A-12 had its drawbacks too. It flew so fast that the aircraft was often damaged when it returned to base and needed time to be repaired before its next mission. It was also not as maneuverable as some of the pilots would have liked. At top cruising speed, the aircraft had an eighty-six-mile turning radius. To turn around and head back to base, it often needed to fly to Thailand to avoid flying into Chinese airspace.

As the A-12 flew its missions, the Soviets improved their SAMs and soon the anti-aircraft missiles were flying at altitudes higher than the A-12 and reaching speeds that would allow it to catch up with the aircraft. Within a few years, the A-12 was obsolete and needed to be retired from service. Fortunately, its replacement was ready to take its place. Lockheed's twin-seat SR-71 was nicknamed the "Blackbird" because of its dark color. It was designed by the same team that developed the A-12 and had superior electronics for navigation, sensors, and payloads. It also had advanced radar countermeasures and was made out of titanium. A total of thirty-two aircraft were built and like its predecessor, not one SR-71 was shot down by the enemy.

Before the A-12's retirement, it was flown on three final missions during the Pueblo Crisis in North Korea. The pilot of the first mission identified the Pueblo's location in Wonsan Bay where it was guarded by two North Korean patrol boats and three Soviet-made Komar Class missile boats. The mission also collected intel on the readiness of North Korean forces to determine if they were preparing to attack South Korean and American forces on the border. The second and third missions identified a new SAM site near Pueblo's hidden location and photographed 84 primary targets plus eighty-nine bonus targets for a potential retaliatory strike by American forces.

On June 21, 1968, Frank Murray made the final A-12 flight to a military warehouse at Palmdale, California where the remaining aircraft were gathered for long-term storage. The aircraft remained there for twenty years before finally being sent to museums around the world.

Operation Francis Marion

April 6, 1967 – Kon Tum Province, South Vietnam

With the Americans focusing their efforts on cutting off routes from Laos into South Vietnam, the supply depots along the Ho Chi Minh Trail were getting backed up. Even though it was easy to open additional supply depots in Laos, that didn't solve the problem of equipping and supplying the communist forces already in South Vietnam. The politburo in Hanoi had little choice but to expand the trail southward into Cambodia and look for new routes over the mountains and through the dense jungle.

It was 4th Infantry Division commander Major General William R. Peers's responsibility to make sure that didn't happen. While it was generally understood that cutting off all enemy supplies, weapons, and reinforcements from the north was nearly impossible, Peers was sure as hell going to try.

Westmoreland had made it very clear that Peers and his men were prohibited from entering Cambodia even though everyone knew that the NVA had their base camps and supply depots just across the border and were staging raids into South Vietnam daily. President Johnson and Secretary of Defense Robert McNamara figured the US military had their hands full trying to deal with communist forces in Vietnam and Laos. They didn't want to expand the war into Cambodia. They were also concerned about destabilizing the Cambodian government which was short of being labeled a strong ally. The communist rebels called the Khmer Rouge were gaining power throughout the country. Raids from US or South Vietnamese forces would only strengthen their cause. So, for the time being, it was hands-off Cambodia.

Even with his hands tied, Peers was still committed to completing his assignment. He planned an in-depth defense against the communist incursions from the enemy's Base Area 702 in the north of Cambodia and Base Area 701 in the south. The 1st Brigade, 4th Infantry Division was deployed along Highway 14B and the defensive line of the U.S. Special Forces camps at Plei Djereng, Duc Co, and Plei Me, fifteen miles east of the Cambodian border. The 2nd Brigade was held in reserve.

Serving as a screen for the main force, the 4th Division's long-range reconnaissance teams, along with Special Forces and indigenous CIDG units were deployed just east of the Cambodian border to search for the enemy and their supply lines. The ARVN 23rd Division extended the screen to the south into Darlac Province while the ARVN 22nd Division extended it to the north to Tan Canh Base Camp. The line was longer and less dense than Peers had hoped, but he still felt that the NVA would need to tangle with the Allied forces if they wanted to get their supplies and weapons into South Vietnam.

Pride was also a factor. How could the communist commanders refuse battle and possibly save face when the Americans were so close? Mau had instructed commanders to only attack when they were assured victory against their opponent, but how could a commander possibly know if he would be victorious unless he engaged his enemy and tested his will? It was a Catch-22.

While Operation Francis Marion started on April 6, 1967, not much happened in the first two weeks beyond a few low-level skirmishes. It wasn't until Special Forces units engaged an NVA battalion in northern Darlac Province that things began to heat up. The communists were attempting an end run to slip behind the Allied forces. It didn't work. The NVA were forced back into Cambodia.

A few days later, the same Special Forces units made contact with two NVA companies fifty miles south of Plei Me trying the same strategy hoping to avoid the allied forces by using smaller-sized units. It too didn't work, and the communists once again retreated. After the multiple contacts, Peers wasted no time inserting a Battalion-sized task force from the 1st Brigade into northern Darlac Province. Peers wanted to make it clear to the enemy commanders that he would move his forces where they were needed to cut the communist supply lines. Using helicopters from Pleiku, Peers could move an entire battalion in less than a day creating a powerful force multiplier.

Four days later, the 2nd Battalion, 8th Infantry Regiment ambushed a group of NVA, killing thirteen with the survivors fleeing to a nearby, fortified base camp. Even with air support and artillery strikes the Americans were unable to break the camp's defenses. As the sun set, the Americans surrounded the camp and broke off contact for the night.

The next morning two tanks and a troop of M113s arrived to support the battalion in overrunning the enemy base camp. But when they entered, they found that the NVA had vanished during the night. The Americans wouldn't give up. They sent out reconnaissance units in different directions and discovered a second base camp where the NVA had fled. Firing canister rounds from their main guns, the tanks, followed by the M113s, advanced and quickly overran the NVA defensive positions. By mid-afternoon, the Americans had decimated the NVA 95B Regiment, killing 138 communist soldiers and routing the survivors. Only one American was killed. Peers was letting the communists know that they would pay a heavy toll if they tried to breach the Allied defensive lines.

The communists didn't give up. With the supplies and ammunition situation getting more desperate by the day for their comrades fighting in the South, they had little choice but to break through the American lines.

A week later, a U.S. company was attacked by an NVA battalion near Duc Co. The Americans were lucky to repel the assault and captured several prisoners. During an interrogation, one of the prisoners revealed two NVA battalions from the 66th Regiment had just arrived in the area and were preparing to attack the US Special Forces outposts before attacking Plei Me.

Hearing the report of the impending attacks, Peers wasn't taking any chances. He requested four B-52 strikes southwest of Duc Co camp. The bombardments shook the earth, but when the 1st Battalion, 8th Infantry went to survey the area they found no signs of NVA activity. More B-52 strikes followed and still no NVA were found.

On May 18th, Company B, 1st Battalion, 8th Infantry patrolled a dense jungle in the Ia Tchar Valley near the Cambodian border. When a lone NVA soldier fired on the lead platoon, the entire company pursued him through the jungle. After several minutes of pursuit, the Americans fell into a well-laid-out ambush by a large NVA force. Outnumbered the Americans formed a tight perimeter and called for air and artillery support.

When the jets arrived, the jungle canopy was so dense, the pilots could not effectively identify the Americans' position and therefore were unwilling to drop their napalm canisters and bombs. The risk of hitting their own troops was too great. The incoming artillery bombardment was somewhat more effective, but not by much. Few shells reached the ground with most exploding in the trees and heavy branches causing a cascade of leaves and flying shards of wood launched in every direction causing the Americans to suffer as much as the communists.

Realizing that Company B was pinned down, the Battalion commander sent Company A to reinforce his besieged company. It was slow going for Company A through the heavy foliage. Company B's 4th Platoon radioed that they were being overrun and called in an artillery strike directly on their position. The Battalion commander sent a detachment of helicopters to pick up A Company and transport them to Company B's position. They arrive just as the sun was about to set. Making contact with Company B, there was little either company could do to help the overrun platoon as darkness descended.

The next morning, Company A set out to find the platoon while Company B held their defensive position. When they finally located the platoon they saw that it had been badly mauled by the NVA with nineteen killed, one missing, and seven wounded. They gathered the dead and wounded and carried them back to Company B. Company B had lost an additional ten killed. Four more B-52 strikes drove off the NVA ending the battle. Sweeps of the area uncovered 119 NVA bodies killed in the bombings and battle.

Peers ordered the 3rd Battalion 12th Infantry to enter the valley and support the 1st Battalion 8th Infantry. The 173rd Airborne Brigade was brought into the area as potential reinforcements if required.

For the next five days, it was quiet with no more assaults from the communists. A dense fog capped with low-hanging clouds moved into the valley making observation of the surrounding jungle all but impossible. It was a bad omen. Ground support from American aircraft would be restricted. But Peers refused to give up the ground no matter how dangerous the area was becoming.

On the sixth day, Peers finally ordered the 3rd Battalion 12th Infantry to break camp and move to another position. A barrage of mortar rounds shrieked into the Battalion's position and exploded, killing one and wounding several other Americans. The barrage was followed by an NVA assault by a battalion-sized force. With both sides having difficulty finding targets through the dense fog, the battle turned hand-to-hand with the enemy appearing only a moment before their attack. After two hours of grueling combat, the fog and the clouds suddenly lifted. American aircraft arrived thirty minutes later, releasing their rockets, bombs, and napalm canisters on the NVA position. Helicopter gunships followed the fighters and unleashed their Gatling guns, strafing the NVA as they fled. The battle was over. The Americans had ten killed while the NVA had seventy-nine killed and four captured.

Just as one battle ended another sprang up. The next day, an understrength American company guarding a landing zone on top of a hill was attacked by the NVA battalion. After an hour of devastatingly accurate artillery fire, the communists withdrew leaving thirty-seven dead behind. The understrength Americans had been lucky and only had four killed.

Peers hated the fact that it was the communists that were controlling when and where to attack. The dense jungle in the area made it all but impossible to find the enemy until they suddenly appeared out of nowhere. By then it was too late, and everyone was fighting for their lives.

On May 26th, Company C, 3rd Battalion, 8th Infantry was advancing through a dense jungle when it was hit by sniper fire. The company commander was the first killed. The sniper moved on to kill every officer in the company. A Master Sergeant took command and order his men to form a defensive perimeter. Soldiers continued to fall from the sniper's shots.

The Battalion commander sent three platoons from Company B to support Company C. Only one made it. The rest were stopped by intense enemy fire including mortars and RPGs. The NVA launched several assaults on American positions. At one point, the enemy came within ten yards of the American lines until they were driven back. After multiple attempts and heavy American artillery bombardment, the NVA finally broke off their assaults and retreated into the jungle leaving ninety-six dead and two wounded. By nightfall, the NVA were back in Cambodia and untouchable.

A day later, Peers sent the 173rd Airborne Brigade into the Ia Drang Valley. The Americans and the NVA continued to have battalion and company-sized battles with the communists attacking in human waves, then breaking contact when American artillery and air support became too intense. It was a frustrating pattern for both sides. The NVA needed to break through, and the Americans were on the verge of destroying the NVA units only to have them flee across the border. Like most American commanders, Peers longed for a decisive battle with the communists. And like most American commanders he too would be disappointed. That was Vietnam – one disappointment after another.

Even the B-52s with their massage bomb loads had difficulty destroying the enemy. Time after time, the bombing squadrons were called in, but by the time they arrived, the enemy had moved from the area avoiding destruction. The valleys and surrounding mountains were pitted with deep bomb craters, but no enemy bodies were found when the bomb damage was assessed. The NVA and Viet Cong could not compete with American artillery and air support. But the Americans continually came up wanting when trying to locate and destroy large NVA units. It was a stalemate, but nobody was willing to give in. And so, the war continued, and more blood was spilled. With the Soviets and the Chinese backing the north and the Americans and its allies backing the south, Vietnam was in a perpetual hell and it seemed there was no way out for anyone.

While Operation Francis Marion succeeded at its

main objective of keeping the NVA from crossing the American and their allies' lines and resupplying the Viet Cong and NVA forces already in the south, the operation fell short of General Peers' expectations of destroying a large force of NVA. He wanted communist blood and was determined to get it. What followed was natural to Peers – he planned a new mission called Operation Greeley which would lead to the fiercest battle of the Vietnam War.

The Hill Fights

Khe Sanh, South Vietnam

On April 20th, the 3rd Marine Regiment arrived and took over operational control of the combat base area which was northeast of the village of Khe Sanh. Only seven miles from the Laotian border, the area was pocked with Bru Montagnard villages and coffee plantations. Highway 9 was the northernmost road in South Vietnam and was considered a key supply route by both sides. The entire area was also speckled with steep hills that made excellent firebases for artillery and mortars. Multiple rivers restricted troop movements through the countryside and made Highway 9 even more important for military vehicles, especially armor.

Interrogations of civilians designated communist

collaborators by the Phoenix program had revealed that the Viet Cong and NVA considered control of the area essential to the distribution of supplies, weapons, and ammunition into South Vietnam from the Ho Chi Minh Trail. This meant that the communists were highly likely to fight for control of the area and the US Marines were more than happy to oblige.

The coming weeks had the potential of giving Westmoreland and the Marine commanders what they wanted – a pitched battle where American firepower could make a real difference and destroy a large number of communist soldiers. Their biggest problem was the weather. It was the end of the hot season and the longer they waited for hostilities to begin, the more erratic the weather. The rains for which Vietnam was famous usually started at the beginning of May in the Central Highlands. Artillery could be used no matter the weather, but aircraft could be curtailed by the thick clouds that brought the rain. Unless the communists attacked shortly, the Marines were at risk of losing a major advantage – air power.

To spur the Viet Cong and NVA into engaging, the 2nd Battalion, 3rd Marines commenced Operation Beacon Star on the Street Without Joy area between Quang Tri and Thua Thien Provinces. The Viet Cong 6th Regiment and the 810th and 812th Battalions from the 325C Division were waiting when the helicopters from HMM-164 landed with the first group of Marines. The most experienced Viet Cong fighters in the war, the 325C Division was one of only six "iron and steel" divisions that originally came from the Viet Minh. They were tenacious, disciplined, and extremely patriotic. Many had been fighting for more than three decades, first against the Japanese, then the French, and now the Americans.

On April 24th, 2nd Platoon, B Company, 3rd Battalion, 3rd Marines established a mortar position on Hill 700. Five Marines were ordered to establish an observation post on nearby Hill 861. On their way up Hill 861, the five Marines entered a bamboo grove and were ambushed. Four of the Marines were killed and the fifth escaped by hiding in the dense bamboo.

When contact with the five Marines was broken off, a squad of Marines was sent to investigate. They entered the bamboo grove and rescued the lone survivor. The commander of the squad quickly realized they were in trouble. Still, he refused to leave until they recovered the bodies of the four Marines. Moments later, the squad came under heavy enemy fire and was forced to retreat without the bodies of their fellow Marines.

Another squad was sent to the hill to recover the bodies. They too came under fire, but not before recovering the bodies of two Marines. An evacuation helicopter was sent to recover the squad and the bodies. As it approached the hilltop, the helicopter came under heavy fire and was hit several times. Escorting helicopter gunships suppressed the enemy fire and the evacuation was completed.

1st and 3rd Platoons from Company B were ordered to cut off the Viet Cong from escaping. While crossing over Hill 861, the two platoons came under intense mortar fire and suffered multiple casualties. Medivac helicopters attempted to pick up the wounded but were driven back by enemy machine gun fire. Trapped on the hillside, the two platoons dug in for the night. The Marines had twelve killed and seventeen wounded. It was a brutal day for the Corps.

The next morning, a thick fog surrounded the hills. The two platoons from Company B continued their advance across Hill 861. From Khe Sanh combat base, Company K, 3rd Marines moved to support Company B. About 300 yards from the hill's summit, K Company's 1st Platoon came upon a well-entrenched unit of Viet Cong. As the fight intensified, the 2nd Platoon, Company B was sent to reinforce 1st Platoon. As night approached, the Marines dug in for the night. As the sun set, Company K, 9th Marines was flown into Khe Sanh to support the assault.

At 5 AM, Khe Sanh combat base and 3rd Battalion command post came under intense recoilless rifle and mortar fire. The Marines did not back down and continued their assault on Hill 861 with Company K, 9th Marines joining the battle by mid-day. Even with the reinforcements, the Marines made little progress. Deciding to leave the Viet Cong to be pummeled by artillery and air power, the Marines finally withdrew under the protection of helicopter gunships. As they prepared to break contact with the enemy, Company B was pinned down and the evacuation helicopters were unable to reach them. Artillery was walked in and around Company B's position driving the Viet Cong back. Company B was freed up and fell back on foot to the Battalion command post.

More Marine units were flown in from other combat bases to support 3rd Marines. Additional artillery batteries were also flown into Khe Sanh Combat Base. Aircraft dropped twenty-five tons of bombs and the arti batteries unleashed 1,800 shells on Hill 861 churning up the enemy's defensive positions.

On the afternoon of April 28th, the 2nd Battalion,

3rd Marines advanced up Hill 861 with little opposition. Except for a few snipers, the Viet Cong had withdrawn from the hill during the night. The Marines found twenty-five enemy bunkers and were dogged by the odor of a massive number of dead bodies that had been removed.

With Hill 861 secured, the 3rd Battalion, 3rd Marines advanced on Hill 750 which was to be used as an intermediate point to launch an attack on Hill 881S. The Marines were in excellent condition, but the hills were steep and their thighs and calves burned. Company M, 9th Marines attacked a Viet Cong defensive position on the slope of the hill. With the Viet Cong occupied, Company M, 3rd Marines were able to secure the intermediate position at the top of the hill and dig in.

The next day, 2nd Battalion, 3rd Marines left Hill 861 and advanced toward 3rd Battalion, 3rd Marines position. As they moved, they walked into an NVA bunker complex and suffered nine killed and forty-seven wounded. Instead of continuing their attack, the battalion backed away and let artillery and air support pound the NVA bunkers. It didn't take long before 2nd Battalion returned and overran the NVA positions.

Company M, 3rd Marines, and Company K, 9th Marines advanced on Hill 881S encountering minimal resistance. As they proceeded up the hill, they were hit with heavy mortar fire, then with recoilless rifle and heavy machine gun fire from a number of NVA bunkers strung along the slope. Both Marine companies were pinned down and taking heavy casualties. Gunships and air support were brought in to assault the enemy bunkers with rockets and bombs.

After several hours of battle, the Marine companies were able to disengage and move back down the hill taking forty-three dead and 109 wounded with them. Company M, 3rd Marines was rendered combat ineffective and replaced with Company F, 2nd Battalion, 3rd Marines. The NVA had 163 killed mostly from the gunships and bombers.

The Marines withdrew from both Hills 881S and 881N to allow several heavy aerial bombardments to drop 650,000 lbs. of bombs on the NVA bunkers. The NVA were unwilling to surrender their bunkers and suffered 140 killed greatly weakening their defense positions.

Two days later, the Marines assaulted and captured Hill 881S with only light resistance. The Marines discovered over 250 bunkers on the hill, some protected by eight layers of logs and five feet of dirt. Only fifty enemy bunkers remained intact after the bombing and most of those were abandoned before the Marine ground assault.

Later that morning, the 2nd Battalion, 3rd Marines assaulted Hill 881N from the south and the east. As they charged up the steep slope, the Marines engaged the NVA defensive positions. Once again, the Marines pulled back to allow artillery support to soften the enemy positions. The entire area was hit with an intense rainstorm making a continued assault impossible until the storm subsided. The Marines dug in for the night.

Early the next morning before dawn, the NVA and Viet Cong attacked the American positions near the bunkers. The communists were able to overrun some of the bunkers and took up defensive positions inside. An American rifle squad and a unit of engineers were sent to clear the reoccupied bunkers but were pinned down by heavy machine gun fire. A flareship dropped two parachute flares that lit up the hillside of Hill 881S revealing a mass of two hundred NVA troops preparing to assault the American positions on the slope. From below, a recoilless rifle unit blasted the enemy with over 100 shells and broke up the assault.

As the sun rose, the American helicopters dropped Company H, 2nd Battalion, 3rd Marines uphill from the enemy allowing them to assault the enemy from the rear. By three o'clock in the afternoon, all of the enemy bunkers on Hill 881S had been captured. The Marines had twenty-seven killed and eighty-four wounded, while the NVA and Viet Cong had lost 137 killed and three captured.

Two days later, the Marines assaulted Hill 881N. When they encountered heavy enemy fire near the top of the summit, they pulled back to once again allow artillery and air support to soften the enemy positions. It worked, and before sunset, the Marines drove off the surviving enemy soldiers and recaptured the hill.

Skirmishes continued between the Marines and the Viet Cong and NVA as the Marines searched the area around the hills. Most of the communists had withdrawn to the north crossing into the Demilitarized Zone, while some withdrew all the way to Laos. The Hill Fights ended on May 10th. The Marines had 155 killed, while the Viet Cong and NVA had lost over 940. Ratios didn't matter. The soldiers that died on both sides were not statistics, but real people with family and friends.

Intelligence from after-battle interrogation of prisoners found that the communists were building up stores of ammunition and supplies south of the border.

The 325C Division was moving a large number of troops into the area. Concerned by how easily the intelligence was given by the prisoners, the Marine commanders didn't know exactly what the communists were planning on doing. It seemed like the communists wanted the Americans to know what they were doing. Something big was in the works…

May 18, 1967 – Dong Ha Air Base, South Vietnam

Attacks on American facilities and outposts were increasing in the North near the border. More Marines were being added to defend the American positions in the Central Highlands. This was especially true of the helicopter air bases which seemed to be the focus of the communist attacks.

Dong Ha was intended to form a supporting base for the McNamara Line and to support American Marine forces engaged at Con Thien. Probing attacks on Don Ha Air Base in the Central Highlands were common. As of yet, the communists had been unable to penetrate the Marine's defenses. The Viet Cong and NVA switched tactics and began shelling the base with mortar rounds in hopes of destroying the helicopters and aircraft stationed at Dong Ha. The mortar attacks proved that they did not need to attack the base's heavily defended perimeter to inflict damage. But the mortars were limited in range and number and did little damage to the American helicopter fleet.

It was early morning on May 18th, when the communists launched a rocket attack from the nearby jungle. A month earlier, the Marines at the base had been hit with fifty rockets. The May 18th attack was three times the size of previous assaults. More than 150

140mm rockets hit the base killing eleven Marines and wounding ninety-one. It was a devasting attack.

Building on their successful attack, the communists didn't let up. They launched more assaults using a large number of rockets that destroyed dozens of helicopters and aircraft, also killing and wounding Marines. The communists were hoping to attract more Marines to protect the base and patrol the jungle outside its perimeter. It didn't work.

The Marines decided that Dong Ha could not be successfully defended against enemy rocket attacks and therefore was untenable as a helicopter base. The Marines moved their helicopter facilities back to Phu Bai and Marble Mountain where the helicopters could be better protected.

After having had great success with their rocket attacks, the communists were naturally disappointed. It was doubtful that they could draw more Marine forces away from the big cities into the Central Highlands now that the Hong Ha air base had been reduced to a logistics airfield. The communists would have to go elsewhere to draw the Marines away.

Mekong Delta, South Vietnam

A drizzle pecked at the muddy water. Nguyet and Tuyet wadded knee-deep as they transplanted baskets filled with seedlings into the rice paddy. It was back-breaking work as they each used a wooden trowel to form a hole, then took each seedling and twisted it into the mud. Nguyet was sure that Coyle meant to help when he rented the biggest field near the village for the mother and daughter. The field was too much, but Nguyet didn't want to insult Coyle or abuse his generosity. Nguyet wanted to spend her time teaching her daughter the skills a woman should know to properly raise a family. Instead, she and Tuyet worked long hours to transplant the seedlings that would yield the rice they would eat for the next year and the surplus to sell at market… if they didn't die from exhaustion.

Coyle had also paid for High Yield seed which meant double the rice at harvest. The thought of harvesting and selling all that rice overwhelmed Nguyet. She hoped that Coyle didn't know that rice farmers in the Mekong could plant and harvest two to three times a year because of the abundance of rain. Once she and her daughter completed the first harvest, she arranged for a neighbor with a large family to work the land for the second and possibly the third planting and harvest. She would receive a portion of the rice grown and would need to sell it herself. More work.

As they approached the end of a row, Tuyet looked up for a moment and saw a man appear from a grove of trees. She pointed him out to her mother. Nguyet squinted to get a better look. The man was wearing black pajamas and holding a rifle. He was Viet Cong. Nguyet didn't panic. The Viet Cong were common in the Mekong. The man made a signal with his hand and more rebels emerged from the trees. "Who are they?" said Tuyet.

"Viet Cong. A raiding party," said Nguyet.

"What should we do?"

"Keep working. They will take what they want from the village. There is nothing we can do to stop them."

"Will there be a fight?"

"I don't think so. Our elders are wise. They know they cannot win. Once they have what they want, the Viet Cong will leave and return to the jungle where they are safe."

"How long will they stay?"

"It depends. Probably just a day or two."

"Okay."

"Tuyet, you know not to say anything about who your father was."

"McGoon."

"Yes, McGoon."

"He was an American."

"Yes, but you can't tell anyone that, especially the Viet Cong."

"You said lying was bad."

"I know what I said, Darling. But this is different. The Viet Cong hate the Americans."

"Am I an American?"

"No. You are Vietnamese like me. Do you understand?"

"I think so. What will they do to me if they find out my father was an American?"

"Just keep quiet and stay away from the soldiers."

"Okay."

"It will be alright, Tuyet. We'll get through this."

Nguyet and Tuyet took one last look before returning to work. Over thirty soldiers were moving across the rice fields toward the village with more appearing every minute. Nguyet tried to hide her concern. It wasn't easy.

Pleiku Air Base, South Vietnam

It was early morning when a C-47 taxied off the runway and onto the apron. It pulled up in front of the small terminal below the control tower. The cargo door opened and Granier with his sniper rifle over his shoulder and his rucksack in hand hopped out. He was followed by ten new sniper recruits for the Phoenix program. In addition to his organizational responsibilities in setting up the overall training program, Granier continued training groups of snipers. He saw the snipers as an important part of Phoenix and wanted to ensure the core group was well-trained right from the start. He knew he couldn't train all the snipers that were needed, but he was going to do his darndest to teach as many as he could and hoped that their skills would trickle down to others. Some were raw recruits, while others had already been through the military's sniper school. He preferred the raw recruits. Fewer bad habits.

Granier needed to train his recruits in real-world situations whenever possible. The great thing about the Central Highlands was that there was always something going on, especially lately. There were almost double the number of attacks from last year. Like everyone else, Granier thought it was the communists trying to secure a fast route into South Vietnam for their supplies and reinforcements. It was the number of attacks and their ferociousness that concerned Granier. The Viet Cong and NVA had always fought hard, but lately, they were taking it to a new level. That was good for his trainees. They needed to see the enemy at its worst. It was also best to set the bar high for newbies.

Granier told the recruits to stow their gear and prepare for battle in the next few days. They would wait until a battle developed that Granier thought was worthy of their skills. In the meantime, he would continue to instruct them in the surrounding jungle. He had no fear of the enemy that might be out there and wanted his recruits to see that. Fear was a bad thing. It stifled one's actions and reactions. The recruits needed to learn to let go of their fear and let their training take over like a warrior demon processing their bodies. He didn't want them thinking too deeply about what they were doing. He just wanted them to do their duty. To hunt and kill on command. It wasn't rocket science. It was just the opposite - limited thinking combined with warrior instinct and training. His training.

Granier thought he might have a couple of beers with Coyle while he waited for a battle to form. It wasn't that he liked Coyle, but he could tolerate him. That was more than he could say about anyone else. At least Coyle was good at his job. That was something Granier could appreciate. He strolled into the CIA office on the base and asked if anyone had seen Coyle. He discovered that Coyle was out on a mission training his recruits and wouldn't be back for a couple of hours.

While he waited, Granier looked over the stack of intelligence reports that accumulated every day. It was hard to keep track of everything that was going on all over the country, but that was part of what made Granier good at his job. He knew more than most officers because he worked at it. The hours of research didn't bother him. He didn't have friends because maintaining relationships with them took up too much time. It was better to be a loner.

He was about halfway through the stack of reports when something caught his eye. It was an intelligence report from the Mekong Delta. He asked the base intelligence officer if he knew anything about the report or what was being done about it. Since it wasn't the officer's area of responsibility, he didn't know anything, but said he would find out. It didn't take long, just a couple of phone calls. With a solid reputation for killing the enemy and a knack for completing the toughest of missions, Granier was greatly admired by the CIA officers in Vietnam. They went out of their way to help him when asked. What Granier was told by the officer was disconcerting, to say the least…

Coyle was surprised to see Granier standing on the flight line when he landed and taxied his gunship. Rolling to a stop, he left his co-pilot to button up the aircraft. Coyle stepped out onto the tarmac and said as he shook Granier's hand, "What are you doing here, Granier?"

"More training," said Granier. "Have you looked at today's intelligence reports?"

"No, why?"

"The village where you found McGoon's whore and her daughter… It's been overrun by Viet Cong."

"What? When?"

"Yesterday morning."

"Jesus."

"Yeah, well… there's more. An ARVN battalion is going in tomorrow morning to retake the village. They've ordered up a Spooky to soften any resistance before they go in."

"Oh, shit. I've got to stop it."

"You're not gonna stop anything, Coyle. The ARVN don't give a shit about a whore and her daughter. They sure as hell ain't gonna call off their attack."

"Then I've got to get them out before the assault."

"They're in the Mekong Delta, Coyle. You can't get there in time."

"Yes, I can. If I leave now. Are you going with me?"

"I can't. I've got ten recruits waiting for a battle."

"So, what? Bring them along. You know where there is gonna be a battle."

"I can't do that. They're not a bunch of puppets."

"Bullshit. You can do whatever you want."

"Well, yeah…"

"Granier, I need you."

"Seems like you always need me, Coyle."

"Yeah, well… we're friends."

"Who says?"

"I say."

"We're professional acquaintances. That's as far as it goes with me."

"Call it whatever you want. Are you coming?"

"Dammit. I'll get my gear and recruits. You get the plane. And get your son. We're gonna need a helicopter pilot."

"You want me to bring Scott?"

"Yeah, he's a good pilot."

"There's gotta be someone else we could—"

"Coyle, he's a natural pilot like you and he's got balls of steel. We need Scott."

"Are you sure you can get us a Huey?"

"Yeah, I'm sure."

"Alright. I'll ask."

"Play the father card if you need to. This is gonna be a tricky rescue mission."

Coyle grabbed a jeep and drove to Camp Halloway two miles away. He found Scott in his quarters. When Coyle told his son about the rescue mission, Scott was all over it. Coyle was a bit concerned how easily Scott said yes to a dangerous mission. Scott asked his co-pilot and crew chief to join the rescue mission. Both accepted.

Scott went to his commander and told him that the

CIA had requested him and his crew for a covert mission. The commander cursed but didn't refuse the request. The Huey crew grabbed their gear and headed back to Pleiku in the jeep with Coyle.

Within the hour, Coyle had requisitioned a C-47 with Granier's help, then loaded up the sniper recruits, Huey crew, and Granier. The aircraft took off and headed south.

Granier walked into the cockpit and said, "If anyone important asks, McGoon's whore is a CIA informant that we need to get out of the village before the ARVN assault."

"If the VC think she's an informant, real or otherwise, they'll kill her. She'll never be able to go back to her village," said Coyle.

"Do you really want her to go back?"

"No. I don't."

"Problem solved."

"Yeah, I guess you're right. I'm worried that the VC may realize that her daughter is the child of an American. She's a big girl with white skin."

"Well, there ain't nothing you can do about that at the moment."

"I suppose not."

"How long before we land?"

"Six hours give or take."

"I'm gonna sack out for a few hours."

"Good plan."

Granier left the cockpit leaving Coyle deep in thought.

Saigon, South Vietnam

When they arrived in Saigon, Granier secured the use

of a gunship by claiming it was for a covert mission and that he had brought his own crew because they had top-secret security clearance. Granier's advantage was that nobody wanted to know what he was doing because they didn't want to get caught up in anything unethical or illegal. They just assumed that if it was a CIA mission, it was probably nasty business.

The gunship that was assigned to him was fully loaded with rocket pods and machine guns. That was a problem that Scott quickly pointed out, "We can't take everyone. Too much weight."

"How many can we take?"

"Not including my aircrew, seven or eight tops if they leave most of the gear behind. We could make multiple trips or get another Huey."

"No," said Coyle. "We are out of time."

"We'll make it work with what we have," said Granier.

Granier picked out the best four shooters and left their spotters behind. That meant no security if they got into a firefight. Because the mission was covert, they couldn't call in additional air support or artillery if things went south.

It was far from ideal, but Granier wanted as many rifles as possible to hold back the Viet Cong. Five snipers including himself could do a lot of damage to any enemy assault crossing rice fields where there was little cover.

The team and aircrew loaded up in the Huey and Scott took off. The village was less than thirty minutes away by air.

Scott did a quick pass over the village. It was still dark and there wasn't much to see. He did see plumes of dark smoke rising from the village. He landed a mile away on a road. Granier and his team jumped out followed by Coyle. "Keep your head down, Pops," said Scott. "No hero shit."

"Right. You too," said Coyle leaving the aircraft.

The team double-timed it to a grove of trees next to the village. Granier ordered his men to spread out in case of a mortar attack. They would follow his lead and only open fire after his first shot. Coyle used a pair of binoculars to survey the village. There was no sign of Nguyet or Tuyet. That didn't mean anything, he told himself. It was still early, and they could be sleeping. He saw multiple Viet Cong guards keeping watch in and around the village. Most of their attention was focused on the village and not the surrounding fields. "Okay. I'm going in," said Coyle carrying a submachine gun with an additional ammo bag.

"We've got you covered until you enter the village. After that, it's anybody's guess as to where the Viet Cong might be," said Granier.

"I'll be okay… I think."

Coyle kept low as he left the trees and crossed the rice paddies around the village. Although he did his best to keep quiet, his boots sloshed through the muddy water. He was sure anyone guarding the village could hear him approaching and he half expected to be cut in half by a burst of machine gun fire. He was prepared to dive under the water at the first sign of trouble. He drove out the thought of the floating human feces that was used to fertilize the field from his mind. He'd be sure to keep his mouth shut if he was forced to dive into the water.

As he drew closer to the village, he slowed and adjusted his path to where he remembered Nguyet's hut was located near the center of the hamlet. The Viet

Cong had bonfires burning at both ends of the main road to prevent villagers from sneaking away. He could see the rebel soldiers' long shadows cast against the huts as they walked by the fires. Then it hit him… the smell of death like rotting flesh. He moved closer and saw bodies on the ground. He felt his heart skip. He slipped into the village unseen. It was easier than he had hoped. No palisades were protecting the hamlet.

As he crept between the huts, Coyle kept low and stayed out of any light so that his shadow would not appear. He stole forward until he could see both ways down the main road. He looked toward Nguyet's hut. It was gone. Only smoldering wooden poles and beams remained. He wanted to weep, but there was no time. Dawn was approaching. He slipped across the road and snuck down to the smoldering frame that was once where Nguyet and her daughter lived. He feared what he would find. It was his fault. He should have acted sooner. He sifted through the ashes and found nothing that resembled human remains. Perhaps they had escaped or been captured before the fire consumed them. He had to know for sure.

Coyle looked down both ends of the earthen street and saw a large gathering of soldiers on one end. If Nguyet and Tuyet had been taken captive there would be guards. He surmised that if they were still alive, they were probably being held near those soldiers. He crept toward them keeping low and sticking to the shadows of the huts as much as possible. The sky was lightening. He didn't have much time.

As he slunk across an alley he stumbled on a rock and fell to his knees. A Viet Cong appeared across the street and leveled his weapon as he called out. Coyle knew he could probably shoot the soldier before he could respond. But the crack of his submachine gun was sure to bring more soldiers. At best, he would be driven from the village, and at worst he would be captured or killed. His mind raced for a solution. A muzzle flash from the grove where Granier and the snipers were positioned was accompanied by a distant crack. Somebody had relieved Coyle of the decision. He imagined it was Granier. The soldier jerked, then fell to the ground dead. Soldiers on both sides of the village ran toward the center. If Coyle ran back toward the grove, he might make it with Granier's help, but he would never know what happened to Nguyet and her daughter. Instead, he laid down his submachine gun and put his hands in the air to surrender. The rebels surrounded him. Seeing his fallen comrade one of the rebels threatened to shoot Coyle. A sergeant stopped him. Coyle was American and worth money if captured alive. Another soldier hit Coyle in the side of the head with the butt of his rifle. Knocked unconscious, Coyle crumpled. Two rebels picked up his limp body and dragged him down the street.

Coyle woke to the sound of a nearby explosion. His head throbbed. More explosions. He could see through the cracks in the wall that it was light outside. He vaguely remembered the ARVN assault that was planned for the morning. The preemptory artillery barrage had begun. The gunship would soon follow. He looked around and saw the faces of frightened villagers being held in a large hut. Nguyet and Tuyet were not among them. He remembered the smell of death and the dead bodies lying in the street. Coyle was losing hope.

He could hear the shouts of the Viet Cong

commander barking out orders to his men. He glanced up at the hut's ceiling. It was little more than a few poles and palm fronds. Little protection from the shower of bullets that would soon rain down from the heavens - shrapnel from an artillery shell or a stream of bullets from a gunship. Either way, he was a goner and so were the villagers. He knew that Granier would not attempt to save him. Granier was smarter than that and would not put his trainees at risk for such slim odds.

Children and women were crying. Men whimpered. They sensed what was coming. So, did he. A soldier beat his rifle against the hut wall and told them to shut up. They obeyed. In the new silence between explosions, Coyle heard a strange noise. He turned to see a knife cutting through the thin rope that held the sticks of the wall together in the back of the hut. The rope broke and the wall fell open. Light shown through the hole. Nguyet's face appeared. She motioned for everyone to keep quiet. She was surprised when she saw Coyle's face among the prisoners. His eyes had welled up with tears as he smiled. She smiled back for a moment, then waved for everyone to escape through the newly formed hole. Villagers piled out. Coyle was the last. A shell exploded next to the hut and the front wall and ceiling caught fire. The hut was engulfed in flames as Coyle pushed through the hole.

Coyle mouthed the words, Tuyet? Nguyet pointed to a nearby grove of bamboo where the villagers were escaping. Tuyet was helping them by bending open several bamboo stalks. She was strong like McGoon. She smiled when she saw Coyle. Coyle turned to Nguyet and motioned for her and Tuyet to follow him. She nodded in agreement.

Coyle hoped that Granier and the snipers were still

watching from the grove. He, Nguyet, and Tuyet moved quickly to the edge of the village and looked out at the rice fields. It was a long way over open ground. He heard the familiar sound of an AC-47's engines. He looked up and saw the gunship starting its turn above the village. Time was up. He grabbed Nguyet's and Tuyet's hands and ran into the first rice paddy. Several soldiers shouted from the village and opened fire. The grove of trees in the distance erupted with muzzle flares and rifle cracks as Granier and his team laid down fire on the soldier. The soldiers' rifle fire stopped. *Damn those snipers are good*, thought Coyle as he climbed up the first dike wall. As they crossed the dike a machine gun from the village opened fire. Coyle rushed the girls over the dike into the next rice paddy. They hunkered down, hoping that Granier and the snipers could take out the machine gun which was hidden behind a stack of logs.

Above the sky erupted with the sound of chainsaws running in unison. Streams of red tracer rounds reached down from Heaven and marched up the main road in the village. Stitched with bullets, a half dozen rebels fell dead. But the hidden machine gun persisted unabated. The gunner and loader were well positioned within the cover of the logs and not even the gunship could reach them.

Coyle, Nguyet, and her daughter could not move from behind the rice paddy's dike without being shot by the machine gun.

Granier and his snipers continued to lay down fire on the machine gun, but they didn't have a clear shot.

The gunship returned to other parts of the village where the Viet Cong were hidden. Anyone that was crazy enough to poke their head out lasted four to five seconds which was how long it took the gunship's pilot to acquire the new target and open fire. The pattern of fire was so wide it was impossible to escape once the miniguns were locked on.

Coyle heard the sound of a squadron of ARVN-tracked vehicles approaching the village. Each M113 armored personnel carrier or APC had a Browning .50-caliber machine gun as its main gun mounted on a shielded turret toward the front of the vehicle and two shielded turrets in the back that held M60 machine guns.

When the first ARVN APC appeared from a line of trees, the Viet Cong opened fire with mortars and recoilless rifles. The APC returned fire strafing the village with large caliber bullets, tearing through the wooden hut walls. The ARVN heavy machine gun's bullets would continue through the walls of three or four huts before the shells finally came to a stop. There was little thought given to the lives of civilians in the village. The ARVN gunners were focused on Viet Cong hidden in the village. Collateral damage was just a part of war and expected.

The machine gun firing on the escapees from the village kept on mission and didn't let the approach of the APCs distract it from the hunt. More artillery and now mortar shells rained down on the village and the surrounding rice fields. Multiple explosions sent the brown water and mud high into the air.

Coyle knew it was only a matter of time until one of the artillery or mortar rounds landed close enough to kill all three of them. It made no sense that Nguyet and Tuyet should die alongside him. He believed the Viet Cong machine gun might stop its firing if it hit an American. His life was far more valuable to the VC than two female villagers. Besides, the gunner and loader had other things to worry about like the approaching ARVN troops. Coyle decided to take action. He turned to Nguyet and motioned that he would run back toward the village and they should run to the grove of trees where the American snipers were positioned. Coyle knew that if he died, Granier, even as cranky as he was, would feel obligated to take care of Nguyet and Tuyet. It was an unspoken brotherhood code. Nguyet nodded that she understood. She didn't want Coyle to die. He had done so much for her and her daughter, but she was a mother and do anything to protect Tuyet.

As Coyle readied himself, he peeked above the dike and looked out at the rice field. If he could make it to the next berm on the opposite side of the field, he might survive. It was a long way with no cover. He would give it everything he had. If he was lucky the VC gunner would focus on him and not Nguyet and Tuyet. *Lucky?* he thought. *The machine gun will probably rip me to shreds.* Out of nowhere, the helicopter gunship flown by Scott and his crew appeared from around the grove of trees in a tight turn and flew in between Coyle and the VC machine gun.

Coyle realized what Scott was doing. He was sacrificing himself and his crew for Coyle and the two girls. It wasn't what Coyle wanted. He wouldn't allow it. Coyle sprang from his position and ran across the rice field raising his arms to keep the machine gunner's attention. But the helicopter gunship was a much bigger prize and a much more powerful threat. The gunner shifted his stream of bullets toward the aircraft.

Seeing the stream of tracers heading toward him and his helicopter, Scott fired all the rockets in one of his HVAR pods. The Rockets shot out of the pod one after another.

A barrage of rockets pummeled the logs around the machine gun sending sharp wooden shards in all directions. The gunner and loader were pierced with wooden shrapnel that buried themselves deep in their human flesh. Their machine gun went silent. They were dead.

With the threat gone, Scott turned his aircraft toward Coyle and set it down on the berm between Coyle and the two girls. They ran toward the open doorways as the crew chief fired his M60 toward the village as more VC opened fire with their rifles. The VC redirected one of their mortars in an attempt to take out the American aircraft. Explosion near the berm sent more mud and water into the air as Coyle, Nguyet, and Tuyet piled into the helicopter. Moments later, Scott lifted off the berm and flew over the grove of trees to safety. "You guys alright?" asked the crew chief.

"Yeah. Thanks," said Coyle. "You saved our asses."

"Just another day in the Nam."

"Right… just another day."

Scott dropped off Coyle, Nguyet, and Tuyet, then went back to pick up Granier and his sniper team. When he returned, Coyle was waiting and said, "Thank you. All of you. I knew it was a big ask, but you delivered."

"I understand the PX in Saigon is having a sale on cases of Johnnie Walker," said the crew chief.

"Whatever you want. It's on me."

"He's kidding," said Scott flashing the crew chief a mock angry glance.

"I wasn't kidding," said the crew chief.

"A case of Johnnie Walker. It's the least I could do."

"You don't understand. If you give him a case of whiskey, he'll be worthless for a week. I need him."

"I'll give it to you, and you can dish it out whenever you feel it's appropriate."

"That'll work."

"Granier, anything for you and your guys?"

"No. We needed the target practice under fire. This was good."

"Okay. I need to get Nguyet and Tuyet to Hue and get them settled in. I trust you guys can find your way back to Pleiku?"

"Not a problem," said Granier.

"I'll see you when I get back. Drinks are on me," said Coyle.

Hue, South Vietnam

The Perfume River flowed through the heart of Hue and passed directly in front of the ancient Citadel which was the center of power for all of Vietnam during the Nguyen Dynasty. It was the home of emperors for over a century. In addition to the river, the Dai Noi Citadel had a wide moat that encircled the complex protecting it from invaders and usurpers. The stone walls surrounding the old Imperial city were tall and thick. Inside, five massive stone gates and 1.6 miles of palisades protected the forbidden purple city where the emperors lived. The defense of the citadel was layered with stone ramparts. Any attacker would need to defeat the lancers, archers, and gunners in the gates to gain access to the forbidden purple city. Not an easy task even for the most brave and skilled.

The ARVN and local militia used the Citadel as

their command center and base of operations. The troops felt well protected as did the officers.

Coyle figured that a small house near the Citadel would be perfect for Nguyet and her daughter. Knowing that the Viet Cong and NVA would be idiots to attack the Citadel, he could rest easy that the mother and daughter were safe if they lived near the fortress. He hired a local real estate broker to assist in the search for a house. Even though he felt pressed for time, he didn't rush Nguyet or Tuyet as they walked through each of the potential homes. If his CIA manager didn't like him leaving with little notice, he could always fire him. Knowing his value to the agency, he doubted that would happen, but he didn't want to push his luck. Once he got the girls settled, he would return to Pleiku and do whatever penance was required.

Coyle felt that several of the houses they looked at would make nice homes and the rent was more than reasonable. But Nguyet was strangely picky. He supposed it was a good thing that she was taking the decision seriously. Nguyet asked where Tuyet would attend school and if they could have a piano so her daughter could learn a musical instrument. Coyle agreed to everything. He wanted them happy more than he wanted happiness for himself.

The Viet Cong wanted to cow the populations in the big cities. It wasn't easy. The cities were protected by South Vietnamese soldiers and militias much more than the villages in the countryside. For this reason, the VC used murder, kidnapping, torture, and sabotage rather than confronting the ARVN and militia troops directly. With these techniques, the VC could liquidate their opponents while eroding the morale of the citizens and government employees. Mining highways with explosives that would only go off when a heavy vehicle passed over the mine were used to target civilian buses. The rocketing and mortaring of cities, villages, and even refugee camps were effective operations of the VC Special Activities Cells. Terror tactics were meant to demonstrate that the South Vietnam government was not capable of protecting its citizens. The attacks would sow panic and insecurity. When the time was right, the Viet Cong believed that the people would join their cause to protect themselves.

Using snipers and booby-traps, the Viet Cong also tried to get the American forces to overact and attack nearby villages. It was an effective tactic that attracted the press and created villagers sympathetic to the VC cause.

Surprisingly foreign journalists spent little time covering terrorist attacks unless a Westerner was killed or wounded. The foreign press focused most of its efforts on covering the conventional war in South Vietnam. That's what their readers back home wanted… stories of their soldiers fighting the communists in fierce battles.

In the depths of the Perfume River and under the cloak of darkness, five VC frogmen used the current as they swam underwater to avoid the ARVN patrol boats with their searchlights and shore patrols on the riverbanks. The frogmen had been training for two weeks and knew how to navigate in the dark by having one of them pop his head out of the water for three seconds to study the lights of the tallest buildings on the shore across from the Citadel. Once he had his bearings, he once again submerged, and the group of saboteurs continued its journey. It took over thirty minutes and used up most of the air in their tanks to reach their destination. When the operation was complete, they would escape on land using civilian clothes they had tucked in their wet bags along with their pistols and explosives.

Their scout was the first out of the water. He made as little noise as possible as he climbed out of the water and stepped on shore. The weight of his tank and gear was substantial and he struggled as he climbed the embankment. He reached the tree that would be his cover as he looked around for the shore patrol. The enemy was nowhere in sight. A good sign.

The scout signaled the others still in the river wrestling with the current to keep themselves from floating away. One by one they climbed out and made their way up the embankment to the tree where they removed their diving gear.

Once the entire team was out of the water, they moved into the park that paralleled the river. It was night and empty except for a few couples on benches that were more interested in each other than the strangers that came from the river. There was an undercover VC agent that met them in the park and helped them hide their gear. The team changed into their civilian clothes, then slipped their pistols into their pants' waistbands underneath their shirts. They transferred their explosives into reinforced shopping bags from nearby department stores brought by the operative.

The operative led them to their target – an eight-story hotel overlooking the river. Inside the hotel were the members of the ICC, the international control commission, from Poland, Canada, and India. The ICC had been created as part of the Geneva Accords that split Vietnam into north and south after the Indochina War. Since the start of the Vietnam War, the members had found themselves powerless and unable to control either side. But like most obsolete bureaucracies they continued their visits to both north and south in hopes that one day peace would be achieved, and they could return to their monitoring under a new set of rules. The communists in the north believed that the members of the ICC were spies that reported their findings to the American CIA. They could easily kill them during their northern inspections but did not want to be blamed for their deaths. The solution was to kill them while they were still in the South.

The sapper team followed the operative into the parking structure below the hotel. The operative distracted the guard by asking to borrow his cigarette lighter. While helping the operative light his cigarette, a sapper moved up behind the guard and slit his throat to prevent him from calling out while he died. They quickly stashed his body and moved deeper into the basement.

Each packet of explosives was attached to a large round column that supported the weight of the hotel above. The explosives were connected by a wire which in turn was connected to an electronic detonator with a timing device. Electronic devices had greatly improved their reliability since the recent invention of integrated circuits. It had not been easy stealing an electronic detonator from the American armories in the South. They were closely guarded.

Once everything was in place, the lead sapper set the timer on the detonator. The sappers and the operative moved out of the garage and back onto the street. They strolled down the sidewalk until they were a safe distance and sat at an outdoor café to watch their handiwork as they sipped hot coffee and ate pastries.

Less than a mile away, Nguyet had finally selected a house and Coyle had signed the rental agreement. He would pay the monthly rent by cabling the money. He would also send Nguyet money until she was able to find a good job. They had moved in that very day.

The house was three stories like most of the houses in the downtown neighborhood of a big city. The first floor was a shop or restaurant that the building owner rented out separately from the second and third floors which were fully furnished. On the second floor was a small living room and a kitchen with a table and chairs. On the third floor were two bedrooms and a toilet. For the first time in her life, Tuyet would have her own bedroom with an actual mattress. She cried when she saw it like somehow it was too good for a young farm girl and would be taken from her before she could enjoy it. Coyle reassured her that she could stay as long as she liked.

Coyle wanted to take them out to celebrate, but Nguyet insisted on cooking a nice meal in her new house. It would be bad luck not to eat in the house on their first day. The kitchen was equipped with the latest appliances including an electric refrigerator, a stove, and an oven. There were beautiful dishes, bowls, drinking glasses, and plenty of silverware in the drawers. There was a tea set with delicate flowers painted on the porcelain. Nguyet was overwhelmed by the discovery of everything. She decided she would use every item in the house at least once a week, so Coyle's rent money would not be wasted.

Coyle had decided he would leave tomorrow after taking Tuyet to the local school. He had been away from his base long enough and needed to get back. He sat in the high-backed chair across from the sofa in the living room waiting for Nguyet to finish her cooking. Smelling the aroma, his stomach grumbled. Tuyet giggled. For a moment, Coyle considered what would happen if he didn't go back. What if he stayed with Nguyet and Tuyet? There were always well-paying jobs for pilots and Hue had its own airport. He would make plenty of money to support them. It was strange. The more time he spent around Nguyet and Tuyet, the more he felt obligated to ensure they had a good life and that he protected them. It was a good feeling. In a way, they felt like his family.

It was the nearby explosion and the shaking of the house that snapped him back into reality. Tuyet screamed. She thought the tall house would fall on top of them. Nguyet left the kitchen and comforted her. "Stay here," said Coyle motioning with his hands before exiting.

Outside, Coyle could see a black plume of smoke rising into the night sky. The explosion had been close. He ran down the street until he stood in front of what was once a hotel. Over eighty percent of the building lay in a pile of rubble. There were bodies of civilians buried beneath the demolished concrete. The entire ICC team had gone out to dinner and wasn't in the hotel when the bomb went off. Instead, the sappers had killed five South Vietnamese civilians and wounded another fifteen. Coyle did what he could to help. He couldn't help but think that he had relocated Nguyet and her daughter from the frying pan and into the fire.

When Coyle returned to the house, Nguyet and Tuyet were waiting. He told the truth about what had happened figuring they would find out anyway. He removed his long-expired American pilot's license from his wallet and handed it to Nguyet. Using sign language and pointing in addition to his words, Coyle said, "If something happens like this again, you take Tuyet and go to the Citadel. Show the guards this. They will let you in. You will be safe there until the danger passes."

In Coyle's mind, the Citadel was one of the safest places in South Vietnam. He was wrong…

Hearing later that they had missed their intended target, the sappers and operator would still see the mission as a success since the bomb had gone off and destroyed the western-style hotel. Any chaos was better than no chaos.

Operation Concordia

June 19, 1967 – Mekong Delta, South Vietnam

The Viet Cong had many strongholds in the Mekong Delta. For the US Army and ARVN, the Mekong was one of the most difficult areas to fight in South Vietnam. It wasn't the rivers and swamps that made fighting difficult, but the mangrove roots covering much of the ground around any water source. Every step through a mangrove forest was like trying to escape from a pod of baby alligators nipping at your boots. Ankles and legs were easily broken and face-plants from tripping were common occurrences. The only consolation was that maneuvering through the mangroves was just as difficult for the enemy. Both sides suffered equally.

Another problem with the Mangrove trees is that their trunks were thick, and they made good cover. This helped the Viet Cong more than the Allied forces. The VC could get very close to their enemy without much risk and "grab them by the belt" which limited the Allies' use of artillery and air support. The VC preferred fighting in the mangrove forests to the open rice paddies where they were easy targets for shrapnel.

To battle the VC in the Mekong Delta, the Americans developed the riverine force – a collection of modified watercraft designed to fight on the Mekong's rivers. The American soldiers that operated the riverine's boats were US Navy seamen that had learned how to fight on the rivers. They were supported by a dedicated brigade from the US Army 9th Infantry Division and an all-volunteer Navy gunship squadron known as the "Seawolves."

The Riverine forces had the ability to strike deep in the Mekong Delta. The landing craft were accompanied by boats with Napalm flamethrowers that could attack enemy units in the jungle along the shore and 81mm mortars that could protect the land force up to three miles from the river. After that, it was up to the Seawolves and long-range artillery.

Mid-1967, the Viet Cong had been strengthening their hold on Can Giuoc District in Long An Province. Rather than concede the territory to the enemy, the allies came up with Operation Concordia to be carried out by the US Mobile Riverine Force and a combination of the US 47th and 60th Infantry Regiments and the ARVN 46th Infantry. The allied commanders knew that their men would be assaulting the enemy's territory where they were well-dug in and had prepared ambush positions. The fight for Can Giuoc would be bloody and fierce but was imperative to keep control of the rice fields that were South Vietnam's breadbasket. The area was just forty miles from Ap Bac where the Americans and ARVN had suffered their first major military loss in 1963.

The US 47th Regiment would be the maneuvering force that would hopefully drive the VC. The ARVN 46th Regiment was assigned the blocking position that would prevent the Viet Cong from escaping without a major thumping from Allied forces.

On June 19th, the 4th Battalion, 47th Infantry landed three miles south of Can Giuoc, while the 3rd Battalion, 47th Infantry landed one mile south of Can Giuoc. ARVN 2nd Battalion, 46th Infantry landed near Ap Bac and set up blocking positions. The idea was to set up multiple positions as a net to catch the Viet Cong. It worked.

At 10 AM, intelligence monitoring enemy radio broadcasts located a battalion-sized VC force just east of the ARVN blocking position near Ap Bac. Elements of the 3/47th Infantry were picked up by helicopter and transported south of the reported VC Nha Be Battalion, while elements of the 4/47th Infantry were picked up by Riverine Patrol boats and landed northeast of the VC location. The plan was to send out smaller units to make contact with the enemy and pinpoint their location and size before piling on with larger forces and air support.

After two hours of sweeping the area, the 3/47th came up empty-handed, failing to locate the enemy battalion. As they moved west, Company C from the 4/47th Infantry encountered the VC positions. At the same time, Company A, 4/47th patrolling to the south across a series of rice paddies ran into a well-entrenched L-shaped ambush. Both companies came under heavy attack creating chaos and heavy casualties for the Americans. Artillery and air support could not be used because they could not determine the exact location of both companies and their platoons. Nearby, Riverine patrol boats used their mortars and machine guns to lay down suppressing fire on the enemy giving the US forces a bit more breathing room but not enough to drive the enemy as the Americans had hoped.

Thirty minutes later, the artillery and air support finally pinpointed the location of all the American units and began firing on the enemy. In addition, reinforcements were brought in to support both American positions. Seawolves helicopters pounded the Viet Cong with rockets and strafed their troops with their machine guns as they raced past the enemy positions. While the initial surprise gave the Viet Cong the advantage, it was the momentum of the additional American forces and air support that turned the tables. As the sun began to set, the American companies were assaulting the enemy from all sides. When darkness finally arrived, most of the Viet Cong were able to slip through the American lines and escape. The Americans were able to transport their seriously wounded by helicopter to military hospitals which saved the lives of many. Both sides had been mauled during the encounter.

The next morning when the Americans saw that the Viet Cong had escaped. The 4th Battalion, 47th Infantry, and the 2nd Battalion, 60th Infantry sent out platoons to find the VC. They re-engaged the enemy south of the ambush area north of Rach Gion Ong stream at Ap Nam. The Americans succeeded in destroying an entire VC platoon.

At the end of the short but furious operation, the Americans had forty-six killed and fifteen wounded, while the Viet Cong had 255 killed. It was the Americans that claimed victory since they succeeded in driving the enemy out of the area.

Tuy Hoa, Phu Yen Province, South Vietnam

Located along the coast in south-central Vietnam

between Nha Trang and Qui Nhon, Tuy Hoa was the capital city of Phu Yen Province. With its southern border on the Da Rang River, the city had a total of forty-one square miles and a population of a little over 100,000 South Vietnamese. In the center of the city sat two mountains: Chop Chai Mountain and Nhan Mountain with its Champa Temple on top. In 1966, the South Korean Capital Mechanized Infantry Division, commonly known as the "Fierce Tiger Division," and the 9th Infantry Division known as the "White Horse Division" took over security for Phu Yen Province including Tuy Hoa. In 1967, the Viet Cong and NVA made their play to take over the province by kicking the South Koreans out. The communist leaders had badly miscalculated.

Most of the Americans that had fought alongside the South Koreans thought they were tough, experienced soldiers that knew the art of war well. The Koreans had a no-nonsense attitude when it came to fighting. They were aggressive which at times meant they killed the wrong people and there were several massacres blamed on the South Koreans. It was said that the Viet Cong and NVA feared the South Koreans more than they feared the Americans or any other nation fighting in the war. It was rumored that the South Koreans only took prisoners when they needed enemy soldiers to interrogate. The South Koreans had fought alongside the Americans during the Korean War. There was a bond of trust built between the warriors. South Korean forces were South Vietnam's largest ally with the exception of the Americans. When the Koreans were given a mission, the American commanders had a high degree of confidence that the mission would be a success. Operation Hong Kil Dong was such a mission and became the largest South Korean operation of the Vietnam War.

In early July 1967, American intelligence detected major movement in the north by the NVA/Viet Cong 5th Division, 85th Regiment, and 95th Regiment. While their main force dug in deep, the South Koreans sent out a large number of recon units in a wide pattern to detect the location of the approaching enemy forces. The Americans reassured the South Koreans they would be given all the air and artillery support required to fend off any opposing force. While the South Korean soldiers were always anxious to grapple with their enemy, their leaders would not sacrifice the lives of the soldiers under their command needlessly.

Once the NVA/Viet Cong forces were pinpointed, the American forward observers took over and the South Korean recon units were ordered back to the city as the American heavy artillery began its bombardment.

Flying in North American OV-10A-30-NH Broncos, the forward air controllers located the enemy positions and called in Tactical Fighter Squadrons to bomb the approaching enemy forces. The Americans unleashed hell on the communists using 500 lb. bombs and napalm canisters.

At night, fixed-wing gunships were called in to break up the enemy advance with their miniguns. Mk 24 Flares dropped from the Spookies (AC-47s) and Stingers (AC-119Ks) helped pinpoint the enemy's positions. When an enemy troop truck or anti-aircraft gun was located, the Stingers used their M61 Vulcan 20mm six-barreled Gatling cannons. Once on target, the Vulcan cannons destroyed whatever they hit… without question. Finally, B-52 Arclight strikes were called in from Anderson Air Force Base in Guam and U Tapao Airfield in Thailand. The "Buff's" massive load of 750-pound bombs cratered the enemy's front lines taking a heavy toll.

During that time, the South Koreans fended off enemy probing assaults meant to discover soft spots in the Korean defensive lines. There were none. The South Korean troops were diligent in all aspects of fighting. They knew that probing attacks could be just as important as a human wave assault if they created confusion or misdirection in their enemy leaders.

When the depleted communist forces finally assaulted the South Korean lines, they found a well-armed opponent that would not give up ground easily. As the communists launched their human wave attacks, the South Koreans remained behind their fortifications and in their trenches. Only M113 APCs and M48 tanks remained in the open where they could maneuver to reinforce different parts of the battlefield when help was needed. Tracer rounds crisscrossed the battlefield in the darkness as mortar-launched flares help the Koreans keep a sharp eye out for gathering groups of enemy soldiers about to attack. Mortars and recoilless rifles were used by both sides to take out enemy fortifications and destroy machine gun positions with their gun crews.

The battle for Tuy Hoa and Phu Yen Province lasted for over a month. With their forces exhausted and running low on supplies, it was the communists that finally broke off and headed back north. But unlike their South Vietnamese and American counterparts, the South Koreans did not wait to rest their troops after the intense battle. Instead, they attacked the fleeing enemy forces, engaging and re-engaging time and time again. The Korean commanders knew that the communists could not turn and counterattack while being assaulted by the feisty Korean soldiers. Offense truly was the best defense.

The communists didn't know what to make of the Korean aggression. They knew they too must be exhausted after more than a month and a half of fighting. But the South Koreans didn't let up. The Communists ended up in a full-on rout trying to get away from the tenacious Koreans. At the end of the forty-eighth day, the operation was over. There was no more enemy to fight. The Koreans moved back to their lines where many collapsed and slept for days.

In the aftermath, the South Koreans counted twenty-six of their soldiers killed and many more wounded while the NVA/Viet Cong had 638 killed and eighty-eight captured. In addition, the communists lost 359 individuals and ninety-eight crew-served weapons. The South Koreans had accomplished the impossible – a 24:1 kill ratio against their enemy. The American and South Vietnamese commanders were more than impressed.

Hanoi, North Vietnam

For the North Vietnamese and the Viet Cong, the key to winning the war in Vietnam and reuniting the country under a communist flag was to get the Americans to leave. It was the American military and financial aid that was keeping the South Vietnamese government and its military afloat. Many politburo members and military officers believed that the South Vietnamese military was no longer combat-effective and could not mount any kind of attack without the

Americans' help.

The planning for the General Offensive and Uprising that would later be known as the Tet Offensive, began in the early part of 1967. The planners in Hanoi decided they could win the war with one big punch throughout South Vietnam. Even with their overwhelming resources, the Americans had failed to win the war quickly as they had planned. The American bombing campaigns had also failed to bring the North Vietnamese to the negotiating table. And the American leaders were now facing rising anti-war sentiment at home.

Communist First Party Secretary Le Duan and well-known politician Le Duc Tho believed that the people of South Vietnam were fed up with their government and its ability to protect them against the communists. They no longer had faith that the Americans would save them either. Thousands of civilians in the countryside were supporting and joining the ranks of the Viet Cong each month. The planners believed they had Saigon on its heels, and it just needed one good push to fall. If there was ever a time for an all-out attack it was now the planners argued.

Privately, Le Duan was concerned that if the American bombing continued to destroy North Vietnamese infrastructure and factories at the current rate or even increased, the communist would lose their ability to mount an all-out-offensive and be stuck fighting a guerilla war for another decade. North Vietnam needed to attack the South while they still possessed the ability to do so.

But not everyone agreed. Minister of Defense Vo Nguyen Giap, the brilliant general that planned and won the Siege of Dien Bien Phu which eventually drove the French from Vietnam, was the leader of the opposition. Giap was a national war hero and had immense power and influence in the politburo. When it came to war, everyone listened to the aging General Giap. Giap's position was supported by the well-respected Truong Chinh, the Communist party theorist, and many of the other politburo members. The North Vietnamese opposition to the General Offensive and Uprising argued that even though the North and the Viet Cong were winning in great strides, they could still lose all the ground they had gained if the offensive failed. If they were patient and continued to make headway, they would eventually be victorious, and the South Vietnamese government would collapse on its own. Once that happened, the Americans would have no choice but to withdraw and go home. Patience would win the war and would be far less costly and risky than a General Offensive that committed all of the North's resources leaving little in reserve.

There was a third faction to weigh in on the discussion and was led by the national hero Ho Chi Minh and Foreign Minister Nguyen Duy Trinh. They believed that North Vietnam should negotiate with the Americans and get them to withdraw. Once they had left, the South Vietnamese government would fall on its own accord and the war would be won without the need for massive bloodshed on either side. Many publicly liked this approach, but in reality, few thought it would work.

Le Duan and his supporters took the position that Minister of Defense Giap had developed his strategy from his experiences during the Indochina War. Le made the point that Giap's strategy was based on the past and was using old conservative methods of fighting. Time and technology had moved on. If the communists were going to win, they needed more up-to-date methods and strategies to avoid mechanically repeating the past believing it would win the war. The Americans were not the French and had entirely different motivations for fighting. And the incompetent South Vietnamese government and military did not even exist during the Indochina War.

It was Le Duan and his supporters that finally won the argument domestically and took control of the North Vietnamese government and military. But the fight wasn't over. Like South Vietnam, North Vietnam was dependent on foreign powers for financial and military aid. Le Duan still needed the support of the Soviets and the Chinese for his plan to succeed.

The Chinese advocated for North Vietnam to carry out a protracted war based on the Maoist model. They feared that like the war in Korea, the Chinese military could be drawn into a conventional conflict and could lose a million of its best soldiers. The Chinese leaders also disliked the idea of negotiating with the Americans and their allies.

The Soviets liked the idea of negotiating with the Americans but believed the North Vietnamese should only approach the peace table from a point of strength. The Soviets continued to arm the North Vietnamese so they could fight a conventional war that would better their negotiating position.

For Le Duan and his followers, it was a juggling act where they needed to keep both the Soviets and the Chinese content. It wasn't easy. The only real advantage that Le Duan had was that the Soviets and the Chinese were vying for influence over North Vietnam and did not reveal what they were thinking to each other. The problem was that internal opposition in Hanoi could reveal his plans to the Soviets and Chinese. Secrecy was a big problem that he needed to deal with sooner rather than later. Le Duan was running out of time before he needed to begin the General Offensive and Uprising.

Biding his time, Le Duan waited on July 27, 1967, to take action. Le and his supporters had done their best to convince his opponents in the government and party, that the General Offensive and Uprising was the best way forward. Some were converted to his way of thinking or at least no longer opposed him publicly. But hundreds of pro-Soviet politicians and officials thought they were safe because of their loyalty toward North Vietnam's most powerful ally. They were wrong as were others that miscalculated Le Duan's determination.

Le Duan knew that before the offensive could begin the north needed to be of one mind. There could be no second-guessing at such a crucial time. The leaders needed to be rowing in the same direction so that the troops in the field were focused and confident in their final destination. If the people of the south were to join the revolution, the people of the north and the Viet Cong could have no doubts.

All of the potential troublemakers were identified based on the individual's stance on which strategy the country should follow and their support for the General Offensive. Le Duan and his followers knew that many would remain silent to avoid any confrontation but that wasn't good enough anymore. He couldn't take the risk of anyone in a vital position sabotaging his plans. Hundreds of party moderates, military officers, and intelligent officers were arrested and imprisoned until after the Offensive was well underway. The move cemented Le Duan's strategy of no negotiations with the Americans, no protracted guerilla war, and the focus on the destruction of the South Vietnamese government and military.

While the American bases and firebases would also be attacked, the main focus would be on destroying the ARVN and government installations. For the first time, the destruction of the American forces was to be secondary.

Minister of Defense Giap had lost his gamble to gain control of the North Vietnamese military. He knew that Le Duan would not dare harm him. He was, after all, a national hero. But Giap was not petty when it came to the revolution. He wanted it to succeed and for Vietnam to once again be united. He offered Le Duan his support in planning the campaign and Le Duan gladly accepted his help but within limits. It was well known that Giap had a brilliant mind for strategy but was also not beyond intrigue. It was decided that the government and military leaders would develop the plans for the campaign, then Giap would review them and make his suggestions for modification. Giap also chose many of the targets. But as the beginning of the campaign approached, Giap elected to go to Hungary for a long-overdue medical treatment. It was a wise move. Giap was a powerful foe and opposing Le Duan at such a critical time could easily make Giap a target to be eliminated. He would watch the results of his work from afar.

Before the offensive began, Ho Chi Minh would be sent to China to reassure the Chinese and to be out of the way if things did not go as planned. Le Duan did not want such a powerful voice of opposition in the country during the campaign.

More arrests were made as the kickoff of the campaign drew closer. Le Duan and his followers were taking no chances. After much discussion, it was decided that the Tet Holiday of 1968 would be the launch date for the General Offensive and Uprising. It seemed the more concrete the plans became, the more opposition to them fell away.

Buffalo and Kingfisher

July 2, 1967 – Con Thien, South Vietnam

General Westmoreland believed that the NVA were planning to overrun and seize the two northernmost provinces in South Vietnam. To ensure that didn't happen, Westmoreland sent commanding general Lewis Walt and the 3rd Marine Division. Marine intelligence estimated the Marines were facing a force twice their size with nearly 40,000 enemy troops in two NVA divisions – the 320th Division and the 324B Division.

The Marines established and reinforced seven strongholds designed to hold back the enemy – Dong Ha, Gio Linh, Con Thien, Cam Lo, Camp Carrol, The Rockpile, and Khe Sanh. If the NVA challenged their strongholds, the Marines would exact a heavy toll. Con Thien was the closest stronghold to the DMZ and the most exposed.

It was called Operation Buffalo. The US Marines' objective was to block the entry of NVA crossing the Ben Hai River into the Quang Tri Province, north of Con Thien. The area became known as Leatherneck Square because of the large number of Marines.

On the morning of July 2, 1967, Alpha and Bravo Companies, 1st Battalion, 9th Marines headed up north on Highway 561. They secured their first objective, a crossroad, without any enemy resistance. Moving further north to their next objective the "Marketplace" between Gia Binh and An Kha, they came under sniper fire from elements of the NVA 90th Regiment. The sniper fire intensified as the NVA launched a tri-direction ambush on company B causing heavy American casualties. Alpha Company moved to rescue Bravo Company. For the first time in battle, the NVA used flamethrowers to set the surrounding hedgerows a blaze along Highway 561. The Marines were forced out into the open and subjected to heavy enemy mortar fire. Suffering even more casualties, Marine Companies A and B were unable to link up. B Company's headquarters was wiped out when a single mortar round exploded with the command group killing the company commander, two platoon leaders, the radio operator, and several others.

But the Marines were not alone. Airstrikes pounded the enemy positions preventing them from overrunning the two companies. 1st Battalion's commander Lt. Colonel Richard Schening send C and D Companies supported by four M48 tanks to rescue Alpha and Bravo. Using helicopter gunships and tank fire to break up the enemy formations, D Company was able to secure a landing zone and evacuate the more seriously wounded from both Alpha and Bravo.

C Company pressed forward under heavy enemy fire and linked up with the survivors of Alpha and Bravo. Together they pulled back to D Company. The NVA kept their positions and did not pursue the Marines. They have mauled the Marines enough for the moment and had no desire to turn a victory into a defeat.

On the first day of the operation, the Marines had

suffered eighty-four killed, 190 wounded, and nine missing. What made the losses even more devastating was that many of the Marines had died because their new M16s had jammed during the battle. It was the worst one-day loss for the Marines in Vietnam. The NVA suffered fifty-five killed and the number of wounded was unknown.

The next day a USAF reconnaissance plane spotted 100 NVA moving south from their northern position above Con Thien. US Marine Battery E, 3rd Battalion, 12th Marines opened fire. Their aim was deadly accurate. As high-explosive personnel rounds rained down, the NVA were caught in the open with no nearby cover. Shrapnel shredded their ranks and killed seventy-five enemy soldiers with most of the survivors seriously wounded. It was sweet revenge for the Marines from the previous day.

On July 4th, the Marines returned to the site of the ambushes hoping to recover the bodies of their fallen comrades. The NVA engaged the Marines once again killing an additional fifteen and wounding forty-four.

On July 5th, the Marines tried again to reclaim the bodies of their fellow soldiers. Supported by tanks, they were successful. As they were loading up the bodies on their tanks, a reconnaissance plane spotted more NVA troops heading their way. Artillery and tactical airstrikes were unleashed on the approaching NVA troops. The Americans claimed to have killed over 200 enemy troops but it was difficult to get an accurate count when the enemy dragged off their dead from the battlefield.

On July 6th, the 2nd Battalion, 3rd Marines engaged the NVA north of Con Thien and killed thirty-five enemy soldiers while losing five of their own with twenty-five wounded. The same day, 400 NVA were observed crossing the Ben Hai River and heading directly toward two Marine battalions. The Marines ambushed the enemy force, then called in artillery and airstrikes to destroy the pinned-down NVA. The fight continued until sunset, then calmed down. The next morning, the Americans found 154 dead NVA soldiers. The Marines had twelve wounded. Also on the 6th, the NVA fired eight SA-2s from the DMZ and destroyed an American A-4E providing close air support to the Marines on the ground. The pilot, Major Ralph Brubaker ejected successfully and was rescued by helicopter the following day.

On July 8th, the 2nd Battalion, 3 Marines advanced toward the Cam Lo River and discovered an NVA bunker complex. Air and artillery strikes were called in to soften up the bunkers. Once the air and artillery subsided, Company G attacked the enemy bunkers. The surviving NVA abandoned their position and retreated. The Marines had killed thirty-nine enemy soldiers and lost two of their own with twenty-nine wounded. Later that afternoon, Company G was engaged by another NVA force. Again, relying on artillery and airstrikes, the Americans were successful at driving the NVA from the battlefield. The NVA had suffered the loss of another 118 soldiers while the Marines had fourteen dead and forty-three wounded.

With no more firefights for the next six days, Operation Buffalo ended on July 14th. The total Marine casualties for the entire operation were 159 killed, 845 wounded, and one missing. The NVA had 1290 killed. They also lost 164 bunkers, fifteen artillery pieces, and multiple rocket positions. The Americans claimed victory because they had driven some NVA forces north of the river back into North Vietnam.

July 28, 1967 – Con Thien, South Vietnam

After Operation Buffalo, the Marine commanders developed a new operation with the same objective of stopping the flow of communists into the south by driving the NVA in the area around Con Thien, nicknamed the "barrel," back across the DMZ and into North Vietnam. It was called Operation Kingfisher.

Although the operation started on July 16th, there was little enemy contact for the first twelve days as the Marines patrolled along the DMZ looking for the enemy. Small skirmishes were few and far between. They weren't what the Marines wanted, who were anxious to get at the communists. It wasn't until July 28th, that the conflict intensified.

Supported by five M-48 tanks, three M50 Ontos, and three LVTEs, the 2nd Battalion, 9th Regiment, 3rd Marines Division advanced north along Route 606 which was little more than a cart track leading to the Ben Hai River. When the battalion reached the river, they encountered a concrete bridge that was too narrow for the armored vehicles to cross. Without the bridge, the Ben Hai River was impassible. It was a bad miscalculation by the planners of the operation. Unable to cross the river, the Marines were forced to turn back around and return the same way they came. The Marines knew the enemy would be waiting for them.

The Marines dug in for the night beside the river and waited until morning before starting back. The column of Marines didn't get far before a command detonated mine exploded wounding five Marines. A short time later, a second mine exploded wounding more Marines and triggering an enemy ambush. The communists opened fire with small arms, mortars, and RPG-2 rockets. As always, the NVA hugged the American lines to prevent the use of air and artillery support. The Marine column broke up into multiple defensive positions as they fought the NVA.

Napalm airstrikes were called in to keep the NVA from overrunning the American positions. It was a dangerous tactic. The aircraft dropped their canisters within yards of the Marine positions. The Americans could feel the intense heat from the wall of flames. They knew it was the only thing keeping them alive.

With the enemy momentarily driven back by the airstrikes, the Marine convoy once again formed up and retreated. The Marines were forced to run a gauntlet of mortars, machine guns, and RPGs. The armed vehicles took the brunt of the enemy's RPG fire. The explosions against the steel hulls did not always penetrate the vehicle's armor, but the shrapnel still took its toll on the Marines riding on the tanks and running alongside for protection.

There were other dangers for the Marines walking next to the armored vehicles. Buttoned up inside, the drivers only saw what was in front of them through a porthole. When under attack, the vehicle drivers gave little thought to who might be outside their vehicles. They maneuvered quickly to protect the crew inside and returned fire. More than one Marine was crushed under the heavy treads of the vehicles. The carnage of a crushed comrade was a sickening sight even for a Marine.

Normally an effective weapon with its ability to fire six mounted 106mm recoilless rifles at an enemy position simultaneously, the M50 Ontos had one fatal flaw – the gun crew needed to leave the protection of the vehicle's armor and reload the weapons from the outside. The enemy waited for such an opportunity before spraying the gun crews with machine gun fire and firing their RPGs when the vehicles' hatches were open.

As night fell, the Marines formed defensive positions that protected each other. Marine artillery rained down all night keeping the communists back. In the darkness, the NVA probed the American's lines for weakness. When they found it, they exploited it until the Marines patched the hole in their position's perimeter. Neither side got much sleep. With their morale seriously challenged, the Marines fought on until morning.

As dawn broke, the airstrikes continued dropping napalm and 500-lb. bombs on the NVA positions. The American aircraft bought the Marines time. The Marines on the ground broke contact with the enemy and hightailed back toward their base near Con Thien. The tanks and armored vehicles were loaded down with dead and wounded. The Marines had suffered 214 casualties. Those Marines on the ground acted as escorts but in reality, they sought the protection of the tanks and Ontos heavy machine guns and recoilless rifles. The Marines kept a sharp eye out for enemy RPG teams hidden in the long grass and behind fallen trees. The NVA waited until the armored vehicles passed their hidden position, then fired at the rear of the vehicle where the armor was thinner and more vulnerable. Exhausted, some of the Marines struggled to keep up with their units. Being left behind was a sure death warrant. The North Vietnamese hated the

American Marines and showed no mercy.

Later that day, the 3rd Battalion, 4th Marines linked up with the beleaguered 2nd Battalion, 9th Marines, and escorted their fellow Marines back to the combat base at Con Thien.

When they finally made it back to the safety of their lines, many of the Marines in the 2nd Battalion convoy collapsed to the ground and fell asleep for several hours. Others curled up in a ball and said nothing for several days. They had seen too much and their minds needed to reset. The stress had been unbelievable. They would recover. They were Marines. They just needed a short break before returning to the fight.

During the three-day battle, the Marines had twenty-three dead and 251 wounded. The NVA had thirty-two dead. Both sides claimed victory, but it was the Americans that gave up the ground. Few Marines that had lost friends would call it a victory.

Operation Kingfisher was not over. The Marines were sent out time and time again to find the NVA and drive them from the DMZ back into North Vietnam or Laos.

In the predawn morning of October 14th, NVA artillery hit the 2nd Battalion, 4th Marines position near Washout Bridge. A night LP spotted two NVA companies moving past their position toward the bridge where Marine Company H was located. The Marines used Starlight Scopes to follow the NVA and saw them mass directly in front of Company H's position. They were preparing to attack. Warned of the pending assault, the Marine tank gunners loaded beehive rounds and opened fire on the unsuspecting NVA companies. Thousands of iron fletchings from the beehive rounds cut into the NVA soldiers killing several and wounding a dozen or more. The NVA were lucky that it hadn't been worse. Under attack by the American tanks, the NVA were forced to start their assault before they were fully assembled. The piecemeal attack failed and the NVA withdrew without penetrating H Company's perimeter.

An hour later, the NVA regrouped and attacked Company G. A communist RPG team destroyed two Marine machine gun positions. The NVA charged forward determined to destroy the Marines. They penetrated the wire around the perimeter and overran the Company command post killing the Company commander Captain Jack Phillips, a forward observer, and three Platoon leaders that had just arrived in country. Leaderless, the company struggled to fight off the NVA in their perimeter. Company F was sent to reinforce Company G and drive the NVA from the position. Several AC-47 Spooky gunships arrived and launched flares over the battlefield. Moments later, they opened up with the miniguns sending streams of red tracer rounds into the NVA positions. The NVA were chewed up by the hail of bullets and forced to withdraw. Nobody messes with the dragons.

The Marines had lost twenty-one killed and twenty-three wounded. The NVA lost about the same amount. It was a brawl with no clear winner.

The back-and-forth battles continued with both sides taking heavy casualties and nobody capturing or controlling significant territory. Operation Kingfisher finally ended on October 31st. The Marine casualties for the entire operation were 340 killed and 1,461 wounded. It was a heavy toll. The NVA sustained

1,117 dead and five captured. The number of wounded was unknown, 155 communist weapons were captured. Both sides claimed tactical victories.

The Forrestal

July 29, 1967 – South China Sea

In June, the USS Forrestal, a 60,000-ton supercarrier driven by four Westinghouse Steam turbines, departed its home port of Norfolk, Virginia, and set out for the Gulf of Tonkin off the coast of Vietnam. Designed with an angled flight deck and a steam catapult, the Forrestal was state-of-the-art when it was commissioned in 1955. It carried eighty-five aircraft and was armed with eight by five-inch Mk 42 guns. With 552 officers and 4,988 enlisted onboard, the Forrestal had the ability to launch more aircraft than most nations had in their entire air force. Even after twelve years at sea, the Forrestal was still a force to be reconned against any enemy.

After taking up its station in the Gulf of Tonkin, the crew of the Forrestal launched aircraft from her flight deck for four days straight. The pilots of Attack Carrier Wing 17 had flown 150 missions against North Vietnam. The crew was tired, but morale was high. They were doing what needed to be done to win the war and their aircraft were taking their toll against the communists.

There was a severe shortage of large bombs that could be used by the carrier's aircraft. On July 28th, the

Forrestal was resupplied with ordnance from the ammunition ship USS Diamond Head. The ordnance included sixteen 1,000-pound AN-M65A1 "fat boy" bombs. The bombs were in horrifying condition. Some of the bombs were more than a decade old and came from open-air Quonset huts at Subic Bay Naval Base where they were exposed to heat and humidity. The older bombs were filled with Composition B which was far less stable than the Mark 83 bombs that used Composition H6. The older bombs were coated with rust and grime. They were still stored in their original packing crates which were rotten and moldy. But most dangerous of all, several bombs were leaking liquid paraffin phlegmatizing agent from their seams.

One of the ordnance handlers questioned whether the older bombs could even survive the shock of a catapult-assisted aircraft launch without detonating. Several handlers suggested they jettison the older bombs over the side of the ship. Their concerns were passed up the chain of command to the ship's commanding officer, Captain John Beling. Beling was acutely aware of the ordnance shortage and that the older bombs had been transferred out of storage at Subic Bay. He just never suspected the bombs would be delivered in such a deteriorated condition. With direct orders from CINCPAC to conduct airstrikes the next day, and no replacement bombs available, Beling had no choice but to accept the 1,000-pound bombs in their current condition. Beling figured the bombs had sat dormant for over a decade and would only be on his ship for twenty-four hours, it was a safe bet nothing would happen in that short period.

The crew was not happy about their captain's decision. Agreeing to one of his crew's demands,

Beling ordered all sixteen bombs to be stored on deck in the "bomb farm" area which was between the carrier's island and starboard rail. Standard procedure would have had the bombs stored in the ship's magazine with the rest of the ship's ordnance where an accidental detonation would have destroyed the entire ship.

On July 29th, the crew was preparing multiple aircraft for more airstrikes. Bombs, rockets, and cannon shells were being shuttled from the elevator to the aircraft in turnaround from previous sorties. The aft portion of the flight deck was packed with twelve A-4E Skyhawks, seven F-4B Phantom IIs, and two A-5 Vigilante supersonic bombers. Most of the twenty-seven aircraft on the deck were in the process of being refueled. As some of the aircraft were ready to launch, the ship was turned into the wind creating a thirty-seven-mph headwind.

While loading five-inch unguided Mk-32 Zuni rockets into an F-4B Phantom II's four-tube LAU-10/A underwing rocket pod, a sailor mishandled one of the five-inch rockets. The Zuni rockets were protected from launching prematurely by a safety pin that was only removed prior to the aircraft being launched from that catapult. The sailor had mistakenly removed the safety pin. It was the kind of slip-up that happened in the high-pressure environment of war.

At 10:51 AM, the aircraft switched from external to internal power. As usual, there was a power surge during the crossover, but with the safety pin missing, one of the Zuni rockets accidentally launched.

The rocket traveled 100 feet across the flight deck, severed the arm of a crewman, and slammed into a

400-gallon external fuel tank on an A-4E Skyhawk piloted by Lieutenant Commander Fred White. Rupturing the wing-mounted tank, the missile continued to fly out of control until it made contact with another A-4E Skyhawk piloted by Lieutenant Commander John McCain. The safe-distance mechanism on the Zuni rocket's warhead prevented it from detonating but when the rocket hit McCain's aircraft it broke into pieces. Burning pieces of solid rocket propellant tumbled across the deck and ignited the highly flammable JP-5 fuel from White's ruptured tank. The fuel exploded engulfing both aircraft and causing an immediate conflagration on the flight deck.

Informed of the fire, Beling looked out from the ship's control tower and saw the thick black smoke and flames around the two aircraft, both loaded with bombs and rockets. Without even considering the sixteen 1,000-pound bombs stored on the flight deck, the captain knew his ship was in trouble. He ordered fire quarters, then general quarters to be sounded.

Things became worse by the minute as the fire spread across the flight deck engulfing a third Skyhawk next to the jet blast deflector. Within eight minutes, Beling changed the carrier to condition zebra requiring all hands to secure the ship for maximum survivability which included closing all the fire-proof steel doors that separated the carrier's compartments.

One of the old 1,000-pound bombs was dropped onto the deck from White's Skyhawk. It rolled between McCain's and White's A-4s and was engulfed in flames from the burning jet fuel. Undoing his safety harness, McCain heard the heavy metal thud of a bomb hitting the deck and looked out his cockpit canopy. The bomb was on fire as was the deck surrounding his aircraft. If he stayed in the cockpit, he was sure the bomb's imminent explosion would kill him if the flames didn't get to him first. Neither was an option he relished.

Damage Control Team No. 8, led by Chief Gerald Farrier, was the first to arrive on the scene. Without taking time to put on his protective gear, Farrier saw the burning bomb and acted. He picked up a PKP fire extinguisher and smothered the bomb with the fire suppression chemical agent. Hoping to stop the fire from spreading and buying time for the pilots to escape their aircraft, Farrier fought the fire as his skin blistered. Based on his training, he believed that he and his team had ten minutes before the flames split open the bomb's casing and detonated. But that estimate was based on a normal bomb in good condition. Farrier watched as the bomb's casing melted away and he knew the bomb was about to explode. He waved for his team to run for it while he stood his ground and kept cooling the bomb with his extinguisher.

Unsure of how long he had before the bomb exploded, McCain opened his aircraft's canopy. Black smoke filled the cockpit making it impossible to breathe. It didn't matter. He didn't have long to live as the flames billowed upward. He crawled over the front of the canopy and slid down on the aircraft's nose. He stood up on the Skyhawk's refueling probe and jumped down onto a clear patch of the burning flight deck and tumbled. He climbed to his feet and ran toward the island until he saw twelve more 1,000-pound bombs stored in the bomb farm. Bad idea. He turned and ran back across the flight deck toward the elevator. He stopped dead in his tracks when he saw a pilot engulfed in flames emerge from the black smoke. McCain moved toward the man unsure what he would do once he reached him. He never got the chance.

Despite Farrier's efforts, the bomb exploded one minute and thirty-six seconds after the start of the fire. Farrier and all but three of the men on his fire crew were killed instantly. Two hose teams were decimated. Twenty-seven men near the blast were severally injured. Many of the pilots trying to escape their aircraft were killed or missing. White escaped his burning aircraft but was killed by the bomb just a few feet away when it exploded.

McCain was blown off his feet and flew ten feet landing and tumbling across the flight deck like a tumbleweed. He looked up at where the burning pilot had been. He was gone. When McCain tried to stand, he felt a searing pain. He had been hit by shrapnel from the bomb. He sat back down on the hot deck and waited for a medical team to reach him. It didn't take long. He was carried below deck to the medical bay. McCain was not sure that below deck was the safest place at the moment, but he was in pain and in no condition to flee elsewhere.

The detonation of the old bomb had destroyed McCain's and White's aircraft and blew a hole in the armored flight deck leaving a large crater of torn steel. Burning fuel poured through the deck fracture and entered the berthing compartments below. Sailors still in the below-deck compartments were burned alive.

All the remaining F-4 Skyhawks were on fire. Damage Control Teams struggled to keep their bomb and rocket loads from exploding. Within the first five minutes of the fire eight 1,000-pound bombs, one 750-pound bomb, and one 500-pound bomb, along with several missiles and rockets exploded from the heat of the fire. Sailors fighting the fire were tossed through the air like ragdolls. Some were hurled overboard beyond the deck nets. Others were pelted with hot shrapnel from the bombs and exploding fuel tanks. The detonations prevented fire suppression during the first critical minutes needed to keep the fire from spreading. The explosions tore seven holes in the flight deck. Forty thousand gallons of burning jet fuel flowed from ruptured fuel tanks across the deck and into the fissures above the aft hangar bay and berthing compartments. Over fifty night crewmen sleeping in the berthing compartments were killed by the burning jet fuel and the black smoke it emitted which suffocated many of the sailors. An additional forty-one crew members were trapped and killed in the internal compartments located in the aft portion of the carrier.

Sailors all over the ship rallied to fight the fire to keep it from spreading further and causing further damage. They pushed burning aircraft, bombs, missiles, and rockets over the side before they could explode from the heat. Inexperienced sailors took over positions on the decimated hose teams and mistakenly washed away the foam being used to smother the flames. As more bombs and rockets exploded, sailors fighting the fire on the flight deck were blown overboard while others caught fire and jumped into the ocean. Nearby ships pulled alongside the Forrestal and fished the men from the water.

The destroyer USS George K. MacKenzie pulled alongside the Forrestal and directed its fire hoses toward the carrier's flight deck. Another destroyer, USS Rupertus, maneuvered to the opposite side of the carrier and directed its own fire hose teams toward the burning flight and hangar deck on the starboard side. The Rupertus moved to within twenty feet of the

Forrestal and stayed on station for ninety minutes battling the fire. The additional hoses from the two destroyers dampened the fire and lowered the heat on the flight deck.

At 11:47, the Forrestal reported that the fire on the flight deck was under control and thirty minutes later the firefighting teams put out the last of the flight deck fires. But the battle was not over. Forrestal firefighting crews continued to fight the flames below deck. The ordnance crew continued to find smoking bombs below deck. They quickly defused the bombs and cast them over the side into the ocean. Spotting unexploded bombs below deck, volunteer ordnance specialists were lowered through the holes in the deck with the fires still burning. They defused the bombs that had fallen through the holes and landed on the decks below. Ropes were used to hoist the unexploded ordnance back to the flight deck and the bombs were jettisoned over the side of the ship.

While the medical teams did their best to save their comrades, they were overwhelmed by the sheer number of casualties and the seriousness of their wounds. As much of the danger passed, the Forrestal rendezvoused with the hospital ship USS Repose and transferred its dead and wounded.

The firefighters combed through the burned-out compartments below deck searching for survivors. While they found some survivors, most of the crewmen were dead. As rigor mortis set in, the firefighters did their best to maintain what dignity they could for the charred remains of their fellow seamen.

At 5 PM, Forrestal mustered its crew still onboard and on other ships. It took many hours to make even a partial accounting for the ship's crew. Many were missing, having been blown overboard, while others had been transferred to other ships. Many of the Forrestal's internal compartments were still burning and too hot to enter. Crew members cut additional holes in the flight deck to allow hose teams to pour more water into the smoldering compartments below the deck. At 4 AM the next day, eighteen hours after the fire had begun, the last of the fires on the Forrestal was extinguished.

When the fire was finished, it had left 134 men dead and 161 wounded. The fire aboard the Forrestal caused the greatest loss of life on a U.S. Navy ship since the end of World War II. Of the seventy-three aircraft on the carrier, twenty-one were destroyed including seven F-4B Phantoms, eleven A-4E Skyhawks, and three RA-5C Vigilantes. Another forty aircraft were damaged by the fire and exploding ordnance.

The Forrestal sailed under its own power to Naval Air Station Cubi Point in the Philippines. The damage was massive. After basic repairs, the Forrestal returned to the United States. It would undergo extensive repairs for five months before it was once again ready for service.

A Naval investigation panel ruled that a mishandled Zuni rocket was responsible for the fire and newly developed ordnance safety procedures and a new deck-edge spray system for carrier flight decks were put into place. While being found not responsible for the disaster, Captain Beling was relieved of his command of the Forrestal and spent the rest of his career behind a desk doing staff work.

A new firefighting school at Naval Station Norfolk was named after Chief Gerald Farrier, the damage control team commander that was killed aboard the

Forrestal while trying to save the lives of the pilots escaping from their burning aircraft. The Farrier Firefighting School hosts an annual memorial honoring the sailors that died aboard the USS Forrestal. It was one of America's greatest tragedies.

August 30, 1967 – Bien Hoa Air Base, South Vietnam

As the Vietnam War progressed, so did the US Military-Industrial Complex. Conflict in Vietnam was complicated by the dense jungles, mountains, and communist tactics. Like any country in which the American military fought, it took time to learn the lay of the land and the enemy it was fighting. Eventually, with the help of US industries, the military caught up and surpassed its enemies. It was dangerous to underestimate the Americans with their ingenuity and industrial might. The Nazis and the Japanese had learned that lesson the hard way in World War II. And so it was that in the late-1960s, American military equipment suppliers began introducing new powerful weapons to take on the North Vietnamese and Viet Cong.

After having developed the UH-1 Iroquois transport helicopter ("Hueys") which became the icon of the Vietnam War and made the concept of air cavalry a reality, Bell Helicopter turned its engineers on the concept of an attack helicopter. While the Hueys were ideal for transporting soldiers across the country, they were vulnerable to ground fire from NVA and VC troops. If a landing zone was contested, the Hueys were almost defenseless. Early attempts to modify the Huey into a gunship with forward-firing machine guns and rockets earned mixed reviews. The additional weaponry and ammunition slowed the helicopter down to the point where it struggled to keep up with the troop transports. America needed a gunship that could pacify a landing zone from the air and loiter over the battlefield as the conflict progressed.

While the Marines and the Army recognized the need for a purpose-built rotary aircraft, the actual development was complicated by inter-service politics. The USAF saw armed aircraft as their bailiwick and did not appreciate the interference from other services beyond transport helicopters. The Army and Marines were concerned that the USAF did not take close air support missions seriously, especially with response times of thirty minutes or more for their fixed-wing aircraft.

As the military branches squabbled amongst themselves, Bell Helicopter secretly developed a mockup they named, "Iroquois Warrior" and displayed it for Army officials to see. Other manufacturers complained to the Pentagon that Bell was circumventing the competitive bid and design process. The moxie that Bell executives showed against their rivals had to do in part with Lady Bird Johnson being a majority stockholder in the company. The moxie worked and so did the innovative design. The Army awarded Bell a proof-of-concept contract. The result was the Bell AH-1 Cobra series.

The Cobra or "Snake" as some called it was a redesign of the UH-1 using the same engine, transmission, and rotor system which were already well-proven in battle and reliability. But that was where the differences ended. The newly developed gunship had a narrow fuselage with an armored tandem cockpit for the pilot and gunner. It was equipped with stub wings with mounts for various weapons and a chin-mounted gun turret under the cockpit. The Army was impressed and submitted few revisions beyond the addition of skids as landing gear. They wanted Bell to begin manufacturing immediately. Secretary of Defense McNamara was particularly supportive of the gunship. The AH-1 Cobra would fulfill the mission of a dedicated armed escort for transport helicopters.

The first six AH-1 Cobras arrived at Bien Hoa Air Base in South Vietnam on August 30, 1967. The curious airmen at the base gathered around the new aircraft. Nobody had seen anything like it. It seemed a mix of a fixed-wing fighter and a helicopter. The helicopter squadron commanders were anxious to see it in the field.

With its Lycoming T53-L13 turboshaft, 1,100hp engine, the Cobra was fast with a top (Never exceed) speed of 220 mph. It had a service ceiling of 11,400 ft and a 360-mile range. The gunner controlled the M28 turret which would hold either 2 x 7.62 six-barrel miniguns or 2 x M129 40mm grenade launchers, or one of each. The aircraft also carried two rocket pods on its stub wings holding seven or nineteen rockets each. The remaining pylon on the stub wings could carry additional rocket pods, missiles, additional mini-gun pods, or two XM35 armament subsystems with Vulcan six-barreled 200mm cannons.

On patrol, the military quickly realized that the Cobra was more effective in tracking down the enemy if worked as part of a "hunter-killer" team. Paired with an OH-6A Cayuse scout helicopter, the Cobra would lay low at a distance. The OH-6 would fly slow and low to draw fire from the hidden enemy. If the enemy revealed its position by engaging the scout helicopter, the Cobra would spring from its hidden position and strike the enemy. It was an effective method until the enemy realized what was happening and avoided shooting at scout helicopters.

On September 4th, the Cobra drew its first blood when it attacked a sampan carrying four Viet Cong firing their AK-47s at an aircraft they had never seen before. All four VC were killed and the sampan with multiple large holes in its hull, sank to the bottom of the river.

Bell Helicopter built 1,116 AH-1s for the Army between 1967 and 1973. The Cobras racked up over one million hours of flying time. Three hundred of the aircraft were lost during the war due to combat or accidents. The Marines also operated the AH-1G for a short time during the development of the twin-engine AH-1J SeaCobra. Once the new SeaCobras were delivered, the Marines transferred thirty-eight AH-1s to the Army increasing their inventory of gunships. The slim profile gunship proved to be an effective weapon in escorting transport helicopters and securing landing zones which were its primary mission.

Mid-October 1967 – Hanoi, North Vietnam

As it had done in previous years, the American embassy in Saigon had sent a request for a ceasefire during the upcoming holidays of Christmas and Vietnam's Lunar New Year called, "Tet." Tet, meaning festival, was the most important holiday in Vietnamese culture.

Considering the Tet holiday as an ideal period to launch their Total Offensive, the North Vietnamese bided their time hoping to throw off the American's suspicions. By mid-October, the North Vietnamese and the Viet Cong sent word that they would accept the ceasefire as they had done in the past. Nobody was really surprised. The communists needed to rest too.

The Americans and South Vietnamese had little faith that the NVA and VC would fully accept the momentary truce, but even a partial ceasefire was better than none. Many of the soldiers had been fighting almost constantly the past year and desperately needed a break, if for no other reason than to get a new uniform to replace their shredded uniforms. A hot dinner that was not from a bag would also be welcome. R&R passes were also issued to many of the officers in both the American and South Vietnamese militaries. The Nguyen Dan Tet ceasefire in 1968 was set to last seven days.

October 17, 1967 – Binh Duong Province, South Vietnam

The NVA and Viet Cong took heavy losses in infrastructure and manpower in the early part of 1967. The United States military had carried out multiple large ground operations including Cedar Falls, Junction City, and Manhattan. Commanding Generals Giap and Thanh had witnessed the disastrous effects of American battlefield mobility through the use of helicopters. While the field commanders had helped develop some new methods for dealing with the helicopters, they had been losing battles time and time again. The helicopters were taking a huge toll on the communists.

Also in 1967, the Americans expanded their Rolling

Thunder bombing campaign and began destroying Hanoi's limited industrial infrastructure. Seeing their factories go up in flames had a demoralizing effect on the North Vietnamese citizens and military. They were determined not to even consider surrender, but the decrease in the communist military personnel and infrastructure meant the war could be dragged out for years to come. A longer war meant using resources that could be used to help rebuild their country. That was not what the communists wanted.

The leaders in Hanoi began questioning their military strategy. Members of the politburo worried that if the American bombers targeted the Red River dikes, Hanoi and the surrounding farmlands would be inundated with floods triggering even more destruction of their limited resources and potentially causing massive loss of life. Le Duan and his followers were also concerned that the Viet Cong might split with the North and negotiate a separate peace with the government in Saigon which was showing no signs of collapse.

Despite all the setbacks, the generals in Hanoi still believed the war could be won using an attrition strategy. If the communist forces fought as long as possible when they engaged the Americans in battle, they could inflict massive casualties. Once the Americans back in the United States saw enough of their young men being returned in coffins, they would demand their government disengage and leave Vietnam. And once the Americans left and took their aid with them, it was only a matter of time before Saigon fell.

The Viet Cong 7th and 9th Divisions had been thrashed earlier in the year and took time to rebuild.

Now commanded by General Thanh, the two divisions were near full strength and ready to return to battle. Thanh believed in the new strategy and was determined that his forces would inflict heavy casualties on the Americans.

Colonel Vo Minh Triet, commander of the VC 271st Regiment, 9th Infantry Division was ordered to move his troops to the Long Nguyen Secret Zone located between National Highway 13 and the Michelin Rubber Plantation. His regiment was to be resupplied and reinforced in preparation for a major offensive.

At the same time as the VC 271st Regiment made its move, US Major General John Hay, commander of the 1st Infantry Division, launched Operation Shenandoah II designed to clear Highway 13 and engage the enemy between Chon Thanh and Loc Ninh.

As the American forces advanced, they unknowingly cut off the much-needed food supplies for the VC 271st Regiment. Triet had no choice but to march his starving soldiers southward to the Ong Thanh Stream where they could link up local VC resupply units. But when they arrived, the VC found that there was little food available. So short on supplies the 271st Regiment could not move again until rice and other essential supplies were delivered. The only thing they could do was dig in to protect themselves should the Americans attack.

On the morning of October 16th, two American Companies B and D led by Lieutenant Colonel Terry Allen, the commander of the 2nd Battalion, 28th Infantry, patrolled an area southeast of the Ong Thanh Stream. The area was covered by a thick jungle canopy blocking out much of the sunlight. After patrolling for a little over a mile, the Americans came upon a fortified VC bunker. Unsure of the situation Allen ordered his men back and called in airstrikes on the VC bunkers. When the bombing was over, Allen and his battalion returned to the bunkers and came under fire from VC snipers in the surrounding trees. When several of his men were hit by the VC, Allen again ordered his men to pull back and called in more airstrikes, this time using Napalm. Once the second series of airstrikes were over, Allen and his men again returned to the bunker with no resistance. The Americans found seventeen VC bodies. When they moved to the western end of the camp, another firefight broke out with a small company of VC.

As darkness descended on the jungle, Allen broke off the engagement and pulled his men back to their base to avoid fighting the VC at night and to see that his wounded were tended to by the battalion's medics. As they were leaving, Allen once again called in airstrikes and artillery to inflict more damage on his enemy.

That night, Allen decided to return once again to the bunkers in the morning and attack the enemy with a full-frontal assault. When D Company's commander, First Lieutenant Clark Welch, suggested waiting to assault the bunkers until they could get more reinforcements, Allen, who believed the VC had already left the bunkers, dismissed his subordinate's advice. He ordered the commander of Company A, Captain James George to lead the attack in the morning instead of Welch and his company.

During the night, the VC didn't rest. Instead, the 1,200-strong 271st Regiment was joined by another 200 men from the Rear Services Group. They set up a three-sided ambush and waited for the arrival of the Americans.

At 8 AM, the 2nd Battalion, 28th Infantry set out with Company A in the lead, followed by Allen and the Battalion Command Group, then Company D in the tail position. Company B stayed behind to protect the base camp. Allen preferred to watch the battle from a helicopter but decided that the jungle canopy was too thick for a good view and elected to go on foot with his men. As the lead company's commander, George was authorized to call in artillery support from Fire Support Bases Caisson V, Caisson III-S, and Lorraine III. The three fire support bases had a mix of 105mm and 155mm howitzers all within range of the projected area of operation.

Allen decided to change the direction of the assault from the battalion's previous attempts. Company A would now approach from the east while Company D was in a flanking position from the north. As they approached the enemy's position, artillery marching fire was used to protect the Americans from any enemy ambush. Allen ordered cloverleaf patrols to scout the area in front and rear of the battalion in addition to both flanks. He wasn't taking any chances.

At 9:56 AM, the 1st Platoon from Company A discovered a trail that had been used within the last hour. The platoon leader sent out cloverleaf patrols to the east and west of the trail. One of the cloverleaf patrols spotted a group of VC. Hearing of the contact, George ordered the platoon leader to set up a hasty ambush across the trail. The VC never came down the trail. They had disappeared.

Ten minutes later, 1st Platoon reported that the trees around them were moving and they could hear weapons clicking. As George listened on the radio to 1st Platoon's report, A Company's right flank protected by the 2nd Platoon began to receive sporadic gunfire from the surrounding trees. 1st Platoon was suddenly pinned down when the VC from a hidden bunker position opened fire using captured M-60 machine guns. Moments later, 2nd Platoon was pinned down by .50-caliber and 12.7mm machine guns. Unable to get a good understanding of the situation, George moved forward with 3rd Platoon.

George found that both 1st and 2nd Platoons were pinned down. He ordered 3rd Platoon to flank the enemy attacking Company A. As they moved forward with George in the lead, a captured Claymore mine exploded in front of them killing his company's radio operator and severely wounding George and his forward artillery observer.

In the thirty minutes following the explosion both the leaders of 1st and 2nd Platoons were killed by enemy fire and almost all of A Company was wounded or killed. Severely wounded and in great pain, George turned D Company over to First Sergeant Jose Valdez. With most of the company already gone, Valdez organized a rendezvous area to the east for the wounded and other survivors. Fortunately, the enemy fire subsided allowing Valdez and his men to disengage and move off.

Once the survivors had been gathered, Valdez radioed Allen and gave him a report. Allen ordered Valdez to move northward and join Company D which had formed a defensive perimeter. Just as the survivors of Company A approached the perimeter of Company D, Company D came under heavy enemy fire. Allen ordered 3rd Platoon, Company D to help the wounded of Company A enter the perimeter.

When the machine gun fire increased from the southern flank of Company D, the Americans heard the distinctive sound of M-60s. Allen and his command group, positioned in the center of Company D's position, assumed that the M-60 machine gun fire was American and that Company A was just outside Company D's perimeter. To avoid friendly fire incidents, Allen ordered D company to cease fire. He only meant for the soldiers on the southern side of the perimeter to cease fire, but his order was carried around the perimeter and all the soldiers in Company D silenced their weapons.

With the Americans performing a unilateral ceasefire, the VC 271st Regiment gained fire superiority. Taking advantage of the American commander's mistake, Triet order his 2nd Battalion which had been held in reserve to attack the American's perimeter. They attacked the Americans from three different directions adding to the chaos.

To counter the Viet Cong's move, Allen attempted to order more artillery strikes. But the Americans and VC were now entangled in hand-to-hand combat making it impossible for the artillery to fire without killing their own men.

To make matters worse, VC snipers had secretly climbed up in the trees above Company D's position and opened fire. Allen and D Company's commander were hit. In pain, but still able to command, Allen waited until Company A had entered D Company's perimeter, then ordered both companies to withdraw northward toward the Battalion's base. He also ordered Company B at the base to move south to support Companies A and D's withdrawal. The entire battalion was now committed to battle.

Seeing the Americans attempting to escape, Triet ordered his men to attack.

As the enemy gunfire intensified, the Americans scrambled to get away and their rear position soon turned to chaos. The wounded from Company A were slowing the entire battalion down. Disaster struck when Allen was grazed in the helmet by enemy machine gun fire. He spun around and was hit with a second volley of machine gun fire. This time the gunner found his mark and riddled Allen's body with bullets. Allen fell dead.

Watching his enemy escape as a wall of artillery rained down on the Viet Cong, Triet decided to break off the engagement. After only two hours of fighting, his men were exhausted and starving. He did not want to turn a victory into a defeat. No matter the lost opportunity to inflict more enemy casualties, his regiment could not pursue the Americans without being resupplied. Poor enemy logistics had saved the American battalion from complete annihilation.

The short but fierce battle had claimed sixty-four Americans killed, including Allen and the entire Battalion Command Group as well as two missing and seventy-five wounded. Only twenty-two Viet Cong bodies were seen by the Americans. It was hard to say if there were more that the VC had carried away. The Viet Cong claimed victory as did the Americans, but the soldiers in the 2/28th Infantry knew better. They had been ambushed and thrashed by the Viet Cong. As much as they hated to admit it, the battle at Ong Thanh was a disaster.

October 21, 1967 – Washington D.C., USA

The leaders of the anti-war movement were frustrated. While they had increased in number with more and more Americans believing that the war was wrong, American soldiers and Vietnamese civilians were still dying in Vietnam. President Johnson and his cabinet seemed more vested in continuing the war and refused to negotiate with the North Vietnamese or the Viet Cong.

In early January, a group of counterculture celebrities met at artist Michael Bowen's San Francisco studio. Bowen's guests included Allen Ginsberg, - a writer and one of the founders of the Beat Generation movement, Gary Snyder Pulitzer Prize-winning poet and environmental activist, Timothy Leary – psychologist and psychedelic drug advocate, and Jerry Rubin – counterculture icon and anti-war leader. After a long discussion deep into the night, the group devised a plan for a huge protest march to the Pentagon. Snyder would propose to perform an exorcism of the Pentagon, while Bowen purposed to actually levitate the building. It was highly probable that Leary may have brought along party favors for everyone to enjoy during the discussion.

Later, the group was joined by Abbie Hoffman – a political and social activist who co-founded the Youth International Party aka "Yippies," and David Dellinger – an activist for non-violent social change and one of the Chicago 7 put on trial in 1967. The march would be organized by the National Mobilization Committee to End the War in Vietnam, aka Mobe. All in the group were heavy hitters well-known in the counterculture movement. They hoped to attract a large number of young, college-educated students to fill out the protestors' ranks.

After months of planning and mobilizing, Mobe was ready. On October 21st, 100,000 people gathered for a rally in front of the Lincoln Memorial in Washington, D.C. It was a diverse group ranging from clergymen, middle-class professionals, hippies, and black activists. Phil Ochs, the counterculture folk singer, galvanized the rally with a concert performance. Intellectuals and well-known authors like Norman Mailer, Robert Lowell, Dwight MacDonald, Noam Chomsky, and Paul Goodman also attended the concert and rally.

Once the concert and anti-war speeches were finished, 50,000 of the attendees joined the march to the Pentagon. It was a little over two miles through the streets of the nation's capital to reach the Pentagon.

As the protestors approached the Pentagon, they were met by the paratroopers of the 82nd Airborne Division which had formed a human barricade in front of the Pentagon's steps. Undeterred by the military, Abbie Hoffman claimed he would levitate the Pentagon using his psychic energy. He said the building would turn orange and vibrate, at which time the Vietnam War would end. Allen Ginsberg assisted Hoffman by leading the protestors in Tibetan chants.

A number of the protestors became violent confronting the paratroopers and trying to push their way inside the Pentagon. When they were arrested, the crowd surged forward, and the paratroopers stood their ground. One of the protesters placed the stem of a daisy in the end of a paratrooper's rifle barrel. A photographer snapped a photo of the event. The photo would become the icon of the Flower Power movement where protestors would fight the military and police with love and flowers instead of violence.

While areas of the demonstration were peaceful, other areas turned into small riots pulling down barricades and pushing against the police and paratroopers. The civilians working in the Pentagon became frightened and worried that they would be assaulted by the protestors and the secretaries possibly raped. Vastly outnumbering the paratroopers, it was the first-time protestors had gone up against the military using violence. The protestors and the paratroopers who had attached bayonets to their rifles clashed for several hours as the sun set. Around midnight the crowd thinned, and the paratroopers were able to chase the remaining protestors off with tear gas and rifle butts.

The March on the Pentagon became one of the largest anti-war protests to that point in the war. Much to Hoffman and Ginsberg's chagrin, the Pentagon remained in place and kept its white marble color.

McCain

October 26, 1967 – Hanoi, North Vietnam

John Sidney McCain III was born in the Panama Canal Zone where his father, John S. McCain Jr., a naval officer was stationed. His grandfather, John S. McCain Sr. was also a naval officer. Both his father and grandfather were naval academy graduates and rose to the rank of four-star admirals. It was an impressive, if not daunting, legacy to follow.

Like most military families, the McCains followed their patriarch wherever he was posted. It meant moving a lot. The younger McCain attended a total of twenty schools all over the United States before he graduated. Following the footsteps of his father and grandfather, McCain applied and was accepted into the United States Naval Academy. He learned to box as a lightweight and earned the nickname "John Wayne." He was popular and a natural leader. McCain graduated from the academy in 1958. His class rank was 894 out of 899 because he had difficulty with mathematics which he barely passed each year and the number of demerits he had collected from arguing with higher-ranking personnel. He was smart but unwieldy, unafraid to challenge authority when necessary.

He spent two and a half years at Pensacola training

to be a naval aviator. When he completed flight school in 1960, McCain became a ground-attack naval pilot. He was assigned to fly the A-1 Skyraider, a beast of an aircraft that carried a massive bomb load. He served aboard the USS Intrepid and USS Enterprise in the Caribbean and Mediterranean Seas. His commanders considered him a reckless and careless pilot. He crashed three times but was not seriously injured. His aviation skills improved over time and practice.

Feeling he was finally ready, McCain requested a combat assignment and was sent to serve aboard the aircraft carrier USS Forrestal headed for Vietnam. He switched aircraft to the A-4 Skyhawk, a subsonic light attack aircraft with a delta wing and a single-engine turbojet. He was thirty years old lieutenant commander and going to war in a jet. For McCain, life couldn't get much better.

But things did not go well aboard the USS Forrestal which was a key element of Operation Rolling Thunder. McCain and his fellow pilots became frustrated by Washington's interference and micromanagement of the war. He later wrote, "In all candor, we thought our civilian commanders were complete idiots who didn't have the least notion of what it took to win a war."

A short time later while refueling and rearming on the Forrestal flight deck, McCain barely escaped one of the worst naval disasters in US Naval history when his Skyhawk was hit by an accidentally launched Zuni rocket from another aircraft. Although he escaped his burning jet, he was wounded when a nearby bomb detonated from the fire's heat while he was helping other pilots escape their aircraft. McCain was struck with hot shrapnel in his legs and chest. After recovering from his wounds, McCain volunteered to serve aboard the USS Oriskany which was also part of Operation Rolling Thunder. Once onboard, McCain was awarded the Navy Commendation Medal and the Bronze Star Medal for previous missions he had flown over North Vietnam.

On October 26th, McCain was on his twenty-third bombing mission when his A-4E Skyhawk was hit by a missile over Hanoi. With his aircraft critically damaged and breaking apart, he ejected. He broke both his arms and one of his legs as he exited the aircraft's canopy. In severe pain, he watched as he descended into the city and landed in Truc Bach Lake in the center of the capital. With both arms disabled, he was unable to free himself from his parachute and began to drown. Several North Vietnamese that had seen him descend paddled out in a boat and fished him out of the lake. When they reached the shore, several angry Vietnamese grabbed him from the boat. They hated the American pilots that had been bombing their city and killing their neighbors and family. One of them crushed McCain's shoulder with the butt of his rifle, then bayoneted him. A Vietnamese officer arrived and ordered the crowd to stop beating the American pilot. Barely conscious, McCain was loaded onto a cart, then transferred to a military vehicle, and transported to Hanoi's Hoi Lo Prison nicknamed the infamous "Hanoi Hilton."

McCain was seriously wounded, but his captors refused to treat him. Instead, they interrogated and beat him when he gave them nothing. He was finally given medical care when an intelligence officer discovered that he was the son of an American admiral.

The officer had guessed correctly that McCain's capture by the North Vietnamese would make headlines in all the major American newspapers.

McCain was treated for his wounds and spent the next six weeks in a hospital. The care he received was well-below Western standards and many of the medical staff had friends or family that had been killed by American bombs. Many refused to care for him and only under the threat of punishment would they do their jobs. They were not gentle with McCain. He lost fifty pounds. He was in a chest cast for his fractured shoulder. His grey hair turned white.

A French journalist was allowed to film an interview with McCain. After the journalist left, the aviator was beaten by the North Vietnamese for not showing enough gratitude toward his captors.

Once released from the hospital, McCain was sent to another prison on the outskirts of Hanoi where he would be safer from the bombing. The North Vietnamese did not want to lose their prize prisoner. But McCain was still in bad shape and weak from his rapid weight loss. He was placed in a cell with two other Americans. They did not expect McCain to live out the week. Three months later, McCain was placed in solitary confinement where he would remain for the next two years.

A few months into his confinement, McCain's father was promoted to commander of all U.S. Naval forces in Vietnam. The North Vietnamese offered McCain an early release because they wanted to appear merciful to the international press. The North Vietnamese also wanted to demonstrate that elite American prisoners were willing to be treated preferentially. Seeing through their deception, McCain refused repatriation unless every American soldier captured before him was also released. The military code of conduct for POWs clearly stated in Article III: "I will accept neither parole nor special favors from the enemy." In addition, American officers had agreed among themselves that to prevent the enemy from using prisoners for propaganda purposes, officers would only agree to be released in the order in which they were captured. McCain stayed in solitary confinement. His captors were angry at his stubbornness.

McCain became even more ill when he contracted dysentery and suffered from heat exhaustion in his cell. His wounds from the crash were still not fully healed and caused him a great deal of pain. When McCain didn't give in to their request, the North Vietnamese were unsympathetic and subjected him to a program of severe torture. He was bound and beaten every two hours.

After weeks of torture and suffering further wounds, McCain decided to commit suicide. As he prepared to take his life, the guards interrupted him and foiled his attempts. To stop the beatings which were getting more severe by the day, McCain made an anti-American propaganda confession. He felt his statement was dishonorable, but he later wrote, "I had learned what we all learned over there; every man has his breaking point. I had reached mine."

Refusing to sign additional statements, McCain received two to three beatings per week. McCain also refused to meet with anti-war groups seeking peace with Hanoi.

McCain remained a prisoner of war for five and a half years until he was finally released on March 14,

1973. His wartime injuries had left him permanently disabled, unable to raise his arms above his head.

On arriving in the United States, McCain was reunited with his family including his wife Carol and his three children. McCain went through months of physical therapy to gain back more motion in his leg and arms. With plans to run for Congress, McCain finally retired from the Navy on April 1, 1981. He moved to Arizona and was elected to the U.S. House of Representatives. Later, he became a U.S. Senator continuing a life of service to his country.

November 2, 1967 – White House, Washington DC

President Johnson no longer trusted his secretary of defense, Robert McNamara. McNamara had grown distant and his assessments of the progress in the Vietnam War were negative. He no longer believed the war could be won.

Based on the reports from Westmoreland and MACV, Johnson believed that they were winning the war. But the American people had lost faith in the war and were turning against him. He needed to reverse this trend before it was too late.

The president held a secret meeting, without McNamara, in the White House. History would later nickname Johnson's panel of supporters "The Wise Men." The participants included: Dean Acheson, McGeorge Bundy, Clark Clifford, Henry Cabot Lodge Jr., and Maxwell Taylor. Johnson trusted their advice and asked them if there was a way to shore up support for the war and unite the American people.

This was the moment the Wise Men had been

waiting for. They had the president's ear without McNamara. They urged Johnson to continue the war as it was being fought but to give the American people more optimistic reports on the war's progress. They wanted Johnson to tell the American people that the US military along with its allies was winning the war in Vietnam. With no other ideas on the table, Johnson bought into the concept of an alternative truth based on a more positive perception of how things were going in Southeast Asia. It was what he wanted to hear… that there was hope. From that point forward, the President of the United States would lie to the American public and himself. And what was just as important… was that Johnson had help with his deception. Most in the chain of command determined that not being a team player and pissing off the boss was not a good career move.

November 11, 1967 – Saigon, South Vietnam

After discussions with the Pentagon, MACV revised its estimate of the number of NVA/VC forces in South Vietnam to 242,000 men versus its previous assessment of 299,000 men. When reporters asked the generals to explain the decrease, they stated that the revised estimate was based on new data of heavier casualties than originally reported and plummeting morale of the communist troops that were deserting.

But the reality of what MACV had done was different than what they had told reporters. To get the new, more optimistic enemy troop estimates, the staff at MACV changed some of the categories normally counted as part of the Viet Cong troop levels. Old men, women, children, and non-combatant villagers were excluded even though they created the boobytraps and planted the mines that killed one-third of the American casualties and hid the supplies, weapons, and ammunition used by the communist troops.

The CIA privately disagreed with the new estimates. Based on the data that their officers collected, the CIA believed that the enemy's strength was closer to 600,000. To hedge their conclusions and give MACV a way out, the CIA wrote in their reports the disclaimer that "we lack precise basic data on population size, rates of growth, and age distribution for both North and South Vietnam. Our data and conclusions are therefore subject to continuing review and revision, especially since capabilities do not remain static." The CIA was a team player and sought not to negatively affect the war effort.

In Saigon, General Westmoreland told journalists that the body counts that his field commanders had been reporting were very, very conservative. In Westmoreland's mind, he was only saying what his Commander and Chief wanted him to say. He was a soldier and obeying orders. He went on to say, "The body count estimates that have been reported probably only represented fifty percent of the enemy that had been killed."

The shift in reporting strategy worked. After the MACV revised estimates were reported in the American media, the American attitude shifted. A Gallup poll concluded that fifty-nine percent of Americans favored continuing the war with fifty-five percent saying that the United States should increase its military effort and involvement. America was back on board with the president and his strategy.

Quigley

Saigon, South Vietnam

By 1967, Malcolm Browne, AP's Pulitzer Prize-winning bureau chief, had left the Associated Press to once again become a freelance journalist. As AP's bureau chief, Browne was replaced by Edwin White, a ten-year veteran journalist known for his calm demeanor even during the most chaotic times. For some odd reason that was never disclosed, White's associates called him "Quigley."

Karen entered his office and said, "You wanted to see me?"

"Yeah. Pull up a chair," said Quigley.

Karen obeyed her boss. She did not know Quigley well and wondered if she might be in some kind of trouble although she didn't know what it might be. Karen was not always good about sticking to the rules, mostly because she rarely knew what they were. Since there was no rule book for journalists in Southeast Asia, the editors practiced a two-step disciplinary code – the first offense was a warning, the second offense was cause for dismissal unless you were well-known and had a wall of awards for your reporting. Awards allowed you to get away with all sorts of shit. No editor in their right mind was going to fire a star journalist unless it was something unforgivable like murder or failing to check your sources on a story. Lying to the bureau chief was also frowned upon but rarely led to dismissal. The chief knew that some dishonesty went along with the job and that the best liars tended to be the best journalists. Allowances had to be made to protect the good name of the corporation and increase profits. "So, what's up, Boss?" said Karen hoping to get right to the point.

"Call me, Quigley. Everyone does," said Quigley.

"Why?"

"Why what?"

"Why does everyone call you Quigley?"

"Oh, well… it's a long story and I don't have time to tell it right now."

"Oh, sure. No problem. What did you want to see me about? Was it the photo of Peterman's ass I posted on the bulletin board? I can explain that."

"Maybe later. Did you really take a shot at Peterman's butt?"

"I'd prefer not to say at the moment."

"Procrastination. That's a sound strategy."

"So, if it's not my Peterman photo, what is it?"

"I need you to show a new journalist around and teach him the ropes. He arrives tonight."

"I'm a photojournalist. Why am I showing a newbie journalist around?"

"It's part of my new program to conserve resources whenever possible. I match two journalists together, then I have two employees covering the same stories. It's a waste of resources. With a photojournalist and a journalist teamed up it wastes nothing. They each have their different jobs to do on every story. You, see?"

"Sure. But I am kinda busy hunting down sources

on the Saigon mafia story."

"Bring him along. He can write the copy."

"It's kind of a big story for a newbie."

"It's okay. I've read his stuff. It's fresh."

"Fresh?"

"As in not stale. We are hoping to attract younger readers."

"Yes, sir."

"Quigley."

"Right… Quigley. That name's gonna take some getting used to."

"Take all the time you need. His name is Chris Butler. We're keeping him at the Caravel until he can find some more permanent digs."

"Got it… Quigley."

Karen sent one of the AP's drivers to pick up Stout at the airport and take him to the Caravel. She left the new journalist a message at the front desk telling him to meet her in the lobby restaurant for breakfast at 7 AM the next morning.

After breakfast, Karen and Stout headed over to the U.S. Embassy to introduce Stout to the MACV press officer so he could be embedded with U.S. military units. As they were heading upstairs, they ran into Granier and the new commander of CORDS, Robert Komer, walking down the stairs. Even though it was awkward, Karen stopped and introduced Stout, "Chris Stout, meet Blowtorch Bob Komer, the new head of CORDS, and Rene Granier, his chief minion. Chris is the latest addition to AP's journalist pool."

"Nice to meet you," said Stout offering his hand to shake. Nobody took it.

"What are you doing here, Karen?" said Granier.

"Exercising our First Amendment rights on American soil."

"You're Tom Coyle's daughter, aren't you?" said Komer turning to Karen while Granier looked stunned like a bear hit over the head with a two by four.

Karen said, "Yeah. How did you know that?"

"Coyle's an associate and you're press. Not a good combination in our business."

"Well, if it's any consolation, my father never says anything about his work. Not that I don't try to pry it out of him."

"I would expect nothing less. You're doing your job and we're doing ours. Speaking of which, no time to chat."

Komer headed downstairs. As Granier passed Karen he whispered, "You're Tom Coyle's daughter?"

"Yeah. Do you know him?"

Granier said nothing but looked as if his mind was racing as he followed Komer down the stairs. Karen smiled at Granier's reaction. He always seemed in control and to see him otherwise pleased her.

Walking through the embassy lobby, Komer said, "What the hell was that?"

"Nothing," said Granier.

"Didn't look like nothing. How do you know her? Through Coyle?"

"No. We met up country during an assignment. She's a real pain in the ass."

"Most reporters are. Best steer clear."

"I do. Believe me."

In less than twenty-four hours with the newbie journalist, Karen decided she didn't like him much. She guessed it was because Chris Stout was too much like her when she had arrived in Saigon. He was brash and overconfident. He had only been in country one day and was already acting like he owned the place. And to top it all off… he was handsome and played the role of a gentleman when around her – opening doors and letting her go first. She hated that most of all. It seemed everything that she tried to teach him, he responded with, "Yeah, I know." Or "I am well aware of that." She wondered if she was wasting her time.

Prepared to write him off, she read a couple of articles he had written that had been picked up by national newspapers. She hated the fact that Quigley had been right. Stout's style was fresh and engaging. That was not an easy task in the newspaper business which was very set in its ways. But Stout's writing was different. She felt obligated to help him even if he was an ass.

Karen decided to swallow her pride and let him be a gentleman. There was no use fighting it. He was who he was and she wasn't going to change him. If she did her job right, she might prevent him from getting thrown in jail or mugged. Saigon was not a beacon of liberty like so many Westerners thought. She had learned that the hard way. Hopefully, Stout would learn from her mistakes. Despite his know-it-all attitude, she would try to teach him.

She taught him about the Happy Hour at the Caravel where the Western journalist hung out in the lobby lounge. She taught him to be patient because the Vietnamese and especially government officials moved at their own pace and fighting it solved nothing and just took more time. She taught him who was important and who was a waste of effort. She introduced him to some of her contacts, but not all.

She would give him a head start, but he would have to earn his own contacts. That's what good journalists did... develop contacts. Address book full of them. Every phone number is a precious gem only to be used when absolutely necessary. Nobody liked to be bothered frequently. And for the very best contacts, always offering something in exchange for valuable information – drinks on the rooftop bar at the Continental Hotel, a transistor radio, or an introduction to an American officer. Half the battle was figuring out what they wanted. The bigger the ask, the bigger the gift or favor. It felt wrong to pay for information, but it was all part of doing business in South Vietnam.

Surprisingly, Stout learned and seemed somewhat grateful. The longer they were together, the more Stout seemed to stare at her eyes. It bothered her and she hit him when he did it. She had seen that look before... puppy love. The crush a student gets on a teacher. She didn't need it. All she wanted was to make sure he could survive, then get back to her real work.

Quigley had given them an assignment – a story on the Saigon mafia and their extortion of local businesses. Saigon had a thriving protection racket, especially in the Cholon neighborhood, Saigon's Chinatown. The merchants and the restaurant owners didn't trust the police who were usually corrupt and demanded a bribe to investigate any crime. The only good thing about the assignment was that Cholon had the best restaurants in all of Saigon. Staking out a business, usually meant a long meal at a nearby restaurant or café which didn't disappoint. Vietnamese dishes like "Banh Xeo" crepes stuffed with seafood, paper-thin spring rolls called "Banh Cuon," mouthwatering "Suon Nuong" charcoal-grilled pork chops, and, of course, world-famous "Pho" soup with it savory broth. There were also Chinese dishes that the Vietnamese loved like Peking roasted duck, twice-cooked pork slices, dim sum, and dumplings stuffed with minced meat or diced shrimp always accompanied with a savory dipping sauce. There were so many restaurants and cafes in Cholon that any dip in quality meant instant death for the business. Only those with large crowds of loyal customers survived. That was a good kind of competition.

Karen and Stout sat at a patio table below an awning that kept the sun away. Blocks of ice in front of electric fans kept a cool breeze going while customers ate their meals. Karen's camera sat on the table where she could keep an eye on it. Cameras were valuable commodities on the black market. She had lost several and the film within them from thief passersby. She learned to always keep her camera in front of her where she could see and always keep a fork or knife close by to provide a quick stab to wandering hands. The same was true on the street where motorbike thieves abound. Keep the camera in front rather than the side where it could be snatched, and the camera's strap slashed with a razor-sharp carpet knife held by a passenger on the back of a motorbike. Purses were also a popular target and the reason Karen never carried one when out in the field. And she never left a camera or camera bag in a car in plain view. It was a sure way to return to the vehicle only to find the side window shattered and the camera or bag gone. The thieves had it down to an art, but always looked for easy prey like tourists rather than photojournalists or soldiers that had learned how to protect their cameras and themselves.

Karen and Stout were watching a liquor store across the street that had been caught up in a turf war between two rival mafia gangs. Both wanted protection money and the owner could not pay. He expected that his business would be firebombed within the next few days. He had told the police, but they did little. He had no money to pay a bribe to the investigating officer. He was on his own. Karen and Stout had found the owner through one of Karen's neighborhood informants. She had paid him the reward that he had expected, so he would continue to bring her information in the future. It was a symbiotic relationship.

While sitting at the table enjoying a very long lunch, Karen noticed something strange down the block in front of an alley. A military jeep was parked in front of the alley. An officer and his driver sat as if waiting for someone. Keeping her camera on the table, she snapped a photo. She didn't think much of it but had decided better safe than sorry. Besides, film was cheap, and the AP had its own lab for developing and printing.

After a few more minutes, a Vietnamese man emerged from the alley and approached the jeep.

Karen discreetly took another photo and again didn't think much about it. It had nothing to do with the story they were working on.

The man from the alley had a discussion with the officer, then pulled out an envelope. He showed the contents – cash.

Karen discreetly snapped another photo. Her interest was growing. One never knew where a good story would pop up. Luck was a big part of journalism.

The officer climbed out of the passenger seat and moved to the rear of the jeep. He pulled a wooden crate from the back and opened it. He pulled out one two-part cylindrical fiberboard shipping tube and pulled it apart. He withdrew an M26 grenade from the bottom half of the shipping tube and handed it to the man for inspection.

Karen snapped another photo. Her worst fear was that Stout would realize what she was doing and turn around to see what she was taking photos of. She did her best to distract Stout while she snapped another photo. She even degraded herself and subtly flirted with him to keep his attention away from the camera.

When the man reached for another shipping tube, the officer stopped him. The officer took back the grenade from the man and demanded money. The man hesitated, then handed the officer the envelope filled with cash. Satisfied, the officer allowed the man to inspect a second shipping tube and grenade.

There was little doubt in Karen's mind what was going on. The challenge for her was telling the story through the camera's lens without looking through the viewfinder. She was an experienced photographer, but the jeep was almost thirty yards away.

She was lucky and smart. At the end of each shoot, she would set the camera's focus ring on the lens to infinity and the aperture ring to as narrow as she dared to create a broad depth of field and give the camera a fighting chance of capturing a random image that she might snap. She had developed the habit to allow her to take a photo at a moment's notice and have it be in focus. Things happened fast in Vietnam and there often was no time to fiddle with the right settings on her camera.

It was all an educated guess. She wouldn't know if the images were in focus until the film was developed in the dark room. Flying by the seat of her pants made her crazy. She wanted to control everything possible when she was shooting. But also needed to be ready for the unexpected. In this case, there was nothing she could do without raising the camera from the table and looking through the viewfinder. If she did that, the officer and the man would most likely see her and there would be trouble. Even though it was a common practice, selling military weapons on the black market was a serious and punishable offense. The officer could be court-martialed, and the buyer thrown in jail.

And then, her worst fear came to fruition… "What are you shooting?" Stout asked.

"Don't turn around. Don't turn around," said Karen.

"Why not?" said Stout as he turned around.

"What part of 'don't turn around' did you not understand?"

Catching Stout's movement in the corner of his eye, the officer turned and looked straight at Karen, Stout, and the camera sitting on the table with the lens pointing straight at him. The officer realized what was happening as his face filled with anger. His mind was racing looking for a way out. Then, he found it. He pulled out his service revolver, aimed it at the buyer, and shouted, "Traitor" in Vietnamese.

Realizing what was about to happen, Karen picked up her camera and looked through the viewfinder. To her amazement, the image was perfectly in focus. She pressed the shutter button at the same moment that the officer put a bullet in the shocked buyer's forehead. The buyer collapsed dead. "Jesus," said Stout watching the event unfold.

"We gotta go," said Karen tossing some money on

the table to pay for the meal.

Leaving the buyer's body at the entrance to the alley, the officer retrieved the grenade, then climbed into the passenger seat of the jeep and ordered his driver to pursue the two American civilians.

Stout was frozen like a deer staring into headlights. "Chris! Snap out of it, you idiot. We're gonna die if we don't get out of here," said Karen already moving through the restaurant to the opposite side.

Stout was startled by her harshness but realized she was right. He moved to follow her, keeping his eyes on the approaching jeep. He bumped into a table knocking over glasses and dishes that crashed to the floor. Everyone was staring at him. He ran to catch up with Karen who was already stepping off the patio. "Where do we go?" said Stout.

"We gotta get off the street," said Karen looking around for a solution.

"There are so many witnesses. Do you really think he might run us over with his jeep?"

"No. I don't. I think he'll shoot us."

"In broad daylight?"

"Yes. This is Saigon. It happens all the time."

"We should call the police."

"No. We shouldn't. I'll get us out of this, Chris. Just stay close."

"Yeah, yeah. Stay close. I can do that."

"There," said Karen pointing across the street.

Three street vendors blocked the entrance to an alley with their food carts which had multiple customers gathered around waiting their turn to be served. Stout followed Karen as she ran across the busy road dodging cars and motorbikes. The jeep was closing fast, just ten yards away. Karen and Stout squeezed in between the crowd and carts to enter the alley.

Blocked by the crowd and carts, the jeep driver skidded to a halt. The officer yelled at the street vendors to move their carts. When they didn't move fast enough, he pulled out his pistol and fired two shots in the air. The crowd scattered and the cart owner pushed their carts out of the alley entrance.

Karen and Stout raced down the alley which was a dead-end. They tried to open the back doors to the businesses that lined the alley, but all were locked. A warehouse loading dock was at the rear of the alley. It was their only option. They ran toward it as the jeep sped into the alley threatening to run them down. With just moments to spare, Karen and Stout reached the open warehouse loading door and scurried inside. The jeep kept going and crashed into crates in front of the loading door. The wooden crates cracked and splintered. The jeep flew into the warehouse and the driver was once again forced to slam on the brake to prevent the jeep from crashing into a wall of crates. The officer and the driver jumped out. The officer was armed with his pistol and the driver with his M1 carbine. The warehouse interior was dark with shafts of light peeking through holes and cracks in the walls and roof. Karen and Stout were nowhere in sight. The officer ordered the driver to stop moving as he listened. He heard the scuffling of feet and turned aiming his pistol toward the noise. It was two warehouse workers that quickly disappeared upon seeing the armed soldiers.

Karen and Stout were hiding deeper in the warehouse. Karen was looking for another way out. There was none that she could see. They were trapped.

Karen opened her camera carefully and removed the film. She hid the film canister in the toe of her left boot. It hurt her curled toes, but she didn't care. The film was far too valuable to let it be confiscated during a search. She hoped her boot's leather was thick enough to prevent anyone from feeling the canister. To complete the deception, she loaded another canister of film into the camera and quietly advanced the film, so it seemed like she was in the middle of the roll.

After listening for a few moments, the officer and driver resumed their search and were moving in the direction of Karen and Stout.

It was Stout that figured out a better hiding place. He pointed upward to the top of the wall of crates. Karen nodded. He clasped his hands together and gave Karen a boost up. With her camera and bag around her neck, Karen used the wooden edge of the crates to climb upward until she reached the top. She pulled herself up and over the edge. Laying on her stomach she looked out at the warehouse and caught a glimpse of the officer and driver nearing Stout's location. She turned back to Stout and motioned that they were approaching, and he needed to hurry. Stout's shoes were loafers and not ideal for climbing. In addition, he weighed a lot more than Karen making his footing on the edge of the crate more precarious. Halfway up, the edge of a crate splintered, and Stout lost his footing. He fell to the concrete floor. Karen cursed and tried to locate the officer and driver. It was too late.

The officer and driver rounded the corner of the crate wall and saw Stout sitting on his ass on the floor. Seeing them aim their weapons at him, Stout panicked and tried to make a run for it. The driver squeezed off two rounds from his rifle. One found its mark in the center of Stout's back. He grunted and fell to the floor. Karen gasped but then stopped herself. Stout's groaning had covered Karen's noise. The officer and driver ran to Stout who was seriously wounded. "I can't feel my legs," said Stout.

The officer looked around for Karen and saw nothing. He aimed his pistol at Stout's head. Watching from the top of the crates, Karen shouted, "No."

The officer turned to see that. He said something in Vietnamese and motioned for her to come down. She obeyed and climbed down. The driver kept her covered with his rifle. The officer again raised his pistol and aimed at Stout's head. He fired one round. That was all he needed. Stout was dead. Karen was horrified. She knew she was next. The officer and driver would not leave any witnesses. The officer ordered the driver to retrieve her camera and bag. He brought them back to the officer who searched through the bag, then opened the camera and removed the film. Holding the film cannister he considered for a moment, turned to Karen, and said, "Where?"

Karen said nothing but pointed to the film in his hand. He shook his head, not believing her. She shrugged. He told the driver to search her. The driver shouldered his weapon and patted her down. When he came to her boots, he felt the sides around her ankle but did not touch the toe of her boot where the canister was hidden. The driver told the officer he found nothing on her. The officer ordered the driver to climb up and search the top of the crates where Karen had been hiding. The driver obeyed and found nothing. The officer remained suspicious but seemed satisfied for the moment. He told the driver to load the American's body in the jeep and cover it with a tarp.

The next day, Quigley was in his office editing a journalist's story before it went out on the wire. He wondered why so many reporters in his office didn't know how to spell and even fewer used proper grammar. He considered it unprofessional but didn't have the time or energy to play schoolmarm. Roger, the lab technician, stuck his head through the doorway and said, "Have you seen, Karen?"

"Not my day to watch her," said Quigley. "Why?"

"Yesterday, she had me rush two rolls of film, but she never came by to pick up the contact sheets."

"That doesn't sound like Karen."

"Well, she didn't and it just burns my britches."

Quigley considered for a moment, then said, "Let me know when she picks her contact sheets, will you?"

"Sure. Like I got nothing else to do."

"I'm pretty sure you'll survive."

Roger returned to his lab leaving Quigley deep in thought. He got up, walked over to the receptionist, and said, "Hey, Margaret. Have you heard anything from Karen today?"

"No. I know she's out with that newbie Stout," said Margaret.

"When's the last time you saw her?"

"Yesterday, in the morning."

Quigley grew a bit more concerned and said, "Let me know if she checks in."

"Will do."

"Another thing… would you check the local hospitals and see if Stout or Karen are there?"

"Sure. Are you worried?"

"Not overly. Not yet. But better safe than sorry."

Quigley turned and walked over to another desk

where Jim York was typing out a story. "Jim, have you heard of anything weird going on in the city?"

"Define weird," said Jim.

"Unusual."

"No. Not really. There was a guy killed by an ARVN officer over in Cholon, but I wouldn't really call that unusual."

"That wasn't on Tran Cao Van Street, was it?"

"Yeah, it was. Right by the traffic circle."

"Damn."

"What's up?"

"I don't know. Maybe nothing. I need a translator. Who's available?"

"I think Phan is available."

"Phan… good. Where's Phan?"

"Probably in the breakroom getting a coffee. He's a fiend for coffee."

"Thanks," said Quigley moving off toward the breakroom.

Karen was in a room with an empty rice bag over her head. Her hands were tied too tight behind her back. She could feel them throbbing from lack of blood flow. There wasn't anything she could do about it but suffer. She hadn't seen the officer or the driver since yesterday. She was hungry, thirsty, and needed to pee. She thought about getting free from the rope tying her hands together, then hiding the film in the toe of her boot someplace else in the room in case they searched her again, but she didn't want to be separated from it.

Stout had sacrificed his life for that film. She felt guilty. He was her responsibility and she let him down. She replayed in her mind what had happened again and again trying to figure out if there was something she would do differently that might have saved Stout's life. She should have let him go first climbing the crates, but she knew he wouldn't have allowed it. That was just the way he was. Besides, he probably still would have fallen hitting her on the way down. And maybe they both would have been killed. There was no way to know what would have happened. She decided not to think about it.

She needed to focus on the present and figure a way out of her situation. She wasn't very hopeful. She wondered why they were keeping her alive. There was no way they would let her live after she witnessed two murders. She concluded that the only reason she was still alive was because of the film in her boot. It was a very big loose end. If they discovered where she had hidden it, she was a dead woman. No question about it. She heard the door open and someone walk in...

"We developed the film roll you had in your camera. There was nothing on it," said a faceless male voice with a French accent. "Where did you hide the film?"

"I don't know what you are talking about. I need to pee," said Karen.

"Then pee. Nobody is stopping you."

"Untie me."

"I don't think so."

"Up yours."

"If you don't tell me where the film is, peeing will be the least of your concerns."

"I don't know where it is."

"You're lying. You do understand that we cannot allow such a thing to be seen by the Americans? We have enough trouble with them, and we don't need any more problems."

"If I knew where it was, I would tell you."

"Again, you're lying. This is about to get… unpleasant. You'll soon find that lying is not an effective tactic."

Someone else in the room removed the rice bag from her head. She saw her inquisitor standing before her. He was tall with a slender build, sandy blond hair, and dressed in civilian clothes. He looked and sounded French, a relic from the past. The officer and the driver were also in the room. Karen knew that she would not survive. She had seen his face and the face of the others. She was sad and frightened but fought back her tears. She wouldn't give him the satisfaction.

The inquisitor said something in French to the officer and driver. The officer went outside the room and disappeared. The driver untied the rope around Karen's leg tying them to the chair legs.

He lifted Karen from the chair so she was standing, her hands remaining tied behind her back. The driver took out his knife and stood on the chair. He punched a large hole in the ceiling wallboard and located a beam. He cut another hole on the opposite side of the beam. The officer brought back a coil of rope. The driver threw one end of the rope over the beam. The officer tied the other end of the rope around the rope on Karen's hands behind her back. "What the hell are you doing?" said Karen panicking.

"Torture is simple enough. Torture without evidence of torture is another story. A true art form practiced throughout the ages. What you are about to endure is called "Strappado. It is a favorite of the Japanese." said the inquisitor. "You can stop this at any time by simply telling where you hid the film."

"Then you'll let me go."

"Of course."

"Now, who's lying?"

"Smart girl. Such a shame. But at least the pain will stop if you tell me where the film is hidden."

The inquisitor nodded to the officer and driver. They pulled the rope lifting Karen off the ground with her hands behind her back. She screamed in pain and squirmed to free herself. It was no use. She was just making matters worse. "Don't move too much or you'll dislocate your shoulder," said the inquisitor. "Then you will know true pain."

"FUCK YOU!" screamed Karen as her left arm popped out of its shoulder socket.

Quigley examined the alley entrance where witnesses had reported an ARVN officer killing a man. The police had already removed the body, but there was still blood on the street. Quigley tried to piece together what had happened. At the same time, Quigley's translator interviewed witnesses from the café where Karen and Stout had been sitting. He conveyed the results of the questioning to Quigley and pointed to the end of the alley where the officer, driver, Karen, and Stout had entered and disappeared.

Quigley and his translator entered the warehouse. The translator asked one of the workers what had happened. The worker showed Quigley and the translator where there was blood on the concrete floor and told them that he had heard several gunshots. Quigley was deeply concerned and asked if the worker had actually seen anyone shot. The worker replied he had not but had discovered the blood after the intruders had left. Quigley asked if he could use the phone for a local call. The worker nodded yes and escorted him to the warehouse office.

Quigley called Westmoreland's office at MACV. When the receptionist answered, Quigley introduced himself as the bureau chief of the Associated Press and asked to speak with the general. Instead, he was transferred to a public relations colonel on the general's staff. Quigley was told that Westmoreland was not in the office but maybe there was something the colonel could help him with. Quigley said, "Alright. I am missing two of my people. I believe they are in real danger."

"Could it have been the Viet Cong?" said the colonel.

"It could have been but it wasn't."

"Okay. I'll bite. Any idea who might have taken them?" said the colonel.

"An ARVN officer."

"Why would he do that?"

"They saw something they shouldn't have. A black-market weapons deal involving the officer and a civilian. He killed the civilian when he realized he was being watched, then kidnapped my journalists. He may have shot one or both. There was blood on the floor. A lot of blood."

"Mr. White, that's a pretty serious accusation."

"I realize it is and I wouldn't make it if I didn't think it was urgent."

"I can make some phone calls."

"Okay. Make sure whomever you are calling understands that we have enough evidence to print a story of their obduction and the circumstances around it."

"Are you sure you want me to threaten them?"

"It's not a threat. It's a promise. I will call each one

of our major media outlets and let them know that I personally vouch for the story."

"You'd put your reputation and the reputation of your news service on the line without knowing for sure what happened?"

"I would and I will. There is very little I wouldn't do to get my people back."

Karen woke up in the chair again when the inquisitor popped her arm back into its socket and said, "I imagine that feels better."

It did. "Are you looking for thanks?" said Karen

"No. Just a comment. Are you ready to tell where the film is hidden or shall we continue?"

"I don't know where the film is."

"Then let's continue. You'll find this next part very interesting."

"I doubt it."

The officer and the driver carried in a galvanized washing tub filled with water and placed it in front of Karen. "Waterboarding?" said Karen, tired and in pain.

"No. We don't have time for that. This will be much more effective."

"I don't have anything I can tell you."

"I don't believe you," he said, then turned to the driver. "Take her boots off."

"Why?" said Karen.

"We don't want them to get wet."

The officer brought a coil of electrical wire into the room. On one end of the wire was a switch box connected to an electric plug. He checked to ensure the switch was off, then plugged the electric switch box into an electric outlet in the wall. On the other end of the coil of wire were two wires that had been stripped of their plastic coating. He attached each of the wires to the metal handles on the washing tub. Once the switch was thrown the water and the metal tub would be filled with electric current. The current would travel through Karen's bare feet and into her body electrocuting her and causing painful convulsions. If left on too long, the current would kill her.

The driver used his knife to cut the laces off her boots. He pulled off the right boot first and cast it aside. When he pulled off her left boot, he heard something loose inside. He looked up into Karen's angry face and smiled. He reached into the boot and pulled out the canister of film.

The inquisitor took the canister, held it in front of Karen, and said, "That wasn't so difficult, was it?"

"Burn in Hell," said Karen.

The inquisitor handed the film to the officer and said in French, "Try to be more discreet next time."

"Yes. What should we do with the woman?" said the officer in French as he slipped the film into his shirt pocket.

"That's up to you, but I would be careful. Even without the film, she's seen all our faces and watched you murder two people. That could still be very dangerous."

"Then it's okay if we shoot her?"

"Like I said… it's up to you. I'm just a facilitator."

Karen didn't understand them, but she knew they were deciding her fate. There was only one acceptable outcome of their conversation. She was going to die and there was nothing she could do about it. The inquisitor slipped out of the room and out of sight. He did not want to be a witness to what was about to happen. The officer moved behind her and withdrew his pistol. He pointed it at the back of her head as he heard footsteps approaching from the hallway.

Two ARVN guards entered the room and leveled their guns at the officer and driver who put their hands in the air. One of the guards grabbed the officer's pistol. The guards were followed by an ARVN colonel, the American Press colonel, and Quigley. "Are you okay, Karen?" said Quigley.

"Not really but I'm really glad to see you," said Karen as the American colonel untied her.

"Where's Stout?"

"They killed him."

"Jesus."

Freed from the rope, Karen turned to the officer, retrieved the film canister from his shirt pocket, then spit in his face and said, "You pig. I hope you hang."

"Can I see that?" said Quigley.

Karen handed the film canister to him and said, "I don't know if the focus is good, but that has enough evidence to convict these two."

"Right," said Quigley, then handed the canister to the ARVN general.

"What are doing?" said Karen.

"Keeping my word."

"Stout died for that!"

"Maybe, but I did what was necessary to find and save you."

"Quigley, you can't…"

"It's done."

"I'm not going to be silent."

"No. You won't. But without the film as evidence, you'll have a hard time getting anybody to listen. Sometimes, we have to do things that go against our grain. The important thing is that you are alive."

"And Stout's dead."

"That film won't bring him back."

"But it may bring him some justice."

"I don't think we need to worry about that. It's time to get you to a hospital and get you checked out."

Quigley put his arm around her. She writhed when he touched her shoulder that had been dislocated and said, "A hospital's probably not a bad idea."

They left the room and walked down the hallway. "I'm sorry about Stout, Quigley," said Karen her eyes tearing up.

"I know you are."

"He was my responsibility."

"Yes. But from what I've been able to piece together, I'm pretty sure it wasn't your fault.

"Thanks."

"I'm not looking forward to telling his parents. Any idea where they might have buried him?" said Quigley.

"Not really. I was blindfolded the whole time. If you want, I'll call his parents and let them know what happened."

"No. As Bureau Chief, it's my job. I'll do it."

They exited the building.

Still, inside the room, the ARVN colonel asked for the officer's pistol from one of the guards. The colonel chambered a round and used the officer's pistol to shoot both the officer and the driver in the head. They fell dead, one on top of the other on the concrete floor. The ARVN colonel turned to the American colonel and said, "Will General Westmoreland be satisfied?"

"I'm sure he will. It's better for everyone that the story ends here."

The two colonels shook hands in understanding.

Dak To

November 3, 1967 - Kon Tum Province, South Vietnam

Preparing for their General Uprising still many months away, the North Vietnamese and Viet Cong leaders were determined to draw the American and South Vietnamese forces away from their large military bases and major cities. The actions that were fought as part of the enemy's deception were called "The Border Battles."

During the early part of the war, Special Forces built Civilian Irregular Defense Group (CIDG) camps along the borders of South Vietnam. Their mission was to monitor communist forces infiltrating into the south and to support and train Montagnard villagers who bore the brunt of the fighting in the Central Highlands. Several of the CIDG camps were located around the Dak To Base Camp where there was an airstrip capable of landing large cargo aircraft for resupply and reinforcements.

In the latter part of 1967, communist forces carried out attacks against the American outposts and firebases at Loc Ninh, Song Be, Con Thien, and Khe Sanh. The

American commanders were not sure what was going on. It seemed the communists had changed their strategy and were contesting the areas near the border with regiment and even divisional-sized forces. In addition, they were attempting to hold the territory that they had captured, something they had never done before. MACV received intelligence reports that showed five NVA Regiments and one Viet Cong Battalion were massing near the US Special Forces camp at Dak To in the Central Highlands.

That was what the Americans had been waiting for, a large number of communists in one area where they could be destroyed with American air power and artillery. Watching the buildup of NVA and VC units in the area, Westmoreland took the bait and ordered the US 4th Division and elite 173rd Airborne Brigade to accompany ARVN 42nd Infantry Regiment, 22nd Division, and ARVN Airborne units in search and destroy missions near the border.

Responsible for the defense of the western half of Kon Tum Province, Major General William Peers was the commander of the 4th Infantry Division. Seeing the buildup of communist troops in his area and noticing their unusually aggressive nature, Peers introduced guidelines that prevented his units from being isolated and overrun in the rugged terrain that dominated the province. Battalions were to act as single units instead of breaking down into individual companies when they searched for the enemy. If for any reason a rifle company needed to move independently, it was to operate within one hour's march of the rest of the battalion. That way, if the company made contact with the enemy, it could be reinforced immediately. Peer's new guidelines helped reduce 4th Infantry casualties while operating in what many considered the most dangerous terrain in all of Vietnam.

Dak To was located on a flat valley floor that was surrounded by ridges, many of which rose into peaks with some as high as 4,000 feet. The ridge lines stretched west and southwest towards the tri-border region of Laos, Cambodia, and South Vietnam. The Kon Tum Province was covered with double and triple-canopy jungles. The only open areas that weren't shrouded with dense jungle and where a helicopter might land were covered with bamboo groves with eight-inch diameter stalks. Landing zones that were clear of the bamboo were few and far between making it a difficult area to resupply and reinforce allied forces by air. Almost all troop movement had to be carried out on foot which took away one of the American's key advantages – mobility.

When the enemies were able to find each other in the dense rainforest, the fighting was intense and both sides took heavy losses. But after just a few days, US aircraft and artillery took their toll on the communists as they attempted to destroy the American forces around Dak To. The battles on the hills around Dak To became some of the hardest-fought and bloodiest battles of the Vietnam War.

On the night of 12 November, the NVA launched a rocket attack against the Dak To airfield. They fired forty-four missiles from a nearby hillside. More attacks followed.

On 15 November, three C-130 Hercules transport aircraft were in the turnaround area as an NVA mortar barrage exploded across the airfield. Two of the huge aircraft were destroyed. Additional incoming mortar rounds set the ammunition dump and fuel storage areas on fire. Random explosions from the burning ammunition dump and fuel storage continued all day and into the night.

The NVA kept up their attacks firing more mortar rounds from different positions. One of the NVA mortar rounds exploded on two steel containers of C-4 plastic explosives. Their contents detonated simultaneously, sending a fireball and mushroom cloud high above the valley and leaving two forty-foot-deep craters. It was the largest explosion to occur in the Vietnam War, knocking men off their feet up to a mile away. Located next to the ammunition dump, the explosion demolished the entire 15th Light Equipment Company compound. Surprisingly, no one was killed. Although more than 1,100 tons of ordnance were destroyed by the mortar and rocket attacks, this was as close as the NVA would get to taking Dak To. The rapid deployment of allied forces had upset the North Vietnamese offensive and had thrown them onto the defensive.

To prevent further enemy rocket and mortar attacks on the Dak To airfield and base, the 3rd Battalion, 12th Infantry Regiment was ordered to take Hill 1338. Only six miles away, the hill had an excellent overlook of the base and airfield. It was one of the tallest hills in the area making it an ideal location for a firebase.

Almost immediately, the Americans encountered an elaborate enemy bunker complex with all the fortifications connected by field telephones. For two days, the 3rd Battalion fought their way up the steep slopes of Hill 1338 taking one bunker after another until the Americans finally captured the hill.

At roughly the same time, the 1st Battalion, 503rd Infantry advanced to take Hill 882 southwest of the Dak To base and airfield. The American force had a dozen journalists and photojournalists with them as they crested the hill and encountered a series of enemy bunkers manned by the NVA 66th Regiment. The NVA opened fire with small arms, machine guns, and mortar fire pinning down the 1st Battalion and the journalists. The NVA mounted several ground assaults against the American position. Helicopters were brought in to airlift out the journalists and the seriously wounded. American artillery and air support pounded the enemy bunkers. Four days later, the fighting ceased when the NVA withdrew.

The ARVN units also had multiple engagements against the NVA forces around Dak To. On Hill 1416 northeast of Tan Canh, the ARVN 3rd Battalion, 42nd Infantry Regiment encountered yet another bunker complex manned by NVA 24th Regiment. The two sides fought it out near the top of the hill as Allied artillery and air support hammered the NVA bunkers. The elite, all-volunteer ARVN 3rd and 9th Airborne Battalions joined the fight by attacking the hill from another direction forcing the enemy to divide its forces. Even with the help of heavy artillery and airpower, assaulting any bunker complex was a difficult and costly task. Two days later, the ARVN took the hill and the NVA retreated leaving 248 of their dead behind. The ARVN had lost sixty-six dead and 290 wounded.

Late in 1967, the communists seemed to break off hostilities and withdraw across the border into Laos. The ARVN commanders declared it a win and transported their units back to the home bases for rest and retrofitting.

But the communists had not gone back into Laos. Instead, they had repositioned themselves on the high ground near the Laotian border that they knew the Americans would want to control. The position was known as Hill 875. They dug man-high trenches, and foxholes, and built reinforced bunkers around the entire hill. As the construction of the defenses was completed, the communists brought in large amounts of supplies and ammunition. They were preparing for a long series of battles. There was no way to take the hill except to break through the communist defenses. Then, sure that the Americans would come... the NVA and VC waited.

A decorated veteran of three wars, Brigadier General Leo Schweiter was the new commander of the 173rd Airborne Brigade. Reading the intelligence reports, Schweiter recognized that almost every key terrain feature had been heavily fortified by the communists. They had spent as much as six months building their defenses. They were there to stay. And that was fine with Schweiter and the 173rd Airborne Paratroopers. Using their technological advantages and the bravery of their soldiers, the Americans were there to kill the communists and drive them from South Vietnam. While wary of the enemy's preparations, Westmoreland, Peers, and Schweiter saw the approaching battles as an opportunity to destroy the communists in large numbers. The Americans wanted to fight and so did the communists. But their objectives were different.

The Americans wanted to destroy a large number of communists and cut off the enemy's access to South

Vietnam. The American generals saw that the communists were changing their strategy to secure territory, but the Americans failed to recognize why.

The communists wanted to destroy a major US element forcing the Americans to bring in a large number of reinforcements to secure the area. Those reinforcements would come from the major cities and military bases around South Vietnam weakening the ARVN's defenses during the communists' upcoming General Uprising in the first months of the new year. To the communist leaders in Hanoi, the Border Battles were a series of costly diversions that were key to the success of a much bigger conflict to come.

With intelligence reports indicating that an entire NVA division had been moved into defenses around Dak To, the Americans moved the remaining units of the 173rd Airborne Brigade, the 4th Infantry Division, two 1st Cavalry battalions, plus four ARVN Infantry battalions, and two ARVN Airborne battalions into the area. The Americans and their allies had over 16,000 troops in the valley against 6,000 communist troops in fortified positions. The stage was set for a major pitched battle around Dak To.

On November 3rd, Sergeant Vu Hong, an artillery specialist with the NVA 6th Regiment, defected to the ARVN in the area. Under interrogation, Hong provided American forces with detailed information on the location and objectives of communist forces around Dak To.

On the 4th and 5th of November, while seeking out the enemy, allied forces came into contact with communist forces in prepared defensive positions.

Peers and his field commanders had developed tactics for dealing with the enemy's defensive positions. They combed the hillsides on foot. When they ran into one of the enemy's fixed defensive positions, the Allied forces would back off a safe distance and call-in air and artillery strikes to soften up the communists and destroy their bunkers and trench positions with napalm and artillery strikes. Once the air and artillery strikes were finished, the Allied forces would attack the communists on foot and drive them from the battlefield. It was similar to how they normally operated but with the addition of not heavily engaging the enemy while the air and artillery pounded their positions. There was little need to risk the lives of allied soldiers during the airstrikes and artillery barrages. The Allied forces knew that the communists would not leave their prepared positions and thereby pinned themselves down.

But the communists knew that the allied commanders could not resist overrunning the NVA positions at which time the communists could inflict large, allied casualties. The communists were willing to sacrifice large numbers of their troops as long as they inflicted heavy damage against their enemy forcing them to reinforce. The more allied troops they could draw away from the big cities and into the northwestern region, the higher the probability of success for the General Uprising.

On the morning of November 19th, A, C, and D Companies, 2nd Battalion, 503rd Parachute Infantry Regiment, 173rd Airbourne Brigade stood at the base of Hill 875 preparing to assault the enemy positions on the steep hill. Artillery and airstrike had been pounding the enemy positions for hours attempting to soften up and even drive off the NVA. The problem was that the jungle was so thick, the artillery and forward air observers could not see through the triple canopy to accurately locate the enemy positions or even see the results of the barrage. Regardless, they kept at it. All the trees on the top of the hill had been mowed down by shrapnel and burned off by Napalm.

As the artillery tapered off, the paratroopers advanced up the hill with C and D companies taking the lead and A company in the rear. The paratroopers made it within 300 yards of the summit when they stepped into a clearing of fallen trees from the earlier bombardments.

The NVA commander was a veteran fighter and knew that his men must grab their enemy by the belt or risk being destroyed by American aircraft and artillery. He waited until the enemy paratroopers were just a few yards from his soldiers' trenches before giving the order to fire. Rifle and machine gun rounds ripped through the air killing and wounding several paratroopers and driving the others to seek cover behind fallen trees. Those that found no cover used their helmets to dig fighting holes where they were lying on the steep slope as the NVA kept up a hellish fire and rolled Chinese-made grenades down the hill. Both American lead companies were pinned down and being shredded by the enemy gunfire and grenades.

To make matters worse at the foot of the hill, NVA troops attacked A Company from behind. They too were pinned down and unable to support C and D Companies. The American commanders of all three companies were killed by early afternoon. Most of the platoon leaders and NCOs were also dead or badly wounded. The survivors in A Company dragged their wounded up the hill to make contact with the other two companies.

Taking the rear-guard position, Private First Class Carlos Lozada stayed behind with his M60 machine gun and laid down covering fire to keep the communists back and give his comrades a fighting chance of reaching the relative safety of the other two companies' perimeter. A few minutes later, Lozada was overwhelmed by enemy fighters and shot dead. For his actions, Lozada would be awarded a posthumous Medal of Honor.

Together the three companies formed a defensive perimeter among the fallen trees placing their wounded in the center. They were surrounded and heavily outnumbered. The battalion of paratroopers was in danger of being annihilated. Artillery and air support could not be used to protect them from their enemy. The two sides were too close. The NVA had succeeded at grabbing the Americans by the belt and didn't dare let go. But the American aircraft continued to pound the NVA positions beyond the circle of paratroopers with bombs and Napalm. It did little to help the besieged paratroopers but took a heavy toll on the enemy.

Another American A-4 Skyhawk swooped in and dropped two 500-pound Mark 81 Snakeye bombs. The first hit the enemy trenches on the slope above the Americans. The second bomb made a direct hit on the American position. In an instant, forty-two Americans were killed and another forty-five were wounded. A badly wounded American lieutenant found a working radio and said, "No more fucking planes. You're killing us up here."

The American aircraft backed off. The American artillery continued to pound the enemy positions at a distance. Things went from bad to worse when the Americans ran out of water in the ninety-degree heat, then ran low on ammunition. Helicopters attempted to ferry in supplies and ammunition. After six UH-1 helicopters were shot down or badly damaged, the resupply missions were called off. The paratroopers were on their own. As dark descended on the hillside, the Americans dug in the best they could for the night. Almost everyone was wounded at least once and many had multiple wounds.

On November 23rd, after four days of fighting on Hill 875, two fresh battalions from the 173rd Airbourne Brigade made it to the top of the hill and rescued the surviving Americans of the 2nd Battalion. All were severely dehydrated and on the verge of passing out if they hadn't done so already. The night before, sensing that the Americans would come in force, the NVA had slipped down the back side of the hill under the cover of darkness. They had succeeded at inflicting terrible damage on the American battalion. That was enough for the moment. They retreated into Cambodia and Laos.

The Americans choose to see the battle as a victory because the NVA had given up the hill. But territory was not the communists' objective. The death of many American soldiers was their goal. In that, they had succeeded.

The Americans sat on top of the hill contemplating what had happened and why so many had died for that piece of dirt.

After an hour, helicopters picked up the Americans

and carried them off to another hill. With the enemy gone, Hill 875 was abandoned. It had little strategic value beyond being a good place for the enemies to kill each other. The Americans had lost eighty-seven killed and 130 wounded taking Hill 875.

The cost of the Battle of Dak To was staggering, 376 U.S. troops had been killed and another 1,441 were wounded. The battalion had survived, but just barely. Another seventy-three ARVN troops had been killed. In addition, the Allies had expended 151,000 artillery rounds, flown 2,096 tactical air sorties, 257 B-52 airstrikes, and 2,101 helicopter sorties. Forty helicopters were destroyed.

The U.S. Army claimed to have killed 1,644 NVA troops, but many American soldiers that fought in the battle contested the inflated body count. Westmoreland personally changed the final report to 474 NVA dead which was still more than the American losses. The North Vietnamese claimed 2,800 Americans and 700 ARVN killed during the operation. They did not report any of their own losses.

Succeeding Peers as the commander of the 4th Infantry Division, Major General Charles Stone criticized Schweiter on the battle for Hill 875 when he said, "It had absolutely no importance in the war thereafter. None. It had no strategic value... It made no difference... that the enemy held all those mountains along the border because they controlled no people, no resources, no real growing areas, and suffered a horrible malaria rate. Why go out there and fight them where all the advantages were on their side?"

There was little doubt that the communists had lost a great number of men, but they had succeeded in their objective. By January 1968, one-half of all U.S. maneuver battalions in South Vietnam had been drawn away from the cities and military bases and into the border areas. The 173rd Airborne Brigade was combat ineffective and ordered to repair and refit at Tuy Hoa. It would take almost a year before the paratroopers in the 173rd would return to full strength and see action again.

November 13, 1967 – White House, Washington DC

After a lengthy internal discussion, the Joint Chiefs of Staff recommended to the White House that no ceasefire be agreed to for the Tet holiday period in January 1968 because of "the fraudulent manner in which the enemy has treated past ceasefires."

Upon hearing the recommendation, President Johnson was not so sure. He argued that the American soldiers also benefited from the ceasefire. They needed a rest from the current pace of one battle after another. Even if the North Vietnamese and Viet Cong were not fully compliant, there was little doubt that conflicts decreased during the holiday ceasefires. Something was better than nothing, he argued.

A short time later, the Americans and South Vietnamese accepted the North's ceasefire proposal for Tet. The dye was cast… The communists set the date for the General Uprising to begin on the first day of the Tet Holiday.

Hubris

November 21, 1967 - Saigon, South Vietnam

While the allies and communists were slugging it out in Dak To, President Johnson and General Westmoreland were continuing to execute the new public relations campaign designed to win back more American support for the war. Johnson had seen the success of the MACV enemy troop estimates revised report and decided to push the disinformation even further. In his mind, he was doing what was necessary to keep the United States safe from communism, even if it meant deceiving the American people.

In an address to the National Press Club, Westmoreland was upbeat and optimistic. He assured his audience when he said, "We have reached an important point where the end begins to come into view."

He went on to cite a list of problems plaguing the North Vietnamese and Viet Cong, including an inability to recruit and the decreasing number of supplies and ammunition crossing the border into the South because of American interdiction efforts. Continuing his optimistic theme, he ended his speech by declaring his goal to reach Phase IV of the war, when the communists would be on the run. He said, "I am absolutely certain that whereas in 1965 the enemy was winning, today he is certainly losing. We are making progress. We know you want an honorable and early transition to the fourth and last phase. So do your sons and so do I. It lies within our grasp—the enemy's hopes are bankrupt."

Secretary of Defense McNamara did not take part in the public relations campaign. He was disillusioned by the war that he helped plan and execute. He was quickly becoming a liability in the Johnson White House and was ostracized by his colleagues and the president. He was alone with his thoughts but still expected to carry out his office's responsibility to prosecute the war.

Johnson knew he had to do something about McNamara. The president had changed and no longer wanted dissension in his administration. He wanted everyone rowing in the same direction when it came to the war. Despite what the others in his cabinet said about McNamara's change of heart concerning the war, Johnson felt he owed a debt of gratitude to McNamara who had done so much to carry out Johnson's wishes for Vietnam up to this point. He needed to get rid of McNamara, but in a way that would not destroy the great man's reputation. Johnson still admired McNamara's intellect even if he disagreed with his conclusions about the war. Johnson began calling in favors on McNamara's behalf searching for a suitable job that his friend could jump to and save face. It wasn't easy. McNamara was in a formidable position as Secretary of Defense of the world's most powerful nation.

Johnson found what he was looking for at the World Bank. McNamara was highly qualified to become the head of the institution. Johnson would do what was necessary to ensure McNamara was offered the job and allowed to resign from his current post in the White House while retaining his dignity. It would take time to make the transition, but the writing was on the wall… Robert McNamara was on his way out of the Johnson White House.

December 23, 1967 – Cam Ranh Base, South Vietnam

Flying aboard Air Force One on his way back from Australia, President Johnson made an unannounced Christmas visit to American troops in South Vietnam. General Westmoreland and his deputy, General Creighton Abrams, and Ambassador Ellsworth Bunker were waiting for Johnson at Cam Ranh Base when he landed at 8:40 AM. After waving hello to the troops on the tarmac, Johnson conferred with thirty of Westmoreland's field commanders about the progress of the war. When the meeting concluded, Johnson addressed 2,450 American troops. He took a tour of the base hospital and personally awarded many of the patients Purple Heart Medals. He did his best to shake everyone's hand that could reach him before his departure on Air Force One at 10:25 AM. He was in Vietnam for less than two hours, but it did a great deal to raise morale among the troops throughout the country.

Vietnam

At the end of 1967, the United States had 485,600 troops in country. During the year, it had lost 11,363 killed. It was the costliest year yet in casualties. South Vietnam had 643,000 troops with 12,716 killed during the year. America's allies: South Korea, Australia, Philippines, Thailand, and New Zealand all had troops in country and were fighting the communists.

North Vietnam and the Viet Cong had 278,000 troops in South Vietnam. They had suffered 140,000 casualties by US estimates. China had 170,000 auxiliary support troops in North Vietnam.

The war was far from over.

Letter to Reader

I hoped you enjoyed *Flames of War*. There were a lot of surprises when I was doing the research for the book. I especially liked the stories of Mohamad Ali and John McCain.

The next book in the Airmen Series is *Crucible of War*. The book includes the siege of Khe Sanh, the Tet Offensive, and the Battle of Hue. And, of course, our heroes are right in the middle of it all. I hope you enjoy it. Here is the link for *Crucible of War*.

https://www.amazon.com/gp/product/B0BH8H2VBC

I appreciate you reading my books and supporting my effort to tell the complete story of the Vietnam War. It's been a long haul.

As always, reviews are appreciated.

Regards,

David Lee Corley, Author

DAVID LEE CORLEY
CRUCIBLE
OF
WAR
THE AIRMEN SERIES

Author's Biography

Born in 1958, David grew up on a horse ranch in Northern California, breeding and training appaloosas. He has had all his toes broken at least once and survived numerous falls and kicks from ornery colts and fillies. David started writing professionally as a copywriter in his early 20's. At 32, he packed up his family and moved to Malibu, California, to live his dream of writing and directing motion pictures. He has four motion picture screenwriting credits and two directing credits. His movies have been viewed by over 50 million movie-goers worldwide and won a multitude of awards, including the Malibu, Palm Springs, and San Jose Film Festivals. In addition to his 24 screenplays, he has written fourteen novels. He developed his simplistic writing style after rereading his two favorite books, Ernest Hemingway's "The Old Man and The Sea" and Cormac McCarthy's "No Country For Old Men." An avid student of world culture, David lived as an expat in both Thailand and Mexico. At 56, he sold all his possessions and became a nomad for four years. He circumnavigated the globe three times and visited 56 countries. Known for his detailed descriptions, his stories often include actual experiences and characters from his journeys.